ECHOES

from the Grave

Also by S.D. Tooley

Sam Casey Series

Restless Spirit

Nothing Else Matters

When the Dead Speak

Remy and Roadkill Series

The Skull

Written as Lee Driver

Chase Dagger Series

The Unseen

Full Moon-Bloody Moon

The Good Die Twice

Short Stories

Sara Morningsky, *Mystery in Mind Anthology*

The Thirteenth Hole, *Mystery in Mind Anthology*

Solving Life's Riddle, Amazon Shorts

PRAISE FOR THE SAM CASEY SERIES

When the Dead Speak

"A promising first mystery of particular interest to readers of Native American mysteries."
— *Booklist*

"Tooley's excellent debut novel of mystery and suspense, with its unforgettable characters and vivid story, shows the depth of research into not only police investigation, but Native American culture as well."
— ForeWord Magazine

"…an action-packed mystery that will garner much attention from fans who enjoy a police procedural with a twist."
— *Midwest Book Review*

Nothing Else Matters

"Entertaining reading in what looks to be a solid series."
— *Booklist*

"The author, who spent six years as a casino dealer, effectively blends Native American lore with the world of riverboat gambling."
— *Publishers Weekly*

"…the characterization and the depth of complexity of the man known only as Sparrow is not only stark and brutal, but also heart wrenching. My sincere compliments to the author of this masterpiece."
— Cindy Penn, www.WordWeaving.com

Restless Spirit

"An exciting mix of police procedure, spiritual 'intuition,' creeping suspense, and page-turning narrative."
— *Library Journal*

"S.D. Tooley's gift for combining powerful police drama, Indian mysticism, and mystery results in an exciting, chilling puzzle that is a real page turner."
— *Midwest Book Review*

"Sam Casey is amazing—a beautifully described and magically interesting character… the plot, characters and pacing are all excellent."
— 4 Star Review, *Romantic Times*

ECHOES
from the Grave

S.D. Tooley

Full Moon Publishing

A special thanks to Kenneth J. Schoon for his informative book: *Calumet Beginnings - Ancient Shorelines and Settlements at the South End of Lake Michigan,* Indiana University Press, 2003

Library of Congress Catalog Number: 2007928435

ISBN-10 0-9785402-2-0
ISBN-13 978-0-9785402-2-7

Published August 2007

Printed in the United States of America

Full Moon Publishing LLC
P.O. Box 408
Schererville, IN 46375

www.fullmoonpub.com

For Bill

Prologue

It was dumped on top of a mound of dirt by a yellow giant. The backhoe roared and grumbled nearby, a yellow piece of machinery frozen in place by its driver who wasn't quite sure what he had disturbed. Over the course of the past two hours the flat ground had been transformed into a gouged pit exposing more colorful pieces of history. But it wasn't the color that drew the driver's attention. It was the white objects. Long and short, smooth and jagged, they had been ripped from their resting place and exposed for the world to see.

The backhoe was silenced and the driver climbed down from the cab. He paused at the crest and stared down at the floor of the pit. More objects had broken the surface. Puzzled, he shoved his hard hat up to wipe the sweat from his forehead. A man in a white shirt and tie ambled over. They convened at the base of the mound.

"This doesn't look good," the driver said. "It doesn't look good at all." They knelt down as though praying to the god of backhoes.

The foreman lifted one bone the size of a broken baseball bat. "Could be from an animal."

The driver shoved his hard hat up and snorted. "Like what? A giraffe?"

Beyond the makeshift orange fence used to contain their site were specialty shops, a bank, and two restaurants. Other than the honking of horns, the foreman saw few signs of foot traffic. Their laughter and the way they huddled on the ground, however, were drawing the curiosity of the other workers.

"Breyton will blow another artery if construction is delayed even one day," the foreman said, drilling him with his eyes. He leaned in close and whispered, "Don't breathe a word of this. Go on like nothing's happened and let's remove any suspicious debris before some pedestrian starts getting curious." The sun scurried behind a cloud, fearing witness to such a conspiracy.

The driver of the backhoe stood and stared into the pit. "What if there's more in there? What if we uncovered an old cemetery?"

"Can't be an old cemetery. We would have seen coffins. You see any coffins in there, Baker?" The foreman was aware of a mass of hardhats headed his way. It would be difficult to keep these many mouths shut.

"No," Baker replied. "Don't mean they weren't old and disintegrated. Don't seem right, Joe." He picked through the mound of dirt and gravel until his weathered and calloused fingers found something familiar. He held up an arrowhead which had been crudely shaped from stone and chiseled to a fine point. "I think we're going to have more problems than just some old cemetery bones, Joe."

"All the more reason to hide what we've seen."

As though the object at the top of the mound could hear, it shifted its position sending debris trickling down. Bent cans and twisted metal hurried out of its way. It picked up speed, drawing the attention of the rest of the workers as well as witnesses beyond the orange fence. It slid the last few feet and rested at the foreman's steel-toed work boot. It was a human skull.

1

"Did you know that cremation reduces the average man to seven-and-a-half pounds of bone and ash?" Frank Travis slammed out of the unmarked car. He stared at Jake over the roof of the Ford Taurus. If he was expecting a five-minute debate on the subject of death and dying, Frank had a long wait. The right side of Jake's mouth quivered, the equivalent of uproarious laughter from the former FBI agent. "Buried or burned. There's got to be another way." Frank scratched a finger across his soul patch.

Jake's moment of amusement faded as quickly as it had started. Behind mirrored sunglasses, his eyes made a quick assessment of the area. A temporary fence had been constructed around a two-acre site. Two beat cops were setting up wooden barricades across a sidewalk. Workmen milled around in tight clusters, most directing their attention to something or someone out of Jake's view. He swiveled his head to the strip mall across the street noticing the slow traffic and the gathering of pedestrians. Dispatch reported that the workmen had found bones while digging the foundation for a building. Most of the time people falsely identified animal bones as human. Today, however, Dispatch also reported that some type of argument had ensued with a spectator who was armed. So far, all appeared quiet on the downtown front.

Chasen Heights wasn't known for its tree-lined streets or upscale shopping mall. Hugging the shores of Lake Michigan just south of Chicago, it had a history of strip joints and murder during the Al Capone era. With a population just over one hundred thousand, it was a melting pot of brick bungalows to the south and million dollar homes to the north. The factories and steel mills to the east didn't care much about the average household income. They belched out smoke and ash indiscriminately, making sure everyone got his fair share.

The heat radiated from the ground. It was eight in the morning and already proving to be another hot one. Perspiration glistened on Frank's bald head and dotted his shirt. Jake eyed a man headed their way. The way the man was dressed in a white shirt and tie told him this had to be the foreman or the owner. He slammed the driver's side door and walked over to where Frank was shaking sand out of his Bruno Maglio shoes.

"Never fails," Frank moaned with a shake of his head. "When I wear my shit shoes, it's a dull day. When I wear my two-hundred-dollar loafers, I'm dumpster diving, swimming in a swamp, or knee deep in dirt."

"I have three words for you, Frank: J. C. Penney." Jake turned his attention to the uniformed officers standing at the edge of the pit, fists jammed at their waists. There weren't any visible bodies or blood Jake could see, so why the back-up?

The name *Breyton* was emblazoned on the backhoe, the construction trailer, and a wooden sign near the street. Men in hardhats were clustered around the safety of the trailer and backhoe. Curiosity seekers were three deep behind the fencing.

"I don't dress like a slob in Henley shirts like some people I know." Instead Frank resembled the pastel shades of a Florida skyline in cream-colored suits and bright colored tee shirts. His wife claimed he watched too many reruns of *Miami Vice*.

Fifty feet away a yellow backhoe was grumbling and spewing noxious fumes while the driver leaned halfway out of the cab lobbing obscenities at someone in the pit. They could taste the fumes and dirt in the air.

The worker in the dress shirt and tie switched from a fast walk to a trot as he rushed over. "'Bout time," he grumbled. "Hurry up and get rid of those bones so we can get back to work. And arrest that redskin in the pit."

"Redskin?" Frank asked.

Jake leveled his mirrored sunglasses on the man whose tie

had somehow loosened on the trot over. His shirt was soiled and underarms ringed in sweat. "Why don't you start from the beginning, Mr...."

He waved off the handshakes, displaying the dirt and grime on his hands. "Joe Erskine. I'm the foreman on the job. We're building an executive office building, high-end, elaborate suites. And we are on a tight timetable." They threaded their way through the workers and toward the backhoe where the driver was screaming and shaking his fist. The foreman explained in words that seemed scripted, "We hit a, uh, grave site about an hour ago. Bones, skulls, you know. Site was probably an old cemetery. Either way, this guy shows up out of nowhere and jumps into the pit. Won't let anyone near. If you can haul his ass out of here, we can get back to work. I would have done it myself except he's armed and dangerous."

"Armed with what?" Frank asked.

Whizzzzziiiiiitttt. The sound cut through the humid air followed by a *thrangggg*. The three men stared at the arrow which quivered from the front tire of a dump truck several yards away. A similar arrow was still vibrating in the opposite tire.

"What the fu...?" Frank blurted but Jake already had his Sig Sauer in hand and was moving toward the pit.

Jake didn't have to look twice to recognize the assailant. He lowered his gun and sighed. "Alex, what the hell are you doing?"

Alex Red Cloud wore his heritage with pride. His gray hair was held back in a ponytail. A red bandana was wrapped around his forehead. Although he sported blue jeans and a short-sleeved shirt, anyone who knew Alex wouldn't have been surprised if he had worn moccasins and a breech cloth. He pulled another arrow from his quill and placed it in the bow. Dark eyes seethed with rage as he raised the bow and aimed it toward the crowd.

Two beat cops pulled their weapons.

"Put your guns away," Jake yelled. "Now." After they holstered their weapons, Jake approached the crest. "Alex, come up here and talk to me."

Alex turned his angry eyes on Jake as if it were his fault. His gaze shifted quickly to the backhoe. He raised the arrow at the driver.

"Alex," Jake warned.

Alex's muscles tensed as he pulled back the bow string. The driver leaped from the cab as the arrow slammed into the seat rest.

"Let me try." Frank stepped closer to the pit. "Hey, bro." But Frank didn't get much further. As though materializing from the heat rising off the pavement, a school bus rattled over the curb and through an opened area between two wooden barricades. The audience backed away, shielding their lattes from the grit. Workers picked themselves up and scattered as the bus made a wide turn next to the backhoe. Tires churned up clouds of dust that drifted across the open field. The door opened and a sea of brown faces emerged.

"HEY, HEY," Erskine yelled, waving his arms frantically. "You can't park there."

The women exited the bus first, carrying picnic baskets. The men followed hauling drums and folding chairs. Two of the men were carrying a long folding table. The Natives ignored Erskine's rantings and traipsed down a ramp of dirt past Alex. The beat cops were out-numbered and looked to Jake for direction.

"Stop them," Erskine yelled. His workers ran toward the crowd. Alex raised his bow sending the workers retreating behind heavy equipment.

The driver of the bus climbed down and held out his hand. An attractive woman in a long, colorful skirt stepped off the bus, pulling her shawl closer around her shoulders. Her dark hair hung in a long braid sprinkled with strands of silver. There was a regal air about her that silenced the workers. Her squash necklace and turquoise bracelets may as well have been a symbol of a crown.

"Finally." Jake hurried to the bus. She turned to face him, her smile telling him that everything was under control. That should have been his first clue. The bus driver had a gentle grip on her elbow but she touched him lightly to let him know she needed no help.

Frank rushed to catch up. "How did Abby hear about it so soon and what is she doing on the bus?"

Jake's steps faltered as those questions sank in.

"Jacob, how nice to see you."

It was a strange comment seeing that he had enjoyed breakfast with his mother-in-law less than two hours ago.

A screech of tires turned their attention to the street where a stretch limousine was making its way through the crowd. It careened over the curb and parked next to the bus. The number of onlookers was growing as traffic halted and pedestrians stopped to check out the commotion.

"This is turning into a damn parking lot," Frank said, flicking a dusting of sand from his dark skin.

"I must join the others," Abby said as she patted Jake's hand.

"Hold up." Jake turned his attention to the pit. The Natives were seated on blankets passing around plates of food. Over the chatter from the construction workers and yelling from the foreman, a soft drumbeat could be heard.

"What the hell are they doing?" Erskine demanded.

Jake blocked Abby's path and placed his hands at his waist. "Talk."

"Alex and I were having tea across the street when we heard that they dug up remains. We were curious so we stopped by to watch. There are arrowheads in there, Jacob. We are making an offering to our ancestors." She gathered her shawl tighter and with an *everything-is-fine* smile, made her way into the pit.

Frank stared at the freight train barreling out of the limousine, shoulders hunched, white hair disheveled. Two side cars that were either bodyguards or Chicago Bears linemen hurried to keep up. "Is this the point, Jake, where we admit we have lost control of a situation?"

The smell of money reached the detectives even before the white-haired man pulled up short of them. "Get the hell off my property."

Jake barred the man from following Abby. "This area is off limits." He towered over the man. And although Jake's steely disposition usually unsettled the most ardent criminal, this diminutive pit bull was having no part of it.

"The hell it is. I own it."

"And you are?" Frank prompted.

"Elton Xaviar Breyton the Third." He spoke louder than necessary, as though attempting to impress the audience that was growing beyond the orange fence. "I'm on a tight schedule. So we dug up an old cemetery. Big deal."

"Not quite," a soft voice said from behind them.

The men turned in unison to see a young woman whose mass of long, curly hair was barely tamed by the sunglasses she had slid on the top of her head. The workmen had turned their attention from the threat of death by arrow to a set of shapely legs exposed through a floral sundress that could have used a few more buttons.

"Sam." Frank flashed a broad smile. "Lookin' good."

"Detective Travis. Nice to see you again."

Jake crossed his arms and eyed her through his mirrored sunglasses. "Your trouble radar is obviously still working, Sam."

Breyton took time to assess the entire package, his smile showing appreciation until he spied the strange leather pouch she wore around her neck and the third earring of beads and feathers which brushed her shoulder. As though suddenly realizing she might be an adversary, his smile faded. "How nice we have time for chit chat, but that isn't getting these trespassers off of my property. We've got work to do."

"Unfortunately," Sam said, turning ice blue eyes on him, "you can't make one more tire tread mark, scoop up one more shovel of dirt or string one more utility line."

"Says who?"

"The Native American Graves Protection and Repatriation Act."

"Oh, no." Breyton waggled a finger at her. "That only applies to federal and tribal lands, not private property. I've been in this business long enough to know the laws, little lady."

"Then you also know that in matters of private property it falls under the Illinois State Historic Preservation Law."

Breyton took a step closer to Sam. Jake tensed. "The mayor is a very close friend of mine," Breyton snarled.

"The governor is a close friend of mine." She pushed past him and walked to the edge of the pit.

Breyton flipped open his phone and as he walked away, the detectives heard him grumble, "Pity the sorry fuck married to that bitch."

Jake stared at the man's back wondering how soon until the mayor made a call to Chief Murphy. That was the last thing they needed. He and Frank joined Sam at the crest. The trespassers continued to pass food and pound drums, paying little attention to the cat-calls from the workmen. It was on that ramp that Alex remained standing like a palace guard.

"Who's watching our son, Sam?"

"Jackie."

Jake lowered his head and peered skeptically over his sunglasses at her.

"What? Dillon loves Jackie."

"At his age, he loves anyone with tits." Jake straightened and studied the bronzed faces huddled on the blankets.

"In that case, every man is stuck at the perpetual age of three months."

Frank cackled, a high-pitched giggle that cut through the clamor and drumbeats from the pit.

"We're going to have a problem, Sam," Jake started. "Our visitors are destroying any chances archeologists will have to research the area. They are stepping on artifacts, possibly breaking some and they outnumber us. I would really appreciate it if you could convince them to leave. I don't want to call up reinforcements."

"No problem." Sam called out to the crowd in her native Lakota language. The brown faces turned and spoke to her for several minutes then started to pack up. She turned back to Jake. "Better?"

He pulled a strand of hair from her face and tucked it behind her ear. "What are you doing here anyway?"

She sighed, a bit too long and a bit too resigned.

"Just can't stay away from a crime scene can you?" Jake knew Sam missed being a cop.

"Mom and Alex are here. How could I stay away?"

Breyton rushed over from his limo. "Wonderful. They are finally leaving. They may have won this round but I'm meeting with the mayor this afternoon. Then we'll see." Breyton watched as the Natives loaded their tables and blankets onto the bus. It departed quickly, leaving plumes of dust and exhaust in its wake.

Alex emerged from the pit but remained standing guard. Abby spoke to him for several minutes before making her way over to Jake. Breyton immediately turned on Abby.

"This is all your fault, you squaw bitch."

Sam was too shocked to speak. Jake moved instinctively as he saw Breyton make a move toward his mother-in-law. But Alex was surprisingly quicker. His gray hair was deceiving and the speed at which he charged made Breyton take a step back. The bow and quill dropped away as Alex tackled the beefy man. Both bodies hit the ground with a thud.

"Get him off of me." Breyton kicked and squirmed from beneath his attacker. Two bodyguards rushed to Breyton's aid, pulling Alex's arms behind his back.

"Back off," Jake yelled.

Frank muscled the hulks to one side. "Let him up." He grabbed Alex's arm and pulled him free.

Breyton jabbed a finger at Alex. "I want that man arrested for attempted murder, trespassing, assault, damage to property, and I'm sure I can think of more if you give me time." He brushed dirt from his tailor-made suit. "Matter of fact, I want them all arrested for trespassing."

2

Sam blocked out Breyton's demands and studied the trees in the distance. Not one leaf was moving. She turned her attention to the flagpole by the bank across the street. The flag was limp and motionless yet she was feeling a breeze. And more than feeling it, she was also hearing it. A chorus of indiscernible sounds, layers of whispers. She navigated toward the massive pile of dirt on the side of the pit, stopping just short of the skull lying at her feet. She sifted her hands through the dirt, trying to pick up images of an era gone by, of hunting tribes setting up camp, traders bartering skins and liquor for jewelry and blankets, women sweating over cooking pots made from the stomachs of buffalo, or children playing with sticks. But her mind was as cold as the dirt, reaping little more than a fleeting drumbeat.

The echoes grew louder as a soft breeze whipped up errant tornados of sand. The small whirlwinds twisted down the mound and circled the skull. Sam bent down and carefully lifted the skull. Immediately she saw herself running through the dark, dodging what might have been trees, stealing glances over her shoulder at an unseen attacker.

"Sam."

She clung to the skull as it nearly slipped from her hands. "Jeez, wear a bell around your neck."

"You're touching my evidence." Jake grabbed the skull and placed it back on the ground.

Sam stared past him at the ramp where Alex had stood. The visitors had managed to pack down the plow marks made by the backhoe. She raised a hand to conceal the glare from the sun and scanned the excavated area. Something didn't look right. "Just have one question – where are the bones?"

"The bones?" Jake pulled his sunglasses off and walked partway down the ramp to study the ground. What bones and artifacts had been visible before were now missing. He scrambled up the ramp and pointed toward a squad car where Frank was opening a car door for Abby. "Hold it." Jake motioned at both Alex and Abby. "Get back here."

Sam followed him across the uneven ground to where Abby and Alex stood.

"Where's the evidence," Jake asked. Alex served Jake a dose of cold silence.

"What do you mean by evidence, Jacob?" Abby asked.

"The bones and artifacts. They're gone."

"Hot damn," Breyton cried out. "Now I can get back to work."

"Not so fast. The dirt dug out and piled there," Jake said, motioning toward the mound, "has enough bones, pottery, and arrowheads to halt construction."

"Not to mention the skull," Frank pointed out. "Even without the artifacts, those bones and the skull still have to be examined."

"Shit." Breyton kicked at the dirt.

"I thought they were there, Jacob," Abby replied. She looked puzzled and glanced wearily at Alex.

Jake never knew Abby to blatantly lie. Alex was a different story. In Alex's world, he couldn't be accused of lying if he kept silent. "Russo," Jake barked at a stocky beat cop several yards away, "put an APB out on that bus." He gave Russo the license plate number, then said, "Get Alex over to the precinct." To another officer he said, "Take Abby to the precinct in a separate car."

"Jake, you can't have my mother arrested."

"She isn't under arrest. I have a feeling Alex is going to be a stubborn ass and refuse to speak English."

Sam took a step back. She knew that look. Jake was in FBI mode—barking orders, pacing back and forth, brows hovering just over his eyes. There wasn't an ounce of warmth in that look.

But when he placed his hand on Abby's shoulder, it was a gentle touch.

"I need you to make a list of everyone who was with you here today, Abby."

"I'm sure if they took them, they had a very good reason." It was Abby's way of telling him she had no intention of turning in any of her people.

"I understand their reasoning, Abby. Believe me. But it isn't the way to go about doing things. Everything should have been left intact for the experts." Jake glanced again at the officer. "Take her downtown."

"I can't be of further help to you, Jacob. Besides, my grandson needs me. I will go home."

Abby played her hole card—her grandson, his son. Jake turned away and aimed his wrath at Breyton. "Send your crew home until further notice."

"I will go home?" Breyton parroted in a sing-song falsetto. "That's all the lady says and bingo." He snapped his fingers. "You let her go."

"She didn't do anything."

"You're going to let that Indian go once you get to the station, when no one is around to witness it, right? Is that how this department works?"

Jake mustered as much self-control as possible and took a step closer. "If you don't like the way I handle my investigation, I suggest you take it up with Captain Lamon Robinson." He pulled a business card from his pocket and handed it to Breyton.

Frank leaned close to Breyton and pointed at the business card. "That's Sergeant Jake *sorry fuck* Mitchell." *You dumb ass*. A rolling thunder of laughter erupted from Frank as the realization struck Breyton that Jake and Sam were married.

Breyton kept his eyes glued to the ground as he sandwiched himself between the two linebackers and stalked back to the limo. Car doors slammed and a cloud of dust spurted from the tires as the stretch backed out into the street.

Sam watched him leave but was soon distracted again by the whispers. She turned toward the mound, the skull lying on its side, appearing to stare at her. Oblivious to the activity around her, Sam tried to decipher the sounds.

Woods…

Watch…

No escape...

Were they actual words or just her imagination? What woods and what or who was she to watch out for? Sam knew the message was for her alone. She was the only one who could hear the dead. She was the only one who could help.

3

"Is he talking?" Jake hung up his sportscoat on the hook in back of his door.

"Course not," Frank replied. He was seated in one of the chairs, feet propped on the corner of the desk. "I have lots of unknowns typed on the booking report. Won't even speak to the public defender and his arraignment is tomorrow morning."

"I can fill in some of those blanks. What about the bus?"

"It was rented under the name of the American Indian Cultural Center in Chicago. Bill Lighthorse is the director. Claims he doesn't know who picked up the bus or who was on it."

"Get a list of every member. I want names, addresses, phone numbers."

"We're on it." Just as Jake was about to sink into the chair behind his desk, Frank added, "Don't sit down. The captain wants to see us."

They made their way down the aisle to the back office. A massive form filled a thick leather chair. Captain Robinson flapped a beefy hand, motioning for the detectives to come in. They took a seat while the captain finished a phone call.

Jake no sooner settled into a chair then he felt Frank's eyes on him.

"Out with it."

"Did Sam pick up on something? I saw that strange look."

"What look?" Jake knew what Frank was referring to but had hoped no one else had noticed.

"You know that look, the one when she's off in her special little world." He wiggled his fingers and gave an eerie whistle.

Jake's head hurt from trying to find logical explanations for some of the illogical things he had seen his wife and mother-in-law do. Talking to the dead, communing with Nature. Even Alex's ability to communicate with animals and make it rain were still difficult for Jake to accept.

Jake slid his eyes toward his partner and gave him his customary *I don't have time for this* glare.

Robinson ended his call and lumbered over to close the door. He had a tight-cropped Afro and mocha-colored skin. No one would dare call him overweight to his face. He was two hundred eighty pounds of mean muscle.

"Is this the hot seat, Captain?" Frank asked.

"If mine is hot, yours is hot." Robinson lowered his bulk onto his custom built swivel chair. He no longer had to wedge himself into a standard-sized chair. "Mayor Jenkin's size elevens are up Murphy's ass and I'd hate to tell you what Chief Murphy has up mine. Breyton wants Mr. Red Cloud charged with attempted murder. The only way Breyton will drop all charges is if we look the other way and let him continue his construction."

"Not going to happen," Jake said. "By this time tomorrow an archeological crew will be combing the area."

"Not to mention it will be on the front page of tomorrow's *Post Tribune*," Frank added.

Robinson smacked his hands together as though brushing off dirt. "Then it's out of our hands, the way I like it." His chuckle was honey-lacquered and resonant. The chair creaked and moaned as he leaned back. "Any word on the stolen items?"

"The baby dicks are trying to locate the people who were on the bus," Frank said. "No progress yet." Andy Brainard and Maury Jackson were the newest and youngest detectives in the department and usually inherited all the grunt work. Of course, no one called them that to their faces but on more than one occasion Captain Robinson's office door had been open when he had spouted his favorite term for them.

"I still don't understand why they took them." Robinson's head swiveled on a neck buried somewhere under his size eighteen shirt collar. His dark eyes leveled on Jake, who just shrugged.

"According to Sam, they don't trust the authorities to return the bones in a timely fashion, if at all."

The phone rang and Robinson clamped a mitt-sized hand on the receiver.

"Robinson." He listened briefly, grabbed a pen and took notes, then grunted a good-bye and hung up. "This is yours, Jake." He ripped off the piece of paper and handed it across the desk. "Inga Svenson is in charge of the archeological team and none too happy that our illustrious mayor contacted a well-connected senator to put a rush on this project. She originally couldn't make it here until next month but the senator threatened to withhold funding if she didn't get here tomorrow. She's bringing with her a Dr. Thomas J. Logan, an archeologist with Illinois Central University and our local college here. What are we doing to secure the site?"

"We have a man there at all times," Frank said, "and Breyton assigned his own security guard to watch our guy."

Robinson shoved away from the desk and unfolded his six-and-a-half-foot frame. "Breyton's insurance company is out taking pictures of the damage to the equipment. His lawyer is also taking statements from the men Mr. Red Cloud threatened. He's in a lot of trouble, Jake."

"I know."

Alex Red Cloud was a transplant from the Eagle Ridge Reservation in South Dakota. He claimed the spirits had sent him to watch over *wicasa waken*, their medicine woman—Sam's mother.

"Not to mention," Robinson continued, "he's throwing our lockup into turmoil. I'm told he's chanting and basically driving the other prisoners crazy. With all these charges, you know the bail will be high."

"He won't pay it," Jake said. "I can tell you that right now. And he will refuse to let Sam or Abby pay it. Alex is going to turn this into a cause. He would chain himself to his jail cell if he could."

* * *

"Hey, sport. Have a rough day?" Jake lifted his son from the baby bouncer on the kitchen table. "Bet it was easier than mine."

The infant yawned and stretched, blinking his surroundings into focus. Long lashes fluttered over eyes which had yet to decide what color to settle on. Some days they looked deep blue, other days dark brown. He had lost the alien newborn features of a misshapen head and spindly appendages. Now his body was filling out, the cheeks pudgy and lips in perpetual search of something to suck on. With fingers clenched tightly, the tiny arms jerked involuntarily. Dillon gave what looked like a half smile then promptly closed his eyes. Jake held him close and kissed his head. A breeze filtered through the patio door bringing with it a blend of aromas from the freesias, peonies and day lilies. The smell of fresh cut grass reminded him that the landscapers had been there, a job Alex insisted on overseeing since he felt the crew always trimmed too close around the flowers and not close enough around the fencing.

Abby appeared next to him, her moccasins silent on the quarry-tiled floor. "Want me to put him in his crib?"

"Not yet." Jake pulled out a chair and sat down. His fingers touched the tiny moccasins on his son's feet, a gift from Tim, Sam's teenage computer geek friend who was spending the summer with the FBI helping to test their computer firewalls. The blankets on the bed in the nursery were of Native American design. The dreamcatcher hanging over the crib and the cradleboard made by Cora, Abby's friend back at Eagle Ridge, were all constant reminders of his son's heritage. He watched as Abby flitted around the kitchen. He couldn't think of a time when she dressed in anything but traditional Native dresses, skirts, and moccasins. Even in winter she wore thick, fringed suede boots.

Sam was different, but then she straddled two worlds. She had inherited her blonde hair and blue eyes from her Caucasian father. Her olive complexion and high cheekbones were from her mother. Very seldom had he seen Sam in Native clothing, other than occasionally wearing moccasins. The medicine bundle she wore, which contained her umbilical cord, sage, and blackgold dust, were as close as she came to revealing the Lakota side of her heritage.

Jake kissed his son's head again while keeping his eyes trained on Abby. She had circumvented his authority earlier and made it difficult for him to do his job, something she had never done before. But he had never had a case before with the potential of pitting himself against his mother-in-law.

Abby set a manila folder on the table next to him. "As you know, Jacob, as a member of the Bureau of Indian Affairs, I will need to be apprised of the archeologists' progress." Nodding toward the folder she added, "Perhaps you should read some background on NAGPRA and maybe you will understand better why we feel the way we do." She smiled, almost a smile of sympathy. "After dinner, I'd like to pack a meal for Alex. Would you take it to him, please? I know he won't eat whatever they give him." She lifted her grandson in her arms. "I'll put him in his crib."

Then she turned away. First she took his authority, then his son, leaving him with a folder of information on the Native American Graves Protection and Repatriation Act and an unspoken request to educate himself. He opened the folder and started to read.

Jake placed the picnic basket in front of the desk clerk. "My mother-in-law packed Alex's dinner. I think she packed enough for every prisoner."

Bob inhaled deeply, closing his eyes to savor the aromas. Bald and muscular, with enough Marine tattoos to thwart any threats from prisoners, he was a department relic who was perfectly happy to remain in the dungeons of the precinct building. "Sure smells good."

"Round steak and gravy, mashed potatoes, candied carrots, and hot apple pie. She has six microwave containers here."

"Well, gee, there's even enough for me. What a lady."

"If Abby keeps this up, she'll have people trying to get arrested just to get in jail." Jake pulled Alex's containers from the basket. "Everything is still warm."

"Well then, dinner is served." Bob pawed through the basket for his share. He set it aside then grabbed the keys to lockup. As he opened the door, disinfectant odors swirled around the stale air. One thing Bob was insistent on was that the cells were cleaned often and thoroughly. After all, the scent drifted toward his desk every time the door was opened.

Bob unlocked Alex's cell door, then closed and locked the door behind Jake. Lockup consisted of ten cells bisected by an eight-foot-wide aisle. Since there were two bunks in each cell, prisoners were doubled up. Bob saved himself walking time by filling the cells closest to the door. Alex had a cell to himself across from two occupied cells.

"This is not an everyday occurrence," Bob barked out to the other prisoners. "If I had my way, you'd get McDonald's."

"White Castle is fine with me," said a black youth. Bob pulled his hand away, letting the aromas of a home cooked meal drift into the cell. "Hey, where you'all going with that?"

"Sounded to me like you didn't want this." Bob slipped the meal through the slot in the cell door. "I don't want to hear no arguing or chanting for the next half hour. Got it?" He gave a nod to Jake before returning to the outer office.

"Abby was afraid you'd starve to death." Jake set the plates on the bed and handed Alex a plastic knife and fork. No response, not even a "thank you". Jake pulled up a chair and watched as Alex shoveled in the food. Lockup was quiet for once. Not one complaint about fast food hamburgers and how it was extreme cruelty to force them to eat cold food. It was probably the first time they had a home cooked meal delivered.

"The archeologists will be arriving tomorrow to work the site. It would help if they could see everything that disappeared yesterday."

Alex remained quiet, head down, fork moving in a synchronized rhythm. Jake wondered if withholding the apple pie would get Alex to open up.

"Abby might be arrested if you don't talk. Do you want that?"

Alex kept shoveling. It was an empty threat because Alex knew Jake would never have her arrested. Jake wished he weren't so transparent.

"Landscapers did a shitty job with the yard." Jake watched the fork hover. Alex prided himself on the appearance of the one hundred acres. It was his hand that pruned and pinched, fertilized and coaxed. Alex snapped the lid back on the container and set it aside. Next, he emptied the pie onto a paper plate, closed the lid to the container, then pushed both containers toward Jake. Alex was obviously dismissing him.

Jake stood and called out, "Open up." He waited for Bob to unlock the door. Turning back to Alex, Jake said, "You have my word that the items will never leave Benny's lab. Just tell me where they are."

Alex stabbed the apple pie with the fork and started eating. Jake left the cell.

4

The detectives returned to the site the next morning. Jake studied the two men in dark sunglasses. They were dressed like bouncers in black muscle shirts and black slacks. Their faces were expressionless as they stood guard outside the first ring of barricades. He approached the beat cop whose coffee cup seemed adhered to his mouth. Jake raised his chin in the direction of the guards.

"How long have they been here?"

"Benny the Bruiser and his pal, Popeye? All night." The beat cop never moved the cup. It was an extension of his lower lip. It was unusual to see older men still in the role of beat cop but there were a handful who preferred to be out on the street. Jim Caulfield was one of those men. "I tried to tell them to move along but they said they had orders from Breyton not to leave until their relief gets here." He shook his head and the coffee cup moved in tandem.

"They didn't take anything or move anything?" Jake asked.

"Nope. Stayed outside the perimeter." He drained the cup, wadded it between his thick fingers, and tossed it into a fifty-gallon trash bin several feet away. The boredom of Caulfield's night could be measured by the number of wadded cups and food wrappers lying at the top of the trash. But Jake knew Shorty's Grill didn't deliver.

"You've never left?" Jake's gaze drifted from the fifty-gallon trash can to the face lined with as much street fatigue as age.

Caulfield's puffy eyes caught site of his contribution to the streets and sanitation department. He shook a cigarette from a pack and it adhered itself to the spot on Caulfield's lip that the cup had vacated. "Shorty's my cousin," he explained as he blew out a stream of smoke. "I call, she makes sure I get what I need. I helped her kid out when he started drifting away from the straight and narrow. Her husband was over in Iraq so there was no father figure."

Jake caught wind of the cigarette smoke and unconsciously took a deep breath. He patted his pocket and came out with one of the two cigarettes he allowed himself to carry each day. Caulfield fired up a match and lit it for him.

Traffic barreled down the road with little respect for red lights. The sign in the bank lot across the street flashed an ugly reminder of what kind of day it was going to be. It was ten in the morning and the temperature was already eighty-three degrees.

At the opposite side of the construction site, two squad cars pulled up. Under Frank's direction, the four officers wasted little time setting up another line of wooden barricades along the curb.

"Don't know why they are doing that," Caulfield said through a haze of smoke. "Ain't been no sightseers here. People don't want to see bones. They want blood and guts. Damn idiots."

"They have an archeology crew coming in this morning. We just need to keep the area contained," Jake explained.

Caulfield took a long drag off the cigarette, then dropped the butt in the dirt and smashed it with his shoe. "Nah. Nobody will be interested in that either. It's still blood and guts. Should walk the streets just one night with me. I'll show them idiots blood and guts."

Jake walked over to join Frank just as Dr. Benny Lau, chief medical examiner for Chasen Heights, climbed out of an unmarked car. Benny drew curious stares from the two guards who appeared to make a mental note of everyone who set foot on the property. He was bronze-skinned with coal black hair that fit like a helmet. The colorful Hawaiian shirt and puka shell necklace he wore were not the general attire for a medical examiner.

Frank asked, "Slow day in the lab, Benny?"

"Yes. And my curiosity got the best of me."

A windowless, white van pitted with rust, lumbered over the

dirt road and stopped behind Benny's car. Behind the van a brown truck with an ICU emblem on the side came to a skidding stop sending clouds of gritty sand into the air.

"Looks like the bone people have arrived," Benny said.

"Ten bucks says Inga Svenson is a blonde bombshell with a nice rack and sexy accent," Frank said.

Benny shook his head. "I say she's Margaret Mead's twin sister dressed in denim and a straw hat."

The three leaned against Benny's vehicle, arms folded across their chests. The driver's door on the white van opened and a portly, gray-haired woman stepped out. She held up a hand to shield the sun as she walked toward the men. She paused momentarily to shove her hair under a straw hat while she gazed longingly at the pile of dirt on the side of the pit. There was a certain glaze to her eyes that told everyone she was definitely in her element.

"Gentlemen." She gave a nod and stuck a hand out to Jake. Behind her, two college-aged students were dragging equipment from the van.

"You looked her up on the Internet, didn't you?" Frank whispered.

"So I did," Benny whispered back.

A man dressed in khaki from head to toe with an Australian outback safari hat perched on his head emerged from the truck through a cloud of dust. From the shade of his tan, it was evident that he spent most of his time outside.

"Sergeant Mitchell? I'm Inga Svenson."

Jake was surprised at the firmness of her grasp. He introduced her to Frank and Benny.

Inga pulled on the khaki shirt and dragged the man forward. "This is Professor Thomas Logan. We affectionately call him T.J." Inga looked toward the van and waved over the two college students. She wove an arm through the young woman's. "This is Angel Morgan, a meticulous and bright graduate student." Angel had a splash of freckles across a face that had that just-scrubbed look. A pixie haircut had obviously been chosen for ease of care when on digs, just as cut-offs and a white tee-shirt were picked for comfort. She gave a shy nod at the men.

"And this is Gregory Stiles." A bob of red hair hovered over wire-rimmed glasses. He was tall and lanky and moved with the nervous awkwardness of a marionette puppet. Greg made the rounds of handshakes.

"I understand all the bones and artifacts have been removed from the pit?" Logan cast an accusing glare at the officers as though suspecting they hadn't done their jobs.

"Not everything," Jake replied. He kept his voice even but his eyes told the professor not to try his patience. "One skull and a few bones from the mound were moved to Dr. Lau's lab. However, his people have not removed anything else from the mound. That has been left for you."

"I'd like Greg and Angel to start in the pit," Inga said. "They will set up the equipment and the grid." She nodded toward the mound. "I'll start with what has already been scooped out."

"And I'd like to take the items back to my lab at the local college here in town," Dr. Logan added.

"Out of the question," Jake said. "All the bones and any artifacts we find will be taken to our medical examiner's lab. You are more than welcome to do your examinations there but they will not leave his lab."

"Fine." The professor was not one to back down. "But I want them in an isolated room limited to our access only. No press, no outsiders."

Sam slid onto the wooden seat next to Abby. She whispered to her mother, "Who's the judge?"

The woman seated at the judge's bench was studying case reports through square-cut bifocals. She wore little makeup and preferred *au natural* for her hair since it was more salt than pepper.

The woman suddenly looked familiar to Sam.

"Judge Vera Purdy?" Sam whispered. "Oh, no." Judge Judy was tame compared to Judge Purdy. Sam's eyes scoured the audience. She wasn't sure who was a reporter, a curiosity seeker, or an acquaintance of Breyton.

It was an old building renovated to change one large courtroom to four smaller, cookie-cutter-style rooms, each with seating for fewer than seventy-five people. Builders had kept the seasoned wooden seats, judge's bench, and railings. Since the case had been on the front page of the local newspaper, Sam wasn't surprised the room was packed.

The judge nodded to the bailiff. A side door opened and an officer led Alex to a table.

The bailiff stood and tugged on her suit jacket in an unsuccessful attempt to stretch it over her midriff. "Case Number 12D010720FA015. Breyton Construction vs. Alex Red Cloud on the charge of trespassing, assault and attempted murder."

"Your honor," a tall man in clothes that smelled of money stood. "Attorney Stephen Weber representing Elton Breyton the Third and the Breyton Construction Company."

Judge Purdy glared at another man seated next to Alex. "And you are here for the defendant?"

The public defender straightened his tie and scrambled out of his seat. "Ummm, yes, your honor. Aaron Jacoby. I've been assigned the case. Attorney Johnson is out of…"

"I don't need an absentee list, Mr. Jacoby."

Sam leaned toward her mother. "Is this the best they could do? He looks nineteen. Mom, there has to be an attorney at the Center that can help him."

"No. Besides, he didn't want one. You know Alex. He's stubborn."

The judge looked over her bifocals at the young attorney. "Your client understands the charges against him?"

The legal pup cleared his throat. "I'm not sure."

The judge's right eyebrow lifted slightly. "You aren't sure?"

"He won't speak."

"Does he speak English?"

"I think so."

"You think?" Judge Purdy shifted in her seat and scanned the courtroom. Her eyes settled on Abby.

"Mom?" Sam whispered.

"He asked me not to help," Abby whispered back.

"He didn't ask me." Sam stood. "Your Honor, Mr. Red Cloud does speak English but refuses to. He feels very strongly about…"

"You are out of order, young lady."

"Alex was only protecting the bones and artifacts that were unearthed," Sam argued.

"Protecting them with deadly arrows, I understand."

"They weren't poisonous, your Honor."

Laughter erupted in the courtroom. Judge Purdy pounded her gavel several times.

"If I could just explain for him," Sam started.

"Ainila!" Silence! Alex barked.

Sam shook her head. *"Mak'ya."* Nonsense.

"That's enough," Judge Purdy shouted. Sam reluctantly sat down. The judge turned her attention to Alex. "The charge of attempted murder negates any chance of bond, Mr. Red Cloud. I'll give you one last chance to communicate." The judge peeled off her bifocals and waited. After several seconds she checked her watch, then set her glasses back on her nose. "Very well. I will hold you in contempt of court until such time that you deem this court worthy of your cooperation. I will also instruct the magistrate to check your assets. If you own so much as a truck you will have to hire your own attorney. You will not be entitled to a public defender." She gave a nod to the bailiff. "Next case."

5

Sam opened the front door and found her friend, Jackie, standing on the second stair, baby bottle in one hand, a burp cloth over her shoulder. "How was he?" Sam asked.

"My little angel is wonderful," Jackie gushed. She looked over Sam's shoulder. "Where's Abby?"

"She dropped me off and went grocery shopping. Told me to invite the archeology crew for dinner." Sam trailed Jackie through the study into the kitchen, her eyes glancing down at her friend's feet. "It's so strange seeing you without shoes."

"Your mama has a way of turning a demand into a request that you barely even notice. She told me I would probably be a lot more comfortable climbing the stairs if I didn't have my four-inch hooker heels on. Although she didn't say it quite like that. But the translation is the same: "Don't go carrying my grandson if your toes and heels aren't level with the ground." Jackie cackled, pressing a hand against her massive chest."

Sam grabbed her friend's hand. Jackie always kept her nails long, shaped like talons and painted to match her outfits. They had been reduced to just one inch in length. "What happened to your nails?"

Jackie sighed and held up both hands. "They'll grow. Just had to trim them back a bit."

"Abby?"

"No, me. I was afraid I'd stab the little guy. My mama used to cook hams that weigh more than him."

Sam grabbed two bottles of water from the refrigerator while Jackie grabbed the baby monitor. A soft breeze seeped in through the screen door bringing with it the smells of summer. They stepped out onto the flagstone patio. Planters filled with wave petunias and impatiens in a variety of colors spilled over the edges and down the brick wall. Hummingbirds whirled in suspended animation by a feeder, their tiny wings beating too fast for any human eye to detect. The two women convened around a table shielded from the bright sunlight by a large umbrella.

"I really appreciate your taking time away from the store to help out."

Jackie dismissed her with a wave of a hand. "My girls are pretty good. And if they run into any trouble, I'm just a phone call away." Jackie owned a boutique near the mall which featured tasteful lingerie. The previous owner also provided lunch time specials for busy executives in the way of adult entertainment. Scantily clad women would dance and strip in private rooms. Jackie phased out that part of the business and transformed it into a 900 sex call business that brought in more profits than the clothing.

"I just never..." Sam's eyes scanned the entire length of her friend, from her Donna Summer-type hair that had been twisted and piled on top of her head in a mess of curls to the full Whitney Houston lips. In all the years Sam had known Jackie she had never been out in public without lipstick. Her eyes settled on Jackie's silk blouse spotted with something Sam hoped would come out at the cleaners.

"What? This?" Jackie raised one leg showing her red crop pants. The blouse she wore had geometric designs in red, white and black. "The whole outfit looks like silk but its rayon polyester. It can take wee-wee and spit up and go right in the washer. Bought a whole wardrobe just for him. And these colors are what babies see most. I read that somewhere."

"You are really getting into this. Maybe you should have one of your own."

"Oh, no. It's like Buckingham Palace. Nice to visit but you don't want to own one. Too much upkeep." Jackie pushed the morning paper aside and dragged the baby monitor over. "What happened in court?"

"A disaster." Sam sighed with frustration. She filled her friend in on Alex, his attorney, and her attempts to help. "Short and sweet. Alex refused to speak and was found in contempt of court."

"Attempted murder is a serious charge, Sam. He can't stay silent forever. What about your family attorney? Why let some wet-behind-the-ears public defender represent him?"

"My attorney doesn't take criminal cases. I wanted to find a Native American attorney but the only ones are in Chicago and their case loads prevented them from taking on Alex's case. Now things are really tense between Abby and Jake. Alex won't speak English. Abby won't tell Jake the names of the people who were on the bus or what happened to the bones and artifacts. Because of the murder charge we can't even post bail. Breyton won't drop the charges. It's a nightmare."

Jackie unfolded the morning papers which pictured the construction site on the front page with Breyton jabbing a finger at the trespassers in the pit. "I remember this guy."

"Please, tell me he was one of your customers so I can get creative."

"Creative? I know your version of creative, sweetie. Usually it means blackmail."

"I can do blackmail. I like blackmail." Sam's eyes lit up at the prospect of doing some harm to the arrogant Elton Breyton.

"Rein in your panting, girlfriend. I don't have that kind of dirt on him. I just remember a nasty divorce that was in the paper. He had dumped his wife and latched onto a trophy wife."

Sam studied the vain face on the front page. The limo, the bodyguards, the well-connected construction company that managed to rake in most of the local government contracts. "Why does that not surprise me?" she said.

Sam left Dillon in the capable hands of Jackie with a promise that she would be back within the hour. After packing sandwiches and drinks into a cooler on wheels, she drove to the construction site. She was surprised that all the news vans were gone and assumed they had tired of waiting for some big revelation and moved on to other stories.

She parked in the bank parking lot and dragged the cooler across the street to the construction site. The wheels rattled along the sidewalk. Jake's unsmiling face followed her approach. Her curiosity about the case far outweighed the fact that she was now a civilian and shouldn't be involved in police work. Sometimes Sam didn't have a choice. She was the only link the victims had to tell their stories.

Sam had the unique ability to hear the dead speak. By touching the deceased or something the victim or killer touched, she could pick up clues which ultimately lead her to the killer. Jake wasn't too fond of her gift because it made her more of a target. But Sam couldn't give it back or stop it. It was a gift inherited from her ancestors. Abby's powers were with the living which is why Abby seldom shook hands with anyone, unless she wanted to. Sam's powers were with the dead, and sometimes living, if the person were so evil Sam could sense it…the prickly skin, an icy cold rush, the pounding of her heart, and sometimes an uncontrollable urge to flee. Neither of them could predict when it would happen or how much information they could learn. And whether Sam was still a cop or not didn't matter much. Abby had tried to explain to Jake on more than one occasion that the spirits could care less about jurisdiction.

Frank was just unwrapping a protein bar when she arrived at the back of Benny's station wagon. "Real food?" he said.

"Certainly better than that compressed cardboard you are about to stick in your mouth."

"Is this going to be a daily ritual," Jake asked, "or a one-time fact-finding mission?"

"I'm on a goodwill mission from Abby." Sam scanned the area and saw two workers running string. A gray-haired woman was sifting dirt through a screen outside the pit.

"This is like waiting for paint to dry," Sam said.

Frank dug through the cooler for a sandwich. "Yeah. It's no wonder these people work for a whole year on a dig."

"We don't have a whole year." Jake unwrapped a sandwich and accepted the Pepsi Sam handed him.

"Patience." Benny jotted down notes in a log book. "The dead are not going anywhere. That's why I work where I work and you work with crime. I can afford to be patient." Benny marked a tag and tied it to one of the longer bones.

Sam reached a hand toward the bones but Benny slapped it away. "Where's the skull that was by the mound?"

"Already in the lab along with all the other bones," Benny replied.

That wasn't good. Sam would have to make a trip to the lab. "Why does the set up take so long?" She watched a man in an outback hat shaking a screen over a second wheelbarrow, a look of disgust on his face.

"No different than the time it takes to set up a grid when you find a body," Benny replied.

"We should be out looking for the stolen artifacts and bones." Jake leveled his mirrored sunglasses at Sam. "Unless you might know where they are."

"Can't help you there."

"Not that you would if you knew." Jake didn't make that comment a question.

Sam said, "Did you check out the Cultural Center?"

"We have it under surveillance. They'll turn up."

"Glad you have so much confidence," Frank said. "They are probably right under our damn noses."

Benny waved a wrapped sandwich in the air. "Inga."

The straw hat lifted and a face smudged with dirt smiled. Within seconds a crowd converged upon the station wagon. Inga and her crew used sanitary wipes to clean their hands.

The man in the outback hat brought up the rear. "Really hate to stop," he said. "There's a lot of work to do."

"You have to eat sometime," Sam said.

T.J.'s scowl evaporated as his gaze washed over her. "Especially when the food is brought by the delights of you." He had a sudden Australian accent.

His flirtation was overkill but Sam smiled in spite of herself. She held out her hand. "I'm Sam Casey." With a nod toward Jake she added, "I'm with him."

"Well then. In case things don't work out." T.J. bent and kissed her hand.

"Can it, T.J.," Inga barked. "Come." She motioned to the workers. "Mind our manners."

Inga introduced the workers. "This is Greg, graduate student who is the tops in his class." The lanky guy with the bad hair day gave a two finger salute. Inga motioned toward the young woman pulling up next to Greg. Angel is our resident tomboy. She's also doing post graduate work. And this is Professor T.J. Logan," Inga said with a shake of her head. "Has a bit of a big head since the ladies think he looks like Keith Urban. He agrees so much so that he sometimes breaks into an Australian accent. But don't let his charm fool you. He feels everything belongs to science first."

"Where would science be without the discovery of the Mayan ruins, Aztalan, Spirit Cave, Cahokia or Mesa Verde?"

"Oh, T.J., zip it," Inga snapped. "Pay him no mind. He's ninety percent science and ten percent heart."

"Perhaps we'll have more time to discuss this over dinner," Sam said. "My mother is inviting your crew to our house for a traditional Native feast."

"Sounds like fun," Angel said.

"Wait." T.J. had suddenly lost his accent. "Don't tell me you are related to the bunch that protested the dig."

Jake explained, "Alex is a friend of the family. Naturally, he won't be there but it will give you and Abby a chance to talk about your concerns."

"Well, I don't like to save everything for the last minute," T.J. said, "so whatever we unearth today I will want to take to your examiner's lab and get them logged into my computer."

Inga dismissed him with a wave. "We'll be there."

"Good thing," Frank said. "Because when it comes from Abby, it isn't a request…it's a demand."

"Dinner is at six," Sam added.

"Whoa, we can't allow dogs in here." Bob walked around the desk and admired the Irish setter. "Even if they are cute."

Jake had Poco on a leash, her tail thumping back and forth against his leg. "This is the department's new drug sniffing dog," Jake said. Poco jumped up on Bob, licked his arm as the desk clerk patted her head.

"Yeah, right."

"We need to check out the cells." Jake held up the picnic basket.

"There are rules against bribery, Jake." Bob peered into the basket. "What's on the menu tonight?"

"Chicken and dumplings. They are leftovers from the freezer. Abby is making a traditional meal tonight for her guests. You are missing buffalo steaks and corn bread."

Dave took a long whiff. "Smells heavenly."

"Brownies for dessert."

Bob pulled the keys off the rack. "Is your mother-in-law available by any chance?"

"Not in your wildest dreams." Jake pulled out two containers and set them on the counter. He left the basket with Bob to disperse the meals to the other prisoners and grabbed the two containers for Alex. "How has he been?"

"Still driving the other prisoners nuts with his chanting. He didn't eat breakfast or lunch. Must have known you were coming."

Bob turned the key in the lock and opened the door.

Poco immediately started to whine, sensing Alex's presence. She pulled on the leash and started barking. The whining intensified, her tail beating frantically. Bob set the picnic basket on the floor and unlocked the cell. Poco made a dash for Alex.

"Hey, girl." Alex cradled Poco's face in his hands.

"Yo, the man does speak English," one of the prisoners said. His dark face was wide and pressed against the bars in the cell across the aisle from Alex. His cell mate rose from a cot and joined him at the bars. He sported a bruised cheek, cut lip, and a local softball team jersey. A third man in the next cell paced the floor in spit shine shoes and a tailor-made suit. His eyes were ringed in red.

"Hope you are getting him the hell out of here. I haven't had a good night's sleep since I got here," red eyes said.

The man with the bruised cheek curled his fingers around the bars and yelled across the aisle. "Hey, how come he gets conjugal visits?" Laughter erupted in the cell as the two palm-slapped and knuckle-rapped each other.

Alex ignored them and immediately switched to his Native language as he rubbed Poco's coat with his hands.

"Dinner sure does smell good," another prisoner said.

Bob closed Alex's cell door and proceeded to pass out the dinners. "Now sit down and be quiet."

"Abby invited everyone from the dig over for dinner." Jake handed Alex the container of chicken and dumplings. He instructed Poco to sit, then handed her a treat. "Breyton hired two guards to watch the area at night. Dr. Svenson and her crew have set up their grid. So far they have found bone fragments, arrowheads, and beaded artifacts."

Alex shoveled in the food with a large spoon, glancing every now and then at Poco who had finished her treat and was resting her head and paws on Alex's foot. Jake gave him sufficient time to respond but Alex remained silent.

"Abby told me what happened in court. Breyton was hoping to get some pull from Springfield but you know whose side Governor Meacham is on. Guess it helps when his wife brings her jewelry to you to repair."

No reaction. Alex avoided eye contact with Jake, choosing to stare at Poco or at the cell door. Jake filled the silence with short biographies on T.J., Inga, and the two graduate students.

The entire lockup was quiet except for murmurs of approval on the meals. Alex set the lid on the empty container and placed it on the bed. Poco lifted her head and whined, sensing that Jake was ready to leave.

Alex leaned over and whispered something to Poco.

The steel door slammed shut and Bob entered holding the picnic basket. "Shove all empty containers to the slot in your door, guys. And thank the sergeant for being so good to you. If I had my way, you'd get crusts of day old bread."

Jake clipped the leash on Poco. She looked up at him with those soulful eyes. "Hey, don't blame me if Alex doesn't want to go home." Alex glared at him as Jake pulled on Poco's leash. "Let's go, Poco."

"Hey," the broad-faced prisoner yelled. "Aren't you taking him with?"

Alex stretched out on his cot and started chanting.

Jake had tried Abby's cooking, Poco, even complaints about the poor landscaping. So far nothing worked. But he had a couple more tricks up his sleeve.

6

"You have one beautiful house, Abby." Inga cut herself another piece of corn bread. "And to serve us a traditional Native American meal was so appropriate."

It had taken close to thirty minutes for Inga and the others to view all four thousand square feet of house with its pottery, rugs and furnishings as well the collection of books in the library, the gym equipment and the view from the Florida room.

"This sure beats eating monkey brains in New Guinea," T.J. said.

"Please, professor. Not another one of your stories." Greg grabbed the wine bottle and filled Angel's glass.

Jake drilled a glare at Sam. She recognized that look. He wanted to be anywhere doing anything else than breaking bread with T.J. She saw Abby place a hand on Jake's arm. Her way of saying, "Patience. It will be over soon."

"I want to hear about the Kennewick Man," Angel said. "I wanted to study the pre-Columbian era but could never fit it into my class schedule."

Sam couldn't believe how different everyone looked once they were out of their dusty work clothes. Angel needed very little makeup. Her just-scrubbed, girl-next-door look was appealing, especially to Greg who hadn't kept his eyes off her all night. Both appeared to be in their mid-twenties. Inga preferred a clean work shirt and slacks, minus the straw hat. T.J. looked every bit the professor in a tweed sport coat and starched shirt. And he hadn't taken his eyes off Sam all night.

"The debate has been going on since the remains were discovered in 1996," Abby said. "So you can certainly understand how scientific studies can delay the return of remains to the proper tribe in a timely fashion."

"If I remember correctly, the remains were given back to the tribes in 2000." T.J. stabbed another piece of buffalo steak from the platter in the middle of the table.

"Yes, but in 2002," Sam reminded him, "the Ninth Circuit Court stated that the tribes had gone too far in claiming the remains were pre-Columbian so the remains were not covered by NAGPRA but by the Archaeological Resources Protection Act."

"It's all ridiculous, if you ask me," T.J. said. "It's the old chicken and egg question. Who knows who was here first? It's difficult for tribes to claim any remains over five hundred years old. Tribes have to conduct studies of remains to determine their antiquity in order to claim them yet it is against their religious principles to conduct studies. I for one believe the theory that Kennewick Man is of Japanese descent. The Ainu are an ethnic group with Caucasian-like features that lived on the islands. Besides, scientific studies benefit all people, including tribes. Without these studies, we'll never learn about early populations."

"So you are siding with the Michigan anthropologist who says that modern ethnic characteristics were the same as during the time of Kennewick Man." Inga shook her head. "That is an argument that has been circulating for years."

"It's almost impossible to do a racial composition on a recent corpse," Jake interjected. "So how can anyone assume racial makeup of any remains from that era? This sounds like an argument that can never be settled to anyone's satisfaction."

"Finally, a voice of reason," T.J. said.

Abby sighed. "The important thing is Kennewick Man is being held at the University of Washington in Seattle, still waiting on another hearing, still out of the reach of his ancestors. It has been over ten years. We became mantel pieces stored in cardboard boxes in university storerooms. We won't become souvenirs stored in cardboard boxes in your storeroom, Professor Logan. That is unacceptable."

"What about you, Greg?" Sam asked, attempting to steer the conversation away from uncomfortable subjects. "How did you get selected for this dig?"

"I took a couple of classes from Professor Logan here at Cal-Sag College, then I took my graduate courses at Illinois Central. Professor Logan teaches at both. I met Inga during the Hoxie Farm dig."

"The one right off Interstate 394?" Abby asked. "Were you there when they started the dig in 2002?"

"No, I came a couple years later."

"I was there in 2002." Angel said.

"So you took Professor Logan's class, too?" Sam asked. She saw T.J.'s eyes roll toward the ceiling.

T.J. snorted. "What I remember is you almost compromised the entire dig when you dumped one of the screen boxes during a temper tantrum."

Angel's face flushed. "It was my first dig and it wasn't a temper tantrum."

Silence settled over the table. Greg cleared his throat. "We found over two hundred pieces of trade copper, the most ever found at a dig site."

Abby started to clear the empty plates away.

"I'll give you a hand," Angel offered quickly.

"Thank you. Just stack the plates on the counter," Abby instructed. "I'll load the dishwasher later."

Sam and Jake escaped to the kitchen to retrieve the dessert. Sam studied their guests through the pass-through in the kitchen. Inga had made an impression on Abby. She was very much like Cora, Abby's closest friend on the Eagle Ridge Reservation. She wasn't afraid to speak her mind, very much like Abby. Angel probably needed a little help in that regard. She was noticeably hurt by the professor's comments. But Sam noticed something else in Angel's eyes when she looked at T.J. Longing? Why not? Every other woman appeared to be attracted to the man. She felt Jake's presence behind her and leaned against his chest.

She turned her head slightly and whispered, "Still love me?"

"I'll get back to you on that," he replied which brought a smile to Sam's face. "Dinners here have been anything but boring," Jake added. "But I don't think I've ever heard your mother so…"

"Opinionated? Resolved? Forceful?" Sam smiled. "You've never seen her at a tribal meeting before."

A cry that sounded like a cat mewing erupted from the monitor on the counter. Sam checked the clock above the sink. "Someone's up." She left to retrieve Dillon while Jake heated up a bottle in the microwave.

Sam returned to the kitchen just as T.J. was continuing his barrage. Dillon was more interested in what she was pulling out of the microwave.

"There's nothing worse than having someone compromise a dig site," T.J. grumbled as he refilled his wine glass. "Just like this construction site we are at now."

"How is it any different than scientists taking off with artifacts and bones? Did you feel that was right?" Abby asked.

"Absolutely not. Sheer grave robbing," T.J. replied. "And that prevents people like me from doing our work. We prefer unaltered sites and unblemished artifacts. Every dig tells a story and with just one item out of place, it loses its scientific value. Take your medicine bundle, for example. I can tell yours is far more significant than your daughter's. You are pretty high up in the pecking order. If we found one of those in our dig next to specific bones, we would know this was an important person. But if the bones were removed along with the…"

"We all get the point," Inga said, "but it's no use rehashing it now. The dig has already been compromised."

"Yes," T.J. argued, "but with her standing in the community, she can demand that the items be returned."

"Doesn't help. We have no idea where each bone and artifact were buried anymore than we know about that pile of dirt with everything all scooped up by the back hoe," Greg said.

Sam figured this was just as good a time as any to change the subject which was about to get even more heated. She carried Dillon and the bottle into the dining room.

"Oh, look," Angel cooed. "He is so precious. Can I feed him?"

"Sure." Angel stood and Sam placed him in her arms. "This is Dillon everyone." As expected, the women gushed, the men just nodded. Sam didn't know why she hovered. Angel was an adult and certainly capable of holding a baby. She waited until Angel sat down before returning to her seat. Angel held Dillon in the crook of her arm. "He is so beautiful, isn't he, T.J.?"

T.J.'s look of disinterest told Sam he was either paying some hefty child support to someone or just didn't have any paternal instincts whatsoever.

He glared at Jake. "What are you doing to find the missing bones and artifacts?"

As always, Jake was vague. "We have several stops to make in the morning."

Sam saw Abby lift the knife from the cake plate, her knuckles white from grasping it so tightly. "More cake anyone?" Abby asked.

While everyone else had more coffee or an after dinner drink, T.J. said his thanks and good nights, making a point to stress that he wanted to get an early start tomorrow. Sam walked him to the door and T.J. took the opportunity to grab her hand.

"Tell me." He nodded in the direction of the dining room, where Jake was watching his every move. "Where did you meet him? In a prison?"

"Excuse me?"

"Jake. Was he a prison guard or something? He looks surly enough to have been one."

Sam studied her husband. Yes, he didn't have Hollywood good looks. And his skeptical nature did give the appearance that he was suspicious of everyone and everything. His size alone would make him threatening. Where Frank had to work over the years to add some bulk to his body, Jake's was a gift from Nature. At six-two and just over two hundred pounds, Jake could easily grab T.J. by the collar and lift him over his head. It was the danger he exuded that attracted women. He was the strong, silent type with soft brown eyes that Sam found utterly appealing. She caught herself smiling and only half listening to T.J.

"To get a woman as beautiful as you, he must have laid all this money at your feet." T.J. glanced around the entry, implying the size of the house.

"It isn't his. But how like a man to think a woman has to rely on her husband for financial assistance."

"Really." He was noticeably impressed. "Then he must excel in other areas."

Sam knew exactly where he was headed but she wasn't going to take the bait. "Yes, he does have a great talent." T.J. leaned in close as though she were going to share some intimate secrets. Sam whispered in his ear, "Jake's an excellent shot."

7

The next morning Sam dropped by Benny's office. She expected to find him in the lab set aside for the dig but he wasn't. A printed sign was taped to the door.

Breyton Dig – No Admittance

Through the plate glass window she could see four tables where bones were scattered like intricate jigsaw puzzles. Additional tables lined up against one wall contained pottery, arrowheads and other artifacts discovered so far at the site.

Sam pressed her hand against the glass. She could feel a pull from some unseen force. Whether it was her own desire to seek answers or someone else's need to see justice served she wasn't sure. All she knew for certain was she had to get into the room. She saw Benny's reflection in the glass.

"I'll pretend I don't see you here, Sam." Benny pointed at the sign on the door. "Logan runs a pretty tight ship."

"I find it hard to believe that you haven't been in there."

"Actually, I have the only other key card and the good professor has me signing in and out, in my own lab no less." Benny swiped his card through the reader. The light flashed green and he held the door open. "What T.J. doesn't know…"

Sam smiled and followed him in. Besides Abby and Alex, Benny was one of the few people who understood Sam's *gift*. "You could consider it a business call since I'm representing the interests of the Native American community."

"Chasen Heights doesn't have a Native American community, unless you are counting Alex, your mother, and yourself, which," he added, "does not a community make." He grabbed a clipboard off the wall.

Sam circled the table to stand across from Benny. "Did you clean these up?" All of the bones were stark white, not the typical brown color of bones that had been buried.

"What? And subject myself to the wrath of that egotistical T.J.?" He moved to the next table which contained even fewer bones. "These are just as they were found. Bleached by Nature herself. My guess is the remains were exposed to the sun for a long period of time before someone decided to give them a proper burial. I'm sure we won't be able to locate all of them. Animals might have carted a few meals to chew on."

"Thanks for the visual."

"Either way, no one is allowed to touch them. Professor Logan is waiting for some expensive equipment to arrive to do his formal analyses." He raised the clipboard in his hands. "I have been going over his notes and it's obvious he knows his stuff."

Sam strained to read the notes upside down.

Benny flipped the clipboard up and hugged it to his chest.

"Come on, Benny. Just a little info."

"You tell me." Benny had always been her mentor. When Sam had first joined the force, she would spend evenings at Benny's elbow trying to learn all she could about causes of death, wound patterns, and gun shot residue. And she would soak it up as fast as she could. Her goal had always been to work in Homicide. It was where she felt she could do the most good.

Sam rubbed her hands together vigorously. "Let's see." She scanned each table quickly, focusing only on the pelvic bones since they were among the few skeletal remains found for all victims. "Four tables, four bodies. All female." Sam knew that women had a larger space within the pelvis for childbearing.

"Correct," Benny said.

The intercom on the wall squawked and a female voice said, "Dr. Lau, it's your wife."

"Be right back." As an afterthought, Benny added, "Don't

touch anything."

Sam approached one of the tables and leaned down for a closer look. Most of the rib bones were intact, given the amount of damage a backhoe could cause. However, it did seem that Alex was able to stop the workers before too much damage had been done. She turned to make sure Benny wasn't watching, then walked over to the table with the skull. Cautiously, she lifted it from the table. Immediately she heard soft whispers filling the room, victims struggling for attention.

Watch

Woods

Danger

It almost seemed like a mantra, a similar warning to what she had heard at the dig site. It wasn't so much the words she was hearing as the urgency of the words. Were they the last words of the victims or were they a warning of things to come? Sam couldn't help but feel they were warning her. But why? What does Sam's present life have to do with what happened to Natives two hundred years ago?

"As usual, you still have a problem taking orders."

Sam almost dropped the skull. She hadn't heard Benny return.

"You okay?" he asked.

"Yes." She shook the cobwebs from her head. "It's nothing." Had the woman met a violent death? Been killed by trappers? Hunters from another tribe? Sam dragged her thoughts back to the skull. She moved it from side to side, concentrating on the jaw bone just below the ear. "Confirms female. Women have rounder jaws."

"Allows them to talk more," Benny said with a chuckle.

"What about cause of death?"

Benny nodded toward the rib bones on one of the tables. Sam set the skull down and joined Benny at the next table. Her finger touched a marking on one of the ribs. Puzzled, she moved to the next table and found a similar marking on one of the ribs.

"Stabbed?"

"According to the professor's notes, he is leaning toward penetration by an arrow and I would have to concur. Doesn't look like a knife made the damage." Benny wrapped an arm around her shoulder. "Come on. Let me buy you a coffee."

Sam's gaze drifted back to the tables and wondered what the four women had done to warrant death. Had they tried to escape? Had they refused to be slaves? So far the dead weren't telling her much.

"What do you think of the archeologists?" Sam asked, once they had their cups of coffee and were seated around Benny's desk.

"Inga and T.J. both know their stuff, although T.J. is not too humble. Angel and Greg are pretty knowledgeable and enthusiastic. I can tell they have been doing this awhile. Angel is quite meticulous. She wouldn't give me one item that hadn't been thoroughly brushed and cleaned of minute particles. Greg is pretty inquisitive about the artifacts."

"That's for sure. He really picked Abby's brain last night about some of the items."

"What about Alex? How's his case going?"

"Neither Abby nor I can get Alex to come to his senses. Even if he caves for the judge and starts speaking English, he still has the attempted murder charge hanging over his head."

"Breyton is an ass. He used to get a listing of all the properties in arrears for back taxes. He'd snap up houses out from under little old ladies who hadn't recognized tax bills when they got them." Benny looked at Sam's half empty cup. "Coffee stale? Want me to make a fresh pot?"

Sam winced, feeling the heartburn scorching her insides. "No thanks. The acid is making me a little queasy." Her attention was drawn to the bones across the hall. She wondered if the queasiness had less to do with the coffee and more to do with the warnings.

* * *

"Not a bad looking building," Frank said as they entered the Native American Cultural Center on Lake Shore Drive in Chicago.

A guard sat behind a circular desk in the lobby, his eyes at half mast as the quiet and solitude rendered him near comatose. A large map showing locations of early tribal settlements was on one wall. Glass cases lined the remaining walls displaying various types of pottery, jewelry, clothing, and other artifacts relating to the different tribes. A bronze sculpture of an Indian on horseback guarded the escalator to the second floor.

Jake rapped his knuckles on the desk. The guard's eyes flew open and his body jerked to attention.

"Can I help you?" A name plate on the desk read *Sonny Mehta.*

Jake held up his I.D. and introduced himself and Frank. "We called earlier and spoke to Bill Lighthorse."

"He's expecting you." Sonny jerked a thumb over his shoulder. "Second floor, first door on the right."

The aroma of new wood stain followed them up the escalator. The Cultural Center had moved to its new home four months ago. Overhead track lighting drew their attention to the rugs hanging on the walls.

"Sounds like you had a memorable dinner last night," Frank said with a chuckle.

"It was educational, to say the least. Professor Logan is a work of art but Inga has a way of putting him in his place. He actually made a move on Sam in my presence."

"And he's still breathing?"

Oak flooring met them at the second floor. They walked past additional glass showcases to an office with a door gaping open. The man behind the desk stood slowly. If Alex had a brother, Bill Lighthorse would be his name. His hair was longer and grayer than Alex's and worn in two pigtails rather than one ponytail, the way

Alex preferred. But it was the eyes, narrowed to black beads of distrust and apprehension. His body didn't unfold from the chair, it uncoiled slowly like a snake, not quite sure what to expect. It was a well-practiced movement and Jake suspected it had become a custom.

"Sergeant Mitchell." Bill gave a nod, then shook their hands. "Have a seat."

Jake sat across from Bill. Frank remained standing, choosing to lean against the wall by the door. As Jake engaged the Center's director, it was Frank's job to casually scan the papers lying on the table by the door and on the desk.

"The police have already been here, Sergeant," Bill stated with a shrug. "I'm not sure what more we can do for you." He leaned back in the swivel chair, hands clasped across his stomach. His wrists were covered in silver, turquoise, and coral bracelets.

"Do you know Alex Red Cloud?" Jake asked. Alex had a unique way of combining coral and turquoise in the jewelry he made. One of the bracelets Bill wore resembled Alex's handiwork.

"Of course. I have relatives still living on the Eagle Ridge Reservation in South Dakota." His eyes narrowed even more when he added, "Alex and I were in the same BIA boarding school." For the first time he turned his eyes to Frank. "Do you have any idea what took place at those schools?" He didn't wait for them to answer, just leaned back farther, preparing for a long lecture. "They cut our hair, beat us like dogs. The dorm attendant would rip the clothes off of us and burn them. They washed our bodies with lye soap and refused to let us speak our Native tongue. But Alex always said, 'They think they can take away everything, but they can't take our spirit'."

Jake said, "You are aware of the charges against him."

"I've read the newspapers."

"According to historical documents, this area was inhabited mainly by the Ottawa, Chippewa, Miami, and Potawatomi, not the Sioux." Jake had thought at first that it would be a waste of time for him to read all the papers Abby had left him. In her infinite wisdom she knew they would come in handy.

"All Native people are related."

"If you've read the papers then you also know everything found at the construction site is being delivered to our medical examiner's lab for analysis."

A young boy around six ran into the office. *"Tunkaśila, Tunkaśila."* He halted and stared at the visitors with doe eyes. His coal black hair was in a bowl shape with thick bangs that brushed his eyelids.

"Cody, Grandpa has guests. You should remember to knock."

Cody smiled and edged closer to his grandfather's chair. Bill grabbed the boy's chin and turned his head toward him. "What is this rash? Have you been walking through that poison ivy again?"

"No, *Tunkaśila.*"

Jake's eyes routinely swept over a child's body looking for bruises and questionable injuries. Force of habit. Cody instinctively rubbed at his mouth which only irritated it more. If he had been anywhere near poison ivy, he must have been chewing on it.

"Now what is so important it couldn't wait?" Bill asked. Cody pressed his lips together and stared with apprehension at the visitors. Bill straightened his grandson's shirt collar and tenderly cradled his face. "*Unci* should have your lunch ready. We'll talk later. Now go find your grandmother."

Cody ran from the room in a flash of youthful energy.

"Cute kid," Frank said.

"My daughter and her husband work at the clinic. Grandparents these days do more raising of children than the parents. Cody was a bit of a surprise. His brother, Quince, is fifteen."

Frank asked, "Does Quince by chance play the drums?"

"Not well. Why?" Bill paused, looked from Frank to Jake, his face revealing he had said too much with those two words.

"Was he at the construction site the day Alex was arrested?" Jake asked. Chasen Heights had very few Native Americans and since a few of those at the construction site had appeared to be in their teens, it was a good chance they might have been from Chicago.

The warmth Bill had displayed to his grandson had been replaced by the cold, distant glare that had greeted them.

"Where are most teenagers? 'Nowhere.' 'I don't know.' 'Around.' I'm sure those words aren't uncommon." Bill pressed a button on the phone. "Nona, have you seen Quince?"

The intercom beeped and a voice responded, "Not since breakfast."

Another beep. "Did he say where he was going?"

"Just that he and Andre would be 'hanging out.'" As an afterthought, Nona asked, "Will you be coming home for lunch? It would be nice to have a meal together."

Bill gave a shrug. His visitors for a brief moment were no longer cops but understanding males in the perpetual war between husbands and wives. "Sure. I just need to finish up some business with two visitors."

"Oh, you mean the two detectives? Did you know the sergeant is married to Abby's daughter?"

Bill looked at Jake with a hint of surprise and puzzlement in his eyes. "No, I didn't know that. I'll see you in a little bit." He pushed a button to turn off the intercom and smiled. "Leave it up to gossiping women to know more about what's going on under our noses."

"My hands are tied regarding Alex," Jake admitted. "If you know Alex then you know he is enjoying this one man stand against the establishment."

Bill pushed away from the desk and stood. "Yes, I know Alex but there is no joy when the laws are against you. And I'm sure you know there is no joy in the household when you keep your wife waiting."

"We were hoping you could give us the names of everyone who had been on the bus that day." Jake pushed his business card across the desk. "And anyone else you might suspect had been responsible for the disappearance of the bones and artifacts from the construction site. Since you now know that I'm Abby's son-in-law, you realize I will do everything in my power to see that no agency or university makes claims to those items."

"That's the operative word now, isn't it, Sergeant? Not everything is in your power."

"We should have just gotten a search warrant like I wanted to," Frank said. "We might have found the artifacts."

They pushed their way through the glass doors after being buzzed in by the guard at the medical examiner's office.

"The Chicago police already searched and came up empty. Besides, the Center is the last place they would hide something, Frank. Alex is too smart for that."

They made their way down the hall but stopped when they saw the *No Admittance* sign on the door. The detectives walked further down the hall and entered Benny's office. "What's up with the sign?" Frank asked.

"Take a guess." Benny grabbed his key card and led the two back down the hall. "But when he's away, the curious will play."

They entered T.J.'s playroom of bones and artifacts.

"Four bodies?" Frank asked as he looked at the display tables.

"Yes, incomplete as they are it is my best guess four will be the final number. Logan has only released the bones he has inspected so far." Benny led them over to a table with a sign reading Table One. "Female, around twenty years of age, approximately sixty-four inches tall. We have retrieved most of her bones." Benny turned to Table Two and picked up a bone shaped like a large ear. "This is the clavicle. It is the last bone of the human body to fuse. As you can tell, this one hasn't fused completely so our friend here is somewhere, I'd say, around seventeen, maybe eighteen years old. In addition," he lifted the skull, "no wisdom teeth." He moved to the next table. "All I know about the third victim so far is that it is a female, around sixty-six inches tall. Same with Table Four. As I told your wife…"

"Sam was here?"

"Yes, and it was nice to know that having a baby didn't suck out all her brain matter."

Jake shoved his hands into his pants pockets and tried to rein in his irritation. "Wish you hadn't done that."

"Let her in?"

"Shared information with her."

"Can anyone keep Sam away from anything? Besides, she said she was representing the Native American interests."

"I'm not being territorial here, Benny. Sam's involved in a way. Alex is in prison. Some of the bones and artifacts are still missing. She could be accused of tampering with evidence."

"Come on, Jake." Frank picked up one of the arrowheads from the table. "You know Sam wouldn't do anything to make things worse for Alex." He examined the crude-looking arrowheads and pottery bowls. He glanced quickly at the second table of artifacts, then to Benny. "No clothing?"

"By the sun-bleached condition of the bones I'd say most of the clothes were left to the elements. Some might have been carted away by animals. According to Sam, some Native customs call for leaving the bodies out in the elements to decompose quicker."

"How do you tell how long ago they died?" Frank asked.

"Clothes would have helped, especially period clothes. Now all we can go by are the artifacts. Once Inga gets them all cleaned up, laid out, and researched, she can tell us what century they are from. It looks like three of them might have been shot with an arrow." He showed them the nick on the rib of one of the victims, then nodded toward Table Three. "I didn't find a similar marking on her but maybe when we retrieve the rest of her bones we'll know more." His dark eyes puzzled over what few bones were on Table Three. "I just hope Inga can find more of that victim. I don't like unfinished puzzles."

"What else did Sam do here?" Jake asked.

"Drank some coffee, ate some cookies, worried about Alex and the attempted murder charges hanging over his head." Benny ripped off the latex clothes and tossed them in a barrel. "She still has a cop's instincts, Jake." He paused a moment, then added under his breath, "That and a little something extra."

8

Jake and Frank were summoned to Captain Robinson's office the next morning where Chief Dennis Murphy was pacing in his three hundred dollar alligator skin loafers. His suit was wrinkle-free, as though he had either dressed in the elevator or someone carted him over in a standing position.

"Shit," Jake said under his breath. Their pace slowed, not wanting to give Murphy the impression that they rush every time the chief snaps his fingers. Heads burrowed deep into paperwork as they passed. Janet Gabriello, the department secretary, was the only one brave enough to give them a passing glance, her eyes displaying that withering look of disgust at the visitor from Headquarters. She mouthed, "Good luck," as they slowed their pace even further.

Frank whispered, "He don't look happy."

"He only looks happy in front of a camera," Jake replied.

Murphy checked his watch and continued pacing. Robinson looked bored, his eyes displaying a hint of dizziness from watching the pacing. The desk was clean, void of any paperwork Murphy might pick up to read.

"'Bout time," Murphy barked. "I have a meeting to go to, now take a seat."

"Good morning, Chief," Frank said with a broad smile as he dropped into a chair in front of the desk.

Jake was much slower in taking a seat, his mind running through scenarios. Had Murphy found out about Sam visiting Benny's office? Had Breyton pulled major strings to try to get his construction crew back to work? If Jake had a choice he would say it was Sam. No one ruffled Murphy's professionally styled hair more than Sam. Murphy had a history with Sam's late godfather who was the previous chief of police. Anyone who had been close to Chief Connelley would always be in Murphy's crosshairs.

Murphy, looking tan and rested, leaned against the credenza, fingers gripping the edges. "I need Breyton up and running by the end of the week. All I need to know from you is how you plan to accomplish that."

"What's Breyton's hurry?" Jake asked. "Besides, this could take years, not weeks."

The chief winced at that comment. "I don't want to hear it. Breyton's on a timetable. If he misses the completion date, he loses out on a sizeable bonus."

"Translation," Frank said with a discernible chuckle in his throat, "Mayor Jenkins will miss out on a huge contribution to his upcoming campaign."

Robinson winced and snapped his eyes toward the detectives, pulsing his head back and forth slowly like a metronome.

Murphy pushed away from the credenza. "Don't try my patience. You." He drilled a glare at Jake. "Tell me how this isn't a conflict of interest. Your family friend is suspected of conspiring to steal those artifacts. He's accused of attempted murder. Give me one good reason why I shouldn't pull your ass off this case?"

Jake just stared at Murphy. Silence usually unnerved the chief who preferred insolence so he could rant and rave and get into a shouting match.

Robinson jumped in. "I could give the case to Detectives Jackson and Brainard, although they would have to bone up on, excuse the redundancy, bones, and learn about the Native American history in this region. Maybe Jake's mother-in-law could find time to spend with them to get them up-to-speed. Might delay things a week or two." He paused before adding, "Or more. But, I could make it happen." Robinson waited, avoiding the faces of his detectives, focusing on Murphy who was mulling this over as if he had been given a complex equation.

"No, that won't work. Not at all." Murphy pulled a small

container from his pocket. He held it in front of his open mouth and sprayed. The chief preferred a quick sprits to breath mints. He went back to pacing, checked his watch. Under the fluorescent lights his skin looked more artificial than natural, as was the porcelain whiteness of his teeth. He stopped suddenly and turned again to Jake. "I don't want your wife anywhere near this case or Benny's lab." Whenever possible, Murphy managed to avoid using Sam's name, preferring to call her *your wife*.

Jake shrugged with indifference. "She speaks Lakota and Abby isn't always available to help with the language barrier." He wasn't about ready to tell Murphy that most of the people involved speak English. "We can always try to get an interpreter. Maybe he or she can fit us in their schedule next week."

"Or next month," Frank added.

Murphy held his head as if it were going to explode. They were overloading him with too much information, too many decisions to make. "No," he growled. "Do whatever you have to do. Just wrap things up quickly." He gave a last-minute stare at Robinson while giving his mouth two doses of spray. When there wasn't a response from Robinson, Murphy left.

Frank reached back and shoved the office door closed. "Always a pleasure, Chief."

"You are going to have to watch your mouth," Robinson cautioned. "I can't be around you every minute. You should be more like your partner and hold your tongue."

"Jake holding his tongue is usually a bad sign. That means his fists are about ready to go into action."

Robinson dismissed Frank's comment with a wave of his hand. "Tell me something good."

Jake filled him in on Benny's findings, their visit to the Cultural Center, and the lack of leads in locating the missing bones and artifacts.

"I said good news," Robinson stressed. "That don't sound good."

"I'm planning to have someone else visit Alex to entice him to cooperate with the judge. Don't know if it will work," Jake said. "I'm waiting on a call back from Bill Lighthorse at the Cultural Center regarding his fifteen-year-old grandson, Quince. It's possible the teen was at the construction site that day and might know something."

Robinson scribbled several notes in a file then tossed down his pen. "You know and I know that one week is an absurd estimate for the resolution of this case. The chief is lucky the archeologists aren't insisting on excavating the entire two-acre site. Now, get to that construction site and get a handle on how long this is going to drag on. Then we'll take it from there."

Inga lifted her straw hat and raked an arm across her damp forehead. "T.J. insists on expanding the dig site. Thinks we're going to find some lost Aztec city or some damn thing. Never know with him. He used to be a lot of fun on digs but now he's overbearing."

"I take it you don't agree?" Jake asked.

Inga shook her head. "Not all burial sites are located in former camping or ritual sites. Sometimes they just find a spot and dig a hole."

Frank said, "But they weren't buried immediately. The bones were too bleached according to our medical examiner."

"That's true." Inga's attention was drawn to the pit where T.J. was ranting about something, slapping his hat against his thigh. "There he goes again. I swear, if he wasn't so good at what he does I'd refuse to work another dig with him."

"What's his problem?" Jake moved to the shade of the van, thankful he had chosen to strip off his jacket and leave it in the car. The bed of the van was littered with sand and grime. He thought better of having a seat.

"Probably found some broken piece of pottery or Angel didn't clean something off to his satisfaction. Thought we'd have to pull him off one of the visitors there." Inga nodded toward two Native Americans standing watch. "Blamed them for the broken artifacts. If they hadn't piled into the pit, the artifacts wouldn't have been stepped on. And he's sure those that are intact are in their possession somewhere." She heaved a long, frustrated sigh, and decided the van bed wasn't too dirty for her to sit in. Her slacks were already dust-covered. "He never used to be this way. Getting older and more ornery, I guess. Fact is, he's right, though. Broken artifacts are useless. Stolen artifacts are even worse." She accepted a bottled water from Frank.

"Who has final say on how long you keep digging?" Frank asked.

"It's usually a consensus. This area had a sand spit that separated the Calumet Lagoon from the rest of Lake Michigan. That Lagoon is now the Little Calumet River. It's not unusual to find lots of arrowheads seeing that Indians had a chipping station in this region for making arrowheads. The Calumet Shoreline which runs just south of here was an Indian trail. A lot of fur trade, French exploration. Now, you go east of here to Merrillville, Indiana, and you might find remnants of the thirty-six Potawatomi communities. Sixteen Indian trails converged in that region. We have found birch-bark canoes, spears for fishing, stone hoes, wooden dishes, deer and bison bones. All kinds of remnants of working villages. There isn't anything like that here. It's just strange. I for one feel like we're spinning our wheels."

"Who has authority, Inga, if there isn't a consensus? How do you know when you have found all you are going to find?" In a sense, Jake hated to give Chief Murphy what he wanted. He'd rather let him stew awhile. But he didn't want Alex to spend any more time in jail than he had to. If getting construction back on track meant making Breyton a little kinder and gentler, maybe Breyton might drop the charges.

"I do," Inga said, tipping back the bottle and drinking the last of the water. "But don't think this is like a crime scene where the tape comes down in a few days. You could probably paint the Sistine Chapel in less time."

"It's dinnertime," Jackie announced as she sashayed down the aisle.

Alex slowly lifted his head and groaned. Cat-calls and whistles pealed from the other jail cells.

"Mamasita."

"Baby."

"Whoa, mama."

Bob grinned like a college kid as he unlocked Alex's cell door. "Jake sent your dinner via one spicy courier."

"Now you get up outta that bed or I'm just gonna have to crawl in there after you." She had thought of wearing a maid's uniform under a trench coat but word would get back to Captain Robinson. Seeing that Lamon was a very close friend, she didn't want to put him in an awkward position. Instead, she chose a bronze silk dress worn off one shoulder which revealed her massage cleavage. Jackie smoothed her hands down the curve of her hips.

Alex groaned again and swung his legs around, quickly coming to his feet and moving to the table. *"Wakan sica."* Devil, he mumbled.

"You better have just called me a sexy babe if you know what's good for you." Jackie's dress left little room for movement. She took half steps in her four-inch high wraparound heels. Once Bob set the plates on the table she turned to the men in the other cells. "You hungry, sugars?" She smiled her Whitney Houston smile and did her best Mae West impression. "See anything you'd like to take a bite out of?" The response of hoots and hollers was deafening.

Alex's head dropped to the table and he banged his forehead several times while again mumbling, *"Wakan sica."*

Bob could barely contain his amusement as he distributed the meals to the other prisoners. He told Jackie, "Let me know when you are ready to go."

The door to lockup slammed shut. Jackie took a seat across from Alex who kept his head down, eyes on his food.

"How long you going to keep this up?" Jackie demanded. "You have everyone in that house worried sick."

Alex slit open the cornbread and slathered on butter.

"Do I have to come here every day and spoon feed you?" Jackie waited for a reply. Nothing. "You know," she said, raising her voice a few octaves, "every day I have to come here I'm going to wear less and less."

This got the prisoners going again.

Jackie shoved her chair away from the table and crossed her legs. Her dress rose up to mid-thigh. "I ever tell you about the red teddy I own?"

Alex bent his head down closer to the container. He was shoveling the food in at a faster tempo. When Bob returned, Alex motioned for a pen and scribbled a note in Lakota on his napkin.

"If you send this woman to my jail cell again, I will plead guilty and go on a hunger strike." Sam dropped the napkin on the island counter. "Real funny, Alex." She turned to Abby. "Mom."

Abby raised her hands in supplication. "I give up. You can't embarrass Alex into doing something."

Jake hoisted Dillon onto his shoulder. "I thought it would work. I don't think anyone makes Alex more uncomfortable than Jackie. Hell, she makes me uncomfortable."

"Well, I have no choice but to play hardball with Breyton." She was met with two sets of eyes trained on her. "It's legal," she argued. "Why do you always think the worst when Jackie and I put our heads together?" She was met with silence. "I'll admit. We've bent a few rules in the past."

"Few?" Jake shook his head.

"Taking a dog into lockup isn't exactly according to the rules either."

"That's a far cry from illegal gambling, breaking into wall safes, and taking illicit pictures for blackmail purposes," Jake replied, referring to several transgressions Sam had pursued in the past.

"I didn't know you were keeping a log book."

"Books," Jake said with a half smile. "And you can probably fill them all."

"All of them were for a worthy cause." Sam had known few boundaries in her years as a cop. The former police chief had looked the other way as long as Sam brought him dirt he could use on his adversaries. Unfortunately, the new police chief wasn't that understanding, especially since he had been one of Sam's targets.

9

Sam stood at the top of the stairs and watched the shadowed figure. Jake was seated on a stool in a room above the garage adjusting the digital camera attached to a telescope. The garage had been remodeled in the spring to provide a glass bubble roof for optimum exposure of the sky. That and the Meade 16" telescope were his Christmas presents. He had protested at first, knowing that they could have purchased a luxury-sized car for the price of the telescope and remodeling of the garage.

The house was isolated from main thoroughfares and sheltered from the interference of street lights. The room was sizeable, expanding the width of three-fifths of the five-car garage. A door opened out to a flat roof where Jake could wheel the telescope outside if he wanted to. One could walk around all four sides of this observatory, like the cabin of a yacht. It made for easy washing of the glass bubble.

The room had most of the comforts of home—a couch, chair, small refrigerator, cabinets for supplies and all of his back issues of *Astronomy* magazine. It was a masculine room with lots of wood and leather. On the walls Jake had hung framed pictures from the Hubble telescope.

Jake didn't feel comfortable receiving gifts. Christmas didn't mean presents when he was a kid. His father had spent money on bottles of liquor rather than presents or decorations.

Little by little Sam had discovered hidden secrets and desires about her husband. His knowledge about astronomy and how he had to give up the telescope he owned when he started working at the Bureau were clues dropped sparingly during late night conversations. And now here he was tinkering at four in the morning in his personal mini-planetarium. Unless there was a homicide,

Jake usually wasn't up this early. Every cop needed an outlet, a relief from the pressures and stress. Some did woodworking, or went fishing, and some even built doll houses. She knew Frank pumped iron and took long bike rides.

Jake had always been a loaner, shutting out people and keeping thoughts to himself. Prior to having the planetarium built, Sam would find him at three in the morning out on the patio smoking a cigarette. She could feel the coolness of the sheets and know he wasn't in bed. Rather than disturb him, she would watch from the upstairs balcony. Once she stood for a full hour while he smoked three cigarettes and stared at the flagstone.

His painful childhood would never be uttered in words. Instead, Sam would have to read them between the scars on his back and just below the hairline on his forehead. It was tough sometimes to decipher if it was a recent homicide keeping him up nights or childhood memories.

Her eyes were drawn to the night sky overhead. It was sprinkled with bright pinpoints of light. The Big and Little Dippers and Orion were the only constellations she recognized and she still wasn't sure which ones appeared in which season.

Sam crept closer, assured that not one stair step from the garage had revealed her presence. She held a cup of coffee in one hand, black, no sugar, just the way he liked it.

"What are you doing up?" Jake asked the darkness.

Sam sighed. "Boy, there's no element of surprise where you're concerned."

"I could smell your perfume and the coffee." He grabbed the cup from her hand, took a long swallow, and set the cup on a table a safe distance from the telescope.

Sam ran a hand across his shoulder and slowly swung one leg across his lap to straddle him. His unbuttoned shirt was worn loose as though thrown on as an afterthought. It was a warm night but the breeze from the opened windows provided relief. "I had to get up to feed Dillon, so I thought I'd see if Daddy needed to be fed."

Jake's attention was drawn to a space just above her head.

"Is it bouncing?" Sam patted the springs of hair that were haloing around her head. Her natural curly hair had a habit of springing and coiling as she slept. She had to wash her hair every morning and drench it in conditioner to get it to a manageable state. But at night it seemed to wrestle itself free from the constraint of foreign chemicals.

"Oh, yeah. It's doing a good impression of Medusa."

Jake had said before that her hair was sexy, in a way. It reminded him of Julia Robert's untamed hair in the movie, *Sleeping with the Enemy*. Lucky for Julia, her hair easily straightened once her perm grew out.

Sam's ratty terrycloth robe slid off one shoulder exposing the swell of her breasts. She could see his eyes following the line of her robe. She ran her fingers across his chiseled jaw line and inhaled his woodsy aftershave. "Ummmm. You know, with these cheekbones, I wouldn't be surprised if you had some Native American in your genes."

"Uh, Sam. You know what tonight is?" His hands wandered under the robe and stroked her thighs.

"Yeah. Three planets are conjugating or something and it won't happen again for another hundred or so years."

"Right. And I have to get things set up."

She took a playful bite of his earlobe and whispered, "But that's why we bought that GPS thingie that searches for the satellite and does all the set up." Her mouth found his as her tongue slowly outlined his lips. She felt his hands exploring more territory.

"Sam, you don't have any clothes on."

Sam gasped and drew back. "I knew I forgot something." He placed his hands on her hips and dragged her closer to his waist. She opened her mouth to his kiss as his hands continued their exploring. A moan no sooner escaped her lips then Jake pulled away and pressed a hand to her mouth.

"Shhhhh." His head lifted and his brows furrowed in

concentration. He whispered, "Did you hear something?"

"Just my raging libido," Sam whispered back. Her lips resumed their quest for his but Sam's attempts at garnering his attention were again interrupted.

A loud scrape and pounding was followed by muffled whispers. Both she and Jake pulled away at the same time. Jake stood so fast that if he hadn't had an arm around her waist she would have fallen on her ass. In his right hand was his Sig Sauer. *Where did he keep that?* Sam thought.

"Stay here," Jake whispered.

The sound had come from downstairs. Sam had left the door unlocked but that shouldn't have been a problem. The front gate was closed and the alarm set. They would have heard the alarm if anyone had jumped the fence to their one-hundred-acre enclave. But like hell she was going to stay put. She shoved her arms back inside the robe sleeves and tightened the belt. Jake was already headed down the stairs.

Jake reached the garage and held his hand up to motion her to stay. She could barely see his face it was so dark. The light switch and the controls for the overhead doors were on the wall to Jake's right.

If she remembered correctly, Jake had parked his Riviera outside. Abby's van was in the first space. The '57 Chevy was on the far side next to Alex's truck. And her Jeep was parked next to the van. There was only one open space and that was in the center of the garage. There was another door on the far side but it was always kept locked because they all used the door closest to the house. So the only way out for the intruder would be through Jake.

Sam felt like she had been holding her breath for five minutes. When was Jake going to make his move? Or was he waiting to hear movement? She no sooner thought it, then it happened. A series of whispers was followed by grunting, as though they were lifting something heavy.

Jake hit the switch and light flooded the garage. "HOLD IT. POLICE." There was a clatter as something dropped and several sets of feet scrambled. "I SAID STOP."

Sam stepped up behind Jake as he moved toward the open parking space. Three bronzed faces, all teens, blinked nervously. Sam recognized them immediately as part of the group that was in the pit.

The taller of the three stared back with cold, dark eyes, but remained silent. Behind the youths was Alex's truck, the tailgate down, the tarp pulled back. Jake walked over to the youths and studied the opened blanket lying on the garage floor. He used the toe of his shoe to flip open the blanket even more exposing pottery, jewelry, arrowheads, and bones.

"Shit," he barked. "Don't tell me these bones have been in my garage all this time." He turned to Sam.

"I didn't know about this." Sam didn't like the look in his eyes. The firm set of his jaw told her he was not going to back down.

Jake peeled the cell phone from his waistband and flipped it open with one hand. He told Dispatch to send a squad car but avoided reporting anything more than a break-in. Next, he dialed Benny at home and told him the missing artifacts and bones had been located.

Jake turned angry eyes on the youths but then focused on the face of the taller one. "Where did you get that rash?" he asked, pointing at the youth's mouth.

The teen remained silent as he brushed a hand across his lips.

"You're Quince, Bill Lighthorse's grandson," Jake said, remembering that Cody also had a rash from poison ivy.

"Quince," Sam said. "You are in a lot of trouble. Just tell us what happened. How did the bones get in my garage? How long have they been here?" Quince remained silent.

"We transferred them the same day," the shortest of the three boys blurted. He was moon-faced and nervously rocked from one foot to the other as though itching to make a run for it.

"Shut up, Carter," Quince yelled.

"Why? You're father won't punish you, but mine will. I'll be grounded until I'm thirty."

"It was for a good cause. Your father will understand."

The third teen looked nervously from Quince to Carter, then to the door behind Jake. Perspiration trickled down the side of his face and his eyes searched the ceiling, probably for an alternative escape route.

"There's no way out," Jake said.

"He won't shoot us." Quince made it sound like a challenge. He took a step forward.

"Yes he will," Sam said. The certainty of her words made the three youths halt.

"Sit on the tailgate of the truck and don't move," Jake ordered.

They reluctantly obeyed. Sam returned to the house to open the gate for the squad car. Several minutes later, with Mars lights flashing, one squad car sped up the three-hundred-foot brick drive and squealed to a stop in front of the garage.

Sam returned just as one of the garage doors rolled open. While the teens were deposited into the back seat of the squad car and Jake conferred with the officer, Sam carefully unrolled the blanket until it lay flat. There were enough bones confiscated to make up for most of the missing pieces in Benny's jigsaw puzzles. There were femurs, tibias, ulnas, ribs, and three skulls. Two of the tibias were shattered midway, almost in identical spots. She wondered if they were broken when the teens dropped the blanket. She moved the rib bones aside and picked up a beaded pouch. It was in pristine condition except for the sand debris. She blew the particles off and turned it over. Inga was going to be thrilled.

She set the pouch down and picked up one of the cracked tibias. The moment she clasped her hand around the bone, the whispers were amplified, filling her head, followed by a scream. Footsteps pounded, accompanied by heavy breathing as though someone were running hard and fast. She set the tibia down and picked up one of the skulls. Her fingers no sooner touched the skull then the screams intensified and the garage was thrown into total darkness. On the horizon two full moons slowly rose, growing in size. She closed her eyes to get a sense of time and place, hoping to catch a hint of how they had died. But the vision was fleeting, less than a few seconds.

"Find anything interesting?" Jake squatted and picked up one of the pouches.

"Lots." Sam set the skull down noticing that the jaw bone was round. All of the jaw bones were round, confirming the assessment that all four victims had been women. "How soon is Benny going to get here?"

"About twenty minutes. Abby is calling the relatives."

"Did they say anything more? Do you know if they were bringing the bones here to hide or were they retrieving them?"

Jake stood and held his hand out to help her up. He pulled the collar of her robe closer and tied the belt tighter. "It was pretty clever. With Alex in jail, we wouldn't think to check his truck. While we were running around with Alex and arguing with Breyton, they had all the time in the world to come here."

"But how did they get in? Everything is locked."

"According to Carter, Alex gave them the code. Remind me to change it today. Abby said a couple of the men were kind enough to drive Alex's truck home that day. That's when they probably hid the blanket under the tarp and drove the truck into the garage."

"What better place to hide it than under your nose." Sam looked up at the sky. The stars had faded, chased by the sun which was peeking over the horizon. "Well, at least you have your planet alignment on film. Me?" She looked down at her ratty robe. "I got undressed for nothing."

10

It only took Jake ten minutes to run down the break-in at his garage, discovery of the stolen items, and his opinion on how and when the items were stashed there. Murphy kept his arms folded and scowled through the detailed explanation. Jake left out the part about Sam's seduction and only said they had wanted to witness the rare astronomical phenomena.

Murphy snorted. "Are you that naïve to think Sam wasn't trying to distract you from what was going on downstairs?"

"If she wanted to, she would have tried to convince me not to go out to the garage or told the teens to come back another night." Jake was surprised he was able to keep his cool in Murphy's presence. Murphy took his time considering the explanation which left an uncomfortable heavy silence in the room.

Frank hated silence. "Now that we have accounted for what we hope are the rest of the missing items, things should move along at a faster pace. That should make Breyton happy."

Robinson knew that was all wishful thinking since the timetable could probably be measured in years versus weeks. But he cheerfully rocked in his roomy chair biding his time. When Murphy jerked his attention in the direction of the squeaking, Robinson brought his chair to an abrupt halt.

"Well, it doesn't make me happy," Murphy snarled. This prompted a spritz of breath spray. "The press is going to have a field day. They know Alex is a friend of the family and let's not even get into your wife's involvement. This really puts me in a bad spot and I'm sure that thrills the hell out of her." His face was turning a light crimson at the mere mention of Sam. "Now I have to get out there and make a statement to the press. What the hell am I supposed to say?" He was wearing out a pretty good path in front of the credenza.

"Good police work," Robinson piped up in his Barry White voice. "We had a squad car parked down the street from Jake's house on the remote possibility that they might try to sneak the evidence onto the property. After all, a cop's house is the last place anyone would look, right?"

Murphy stopped in mid-stride and turned. "You did?" He turned to Jake who only lifted one eyebrow in response. The chief took that as a yes and continued his pacing.

Robinson pulled a folder from his In Box and waved a memo at Murphy. "Maybe this is a good time to talk about the outside consultant the city council approved to put on retainer. Who better to help work this case?"

Murphy halted and ripped the letter from Robinson's fingers. "What consultant?"

"You were copied on the memo, Chief." Robinson pointed a thick finger toward the bottom of the page.

Jake hated being blind-sided and knew exactly where Robinson was going with this. Sam could have revealed a major impropriety on the part of Chief Murphy last year. He had withheld information that could have cleared Sam sooner in the murder of another officer which had resulted in her resignation. Although she exposed him in her farewell speech to the Board of Police and Fire Commissioners and Mayor Jenkins, she had managed to keep Murphy's name from the press. It was Jake who had suggested that it was in her best interest to keep an ace in the hole.

Murphy read the memo silently, his lips moving in sinc. "You can't…this couldn't…you don't mean?" He glared at Jake as though he were a stand-in for Sam. "You can't possibly mean Sam Casey?" he stammered.

Robinson rocked back in his chair, hands clasped across his stomach, thumbs twiddling backwards for several beats, then forwards. "Could work to your advantage. Tell the press she has been working with us; and, with her relationship with the Native

American community, she was able to convince the boys to turn in what was taken from the dig site." He pulled another sheet from the same folder. "Matter of fact, I have your entire speech written for you."

Murphy snatched the second paper from Robinson's hand and skimmed through it. There wasn't any need to remind Murphy why he had to play nice. The mayor would be more than happy to do that. "Fine," he barked out before storming out of the office.

Once the door clicked shut, Robinson turned to his detectives. "Any problems with that?"

"Does Sam know this, just in case the press shows up on my doorstep?" Jake said.

"Sam's pretty good at tap dancing. Now tell me what's happening with the teens."

"Two are cooperating. I cut them, released them to their parents. Quince's grandfather asked me to keep him, with the parents' permission." Jake added with a wicked gleam, "We agreed the best place for Quince was in the same cell as Alex. Forty-eight hours with Alex will either straighten out Bill's grandson or have Alex screaming to be released."

If Jake thought Frank had dropped the subject, he was sorely mistaken. They no sooner stepped into the M.E. lab then Frank blurted, "Buried or burned."

Jake slid his eyes from the objects on the tables to Frank.

"I'm serious." Frank turned to Benny as though pleading his case to Jake were a waste of time. "My in-laws are offering to buy us plots next to theirs and want an answer ASAP so Claudia feels we have to hurry up and make a decision—worms or flames. I don't even want to think about bugs crawling all over me."

"I've seen urns shaped like golf bags, pianos, even a TV remote," Benny offered.

"Really?" Frank thought about that. "So maybe I could have

my ashes placed in an urn shaped like a gun."

"Or launched into space like Scotty from Star Trek." Benny walked over to where Inga was busy taking pictures of the latest artifacts recovered from Jake's garage. "Just about half of all funerals involve cremation."

Inga straightened from her picture snapping. "Who's being cremated?"

"Buried or burned?" Frank asked. "Which would you rather be?"

"I'm donating my body to science," Inga replied.

"The Body Farm?" Frank grimaced. "And have people seeing my naked black ass half buried in a swamp or left in a car trunk?"

Jake's reaction was as close to hilarity as he ever got. He had to admit…Frank had a way of making work amusing. He had been through Frank's vegetarian phase which lasted one month. Claudia was always getting Frank to eat healthy but even she had to admit garden burgers and tofu salads just don't taste the same as a filet mignon. Then there were the yoga lessons. Meditation is fine for someone who can clear his mind and focus on a mantra. Frank couldn't sit still for five minutes.

"Nah." Inga waved him off with a flick of her wrist. "They have more bodies now than they can handle. No, I'm donating organs, eyes, tissue, whatever they need. Then they can cremate what's left."

"So you are in the burn category," Frank replied as he made a mental column of checkmarks.

Jake made a slow trek between the tables noticing how each skeleton was missing a few bones and most were missing the skulls. He made his way over to Inga who stopped snapping photos and was marking notes on a clipboard.

"Wonderful display, don't you think?" Inga held up a piece of pottery, its handle shaped like a bird's beak. "This is a Sikyatki vessel from around the eighteen hundreds, I believe. Definitely Southwestern."

"How did it get here?" Jake studied the pottery. The mouth at the top was wide, the vessel itself shallow.

"Probably used in trade. That's what these seashells and beads were used for, too." She motioned toward a section of the table where she had arranged the seashells by size and the beads by color. "I have my books back at the hotel but I'm sure Abby would agree it definitely isn't from the Sioux tribe." She set the pottery down and picked up a beaded necklace in the shape of a Victorian shoe. "These beads are glass and they are mounted on a cardboard framework. Could be Iroquois." She set it down and sighed appreciably as she picked up a necklace made of what looked like claws.

"Are those deer claw?" Jake asked.

"Bear, I believe, with antelope horns and glass trade beads. It was considered a feat worthy of a brave warrior who could kill a grizzly bear. Definitely Plains Indian. Quite valuable. Probably from the eighteen hundreds."

Jake picked up an object in the shape of a turtle. "This a medicine bundle?" Abby's and Sam's medicine bundles were shaped like pouches.

"Yes, Sioux I believe. Deer hide, glass beads. It's called a Natal Charm. Also from the eighteen hundreds." Inga moved to the end of the table and picked up a figure of a man carved from a solid material. "This is a pendant, believe it or not, made of bone. Very old and something I wouldn't expect to see this far north. I think it's from South America. Again, I have to research my books to be sure. I believe it's called a gorget."

Jake picked up what looked like a button with a carved face. Inga gingerly plucked it from the palm of his hand.

"Haven't figured this out yet. I know I've seen them before but it's been years. You know," she set the button back in his hand, "you should ask Abby to stop by and take a look at these when she has time. I'll bring my books from the hotel. Maybe between the two of us, we can make heads or tails out of the history of our ladies there." She nodded toward the four examining tables.

"The rest of these items," Inga said, focusing her attention again on the artifacts, "are cooking and eating utensils made from wood, bones, and horns." The utensils were carved with precision, edges smooth, color a burnish brown.

Frank appeared at the end of the table. "This looks dangerous." He picked up a knife with a carved handle."

"This I really have to research," Inga said, taking it from his hand. "It has a steel and copper shaft with inlaid abalone shell in the handle. It speaks Northwest Coast to me, definitely not Plains Indian."

"But could have been used in trade, right?" Frank said.

"Or a murder weapon," Jake added.

11

Sam clamped on the visitor's badge as she surveyed the fourth floor of Precinct Six. Desks were bumped together in busy clusters, some buried in papers, some neat and tidy as if its occupants were on an extended vacation. The Sixth Precinct was the oldest of the precincts and in desperate need of a facelift. Some thought they should just implode the entire building and start from scratch.

No matter its appearance Sam had to admit she missed the walls in need of paint, the aged tiles, the smell of burnt coffee and perspiration. Old news. She had to get over it.

Ed Scofield, the desk sergeant, eyed her over the tops of his bifocals. Tall and lean with birdlike limbs, he always appeared as though he were a lump of clay that Nature had stretched too far.

"I'm not sure when Jake is gonna get back. What me to raise him on the horn?"

"That's okay. I tried him on his cell but he's not answering so he must be tied up. I have a few minutes to kill before going to visit Alex."

"I understand he's driving all the prisoners nuts."

"And enjoying every minute of it."

A soulful sob erupted from the center of the room. A woman with starched white hair and a navy blue dress was pressing a handkerchief to her mouth. A man in a tattered suit patted her shoulder and whispered in her ear. The dough-faced detective listening to the couple leaned forward, his face camouflaging the doubt in his eyes. He scribbled notes but Sam was sure it was just for show. Sam didn't recognize the detective and could only assume he was on loan from another precinct.

Two office clerks huddled near the file cabinets watching the scene with mild curiosity. Sam guessed by their age and lack of office decorum that they were summer interns. They peppered their curiosity with high school whispers and giggles.

Sam turned to Scofield. "What's with the couple?"

He pulled his bifocals off with a sigh, placed them on the desk. "Fran and William Korwin. They read about the remains found at Breyton Dig. Their daughter, Allison, disappeared over twenty years ago so they travel from city to city with all of her medical records and photos. When they hear about a body being discovered, that's where they go, hoping against hope they can find their daughter."

"How sad."

"Yeah. They've spent their savings on private dicks. Now that they are retired it's *have case number, will travel*."

"Didn't they read that it's an archeological dig probably two hundred years old?" Sam studied the couple again. No wonder their clothes resembled garage sale purchases. They had dedicated their lives to finding their daughter versus taking care of themselves. "How old was their daughter when she disappeared?" Sam watched the woman hold up something which the detective barely glanced at. The woman slowly returned the object to her purse.

"Twenty. On spring break from Ohio State University and headed back home to spend the week with her parents. Supposedly drove Interstate 80 to get to and from college and there have been a lot of women abducted over the years from that stretch of highway. FBI had been targeting over-the-road truck drivers but they've never found the killer."

"I haven't heard of any recent cases, though."

"Nope. The guy has been silent for quite a few years now. He's either dead, in prison for something else or off in another part of the country wreaking more havoc."

"Who's the detective?"

"Jim Jamison from Robbery. Had to pull someone over to explain things to them since everyone else is out in the field. They insist on waiting for the lead detective on the case."

Which was Jake. "If he rolls his eyes one more time I think I'm going to roll him." Sam turned her attention from the grieving parents. "Why don't you tell him to get the couple something to drink and to take his time."

Scofield picked up his glasses and chewed on the arm. He gave her one of those looks that Sam was sure he must have adopted from Jake. It said, "What are you up to?" After a full minute of mentally wrestling with his options, Scofield punched two numbers on the phone. Sam watched Jamison pick up the receiver. "Jim, why don't you get the lovely couple something to drink?"

Jamison jerked his head toward the desk sergeant. When he saw Sam standing there, he looked back to the couple, then back to Sam before getting the gist of what was happening. Sam watched him hang up the phone, ask the couple what they would like to drink, then headed for the break room.

"I like my job, Sam."

She walked away from him with one hand up—a signal that she's heard it all before.

"Hi, Mr. and Mrs. Korwin. I'm Sam Casey. I worked Homicide before and now I'm a private detective." She slid onto the chair before the bewildered couple could object. "Although this is an archeological dig, I would like to hear more about your daughter."

The couple shared a frown. "We're kinda through with private detectives," William said.

Sam couldn't help noticing the fabric frayed at the edge of his suit sleeves. His thinning hair hadn't lost too much of its natural brown color whereas Fran's hair had turned completely white. The hankie she had wadded up in one hand had a crocheted border. Sam could make out the top portion of an initial "A", probably for Alison.

"I understand. I wasn't looking for you to hire another detective. I just thought since Sergeant Mitchell is going to be tied up most of the day and that you have driven so far already, maybe I could make sure the department has its database current."

Sam glanced quickly at Scofield. He was talking to the mail clerk. Sam tapped the computer screen and it came to life. She accessed the missing persons database and typed in Alison Korwin's name.

"Did you know that over two thousand Americans are reported missing every single day?" Sam found Alison's name and tabbed down for *Details*. "Of the close to one million people missing annually all cases except around fifty thousand are under the age of eighteen." Sam turned the screen toward the couple. She hoped she wasn't giving them the impression that their daughter is just another in a growing list of missing persons to be filed away and forgotten. "This is the information in the database on Alison. Is there anything that we could add? Any detail, no matter how trivial, could be crucial."

She let them study the screen for several minutes. Twenty years and they hadn't given up. Sam could see William's calloused fingers, and the dirt under the nails which were permanent reminders of his years of working his farm. They were a middle-class family scraping by each day, probably without a pension, still living in the same farm house where they had raised Alison.

"Her necklace," Dorothy said, jamming her hand into a tapestry purse that looked more like an overnight bag. She pulled out a silver chain and handed it to Sam.

"It was found about ten feet from her car," William explained. "The clasp had been broken so the police thought her…," he hesitated, grasping for the right word to use, "that it had broken off in a struggle."

It was obvious to Sam after twenty years the parents didn't want to put a label on their daughter's case, not without proof. And how could she blame them? She lifted the necklace. A dolphin pendant carved from what looked like Mother of Pearl, hung from the chain.

"Alison loved dolphins," Fran explained. "She is…was studying to be a marine biologist. We bought her the necklace and pendant for her high school graduation. She always wore it." The hankie was pressed to her mouth again.

Sam held the dolphin for several seconds. She didn't expect to glean anything from the pendant. It had been too long, been touched by too many people. "The police checked for fingerprints?" Sam scrolled down the screen. There wasn't any mention of the necklace. A picture of Alison popped up on the screen. Sam heard a collective gasp from the parents and turned to see their eyes transfixed.

"She…is beautiful," Sam said. Alison had long blonde hair and green eyes. She was dressed in jeans and sweater, posed leaning against a white fence. Her nails were long but unpolished, skin clear, makeup barely there.

"We used that photo for her yearbook," Fran said.

Sam printed out the report on Alison. "I'll leave a note about the dolphin for Sergeant Mitchell. He would have to be the one to make changes to the database." *Since I don't have authority to do so and Jake will kill me when he finds out I even accessed the database. But, what else is new?*

Jamison returned and set two cans of Pepsi on the desk. "Mrs. Mitchell." He nodded toward the computer. "Find what you wanted?" he growled. Sam caught a whiff of stale coffee and cigarettes.

"Yes, we did." She stood and thanked the couple for their time. "Maybe this nice gentleman will update the database for you." She wished she could do more for the couple. They should be off golfing or fishing, enjoying their retirement. As she moved away from the desk, Jamison reached over and snatched the necklace from her grasp. "I believe the Korwin's will want their property back."

Sam slid her business card across the desk to William. "Keep in touch." She walked over to the printer by the filing cabinets, grabbed the report she had printed, and walked out.

12

Sam smiled at the teen sharing Alex's cell. He was sitting on his bunk, slouched against the cell bars. The ten foot square room had the bunks set up in an L-shape with a small table and two chairs in the corner by the cell door. Quince gave her a sneer in greeting but she ignored it.

"I see Alex is talking your head off." Sam pulled a chair over and sat down.

"Good thing he keeps quiet. No one can understand him," Quince hissed. "That's rude, dude." He spat the words in Alex's direction.

"You tell him, Tonto," the Hispanic in the adjoining cell yelled.

Quince leered at him. "Shut up, Manuel."

But Manuel ignored him and yelled, "Hey, old man. How do you get such good lookin' women to come visit?" His eyes slowly dissected Sam's body parts. "Baby, yoos got some hot gams."

Sam silently cursed herself for not wearing slacks into a lockup. She ignored the prisoner and said to Quince, "I don't think it speaks of Alex's rudeness as much as it does your ignorance of your heritage." Sam tried to remain pleasant and not let Quince's attitude get under her skin.

"Heritage." Quince said it as though it were the most distasteful word he had ever heard. "You live in the past, you die in the past."

"How many years do you think I would get if I pound some sense into this brat?" Alex asked Sam in their Native language.

"If you get Judge Purdy she'll probably pin a medal on you," Sam replied also in Lakota.

"Shit. Not you, too," Quince griped and slouched even further on his bunk.

Sam handed a Lakota dictionary to Alex. "Mom thought you might be able to use this for your Lakota 101 lessons with the brat."

Alex took the book from her. "It's not heavy enough to beat him with."

Sam laughed at that and laughed even more when she saw how it irritated Quince that he didn't understand them.

"Hey," Manuel yelled. "Like he said. It's rude to speak gibberish in front of other people."

"Yeah, Pepe," Quince sneered. "Like you and your taco friends don't talk in your taco language knowing we don't understand you."

"HEY." This woke up the black teen across the aisle who had a tattoo of a snake around his neck. "Some of us are trying to sleep over here."

"You were born sleeping, you lazy ass," Quince yelled back.

The black teen popped off his bunk as if ejected. "What did you call me?"

The door to lockup opened and a cop with a face like a bull dog stepped in. "Keep it down in here or I just might forget to serve lunch." He glared at them and was met with silence. "That's better." He slammed the door shut and locked it.

"Can't believe my parents are leaving me in here," Quince mumbled.

Sam almost felt sorry for the kid. He had never been in jail before and now felt betrayed by his parents and grandparents. She wasn't sure if his experience would be for the better or for the worse.

She pulled her chair closer to Alex's bunk. "Alex, I can't believe you put us in that position. Giving these kids the code to our gate? Hiding the stolen items in our garage? Jake could have been pulled off the case and you know another detective wouldn't have been as partial to you and Abby."

"They were supposed to drive my truck to their home, unload the items, then return my truck to the garage. That is why I gave them the code. Didn't know if anyone would be home to let them through the gate and parking is not allowed on the street."

Sam felt a headache swelling behind her eyes. The smell of body sweat in the holding cells hung thick in the air. "We have the items back now. When do you plan to start talking English to Judge Purdy so she can at least eliminate the contempt of court charge hanging over your head?"

"What does it matter? I still have the attempted murder charges." Alex shook his head and leaned back against the wall. "We have lost our ancestors and treasures to the bureaucracies again. I'm tired of losing, Sam. All I have left is my fight, whether against the Breytons of the world or arrogant archeologists."

Whenever Sam heard Alex talk like this, she was reminded of the past baggage he carried like a suit of armor. She reached over and patted his hand. She loved the stubborn guy like a father and could only respect his opinion.

"Let me run something by you." Sam reached into her tote bag and pulled out a can of cookies.

"Hey, what about us?" Manuel reached his hands through the bars of his cell.

"Sorry, didn't bring enough." She opened the can and offered it to Quince. He turned his nose up. Sam shrugged it off, grabbed a chocolate chip cookie and handed the can to Alex. "When I touched one of the skulls," Sam continued in their Native language, "I saw a vision of two moons. Do you think that has to do with a harvest season?"

Alex stuffed an entire cookie in his mouth as he thought it over. The aroma of chocolate chip cookies got the best of Quince. He approached slowly, peered in the can, grabbed two cookies, and returned to his bunk.

"Could refer to blue moons, months with two full moons. Doesn't happen that often. Do you know if it was summer or winter?"

Sam thought back to when she held the skull at the dig site and the bones in the garage. "I don't remember feeling a chill so I think it might have been summer."

"Check the computer. It will have dates of all the years that had two full moons."

Quince licked his fingers and strolled back over to Alex. Alex clutched the can and said, *"A'guyani skuyela."*

"Huh?" Quince looked at Sam. "What's he saying?"

"Cookies," Sam said with a smile. "He won't give you one until you ask in Lakota."

Quince rolled his eyes, started to turn away, then gazed at the cookies again. *"Aga yanni skooyella."*

"Close enough," Sam said.

Alex held out the can to Quince. The teen smiled.

Sam dumped her purse on the couch in the study and rushed over to the computer. The desk covered four feet of one wall with an attached hutch and printer table. She tapped the mouse and the screen sprang to life. She signed onto the Internet and did a Google search to look for lunar calendars and blue moons. Alex was probably right that her vision of full moons referred to the rare occasion when one month has two full moons. But where to start? Inga probably hadn't dated the artifacts yet so Sam wasn't sure what century to search.

It didn't take long to locate a Web site from the U.S. Naval Observatory listing the phases of the moon. All Sam had to do was plug in a year and it gave her the dates of the new moon, first quarter, full moon, and last quarter. From there she could easily see which month had more than two full moons. After the site collected the data for a submitted date range, Sam printed out the results. She spent twenty minutes printing out charts then used a yellow highlighter to mark up the pages.

She eliminated any years when the two full moons didn't occur in the summer and all dates after...when? Sam didn't remember when the pioneer settlers started moving in.

Bookcases lined two walls but she wasn't sure where she put the book. Each shelf was labeled. Her eyes scrolled the categories looking for history. Science, politics, photo albums, mystery, legal, finally history. She cocked her head and scanned the spines until she found it—*Calumet Beginnings by Kenneth J. Schoon. Ancient Shorelines and Settlements at the South End of Lake Michigan.*

She carried the book and a notepad to the kitchen where she grabbed her water, then headed to the dining room. One of Sam's favorite places besides the Florida room was the window seat in the dining room. The windows were cranked open sending a fragrant breeze through the house. The balconies off the second floor bedrooms shaded some of the sun's rays.

Post-it notes marked pages where information on Indian trails, settlements, and the different tribes which traveled this area were mentioned.

The Potawatomi had a number of villages in the area until the fur trade ended. Then they left for reservations west of the Mississippi River. The first American settlers to the area arrived around 1835, according to Professor Schoon. The pioneer and stagecoach period started in 1833. Sam would think the Native Americans would have vacated the region so the burial site should date prior to 1833.

She found another entry regarding Fort Dearborn. U.S. soldiers built it in 1803 at the mouth of the Chicago River. Sam wondered how many Chasen Heights residents realized that this area was among the last regions in Indiana and Illinois to be surrendered by the Potawatomi.

Her fingers flipped through the pages, then came to a halt as her eye caught the heading, *Native American Occupation*. According to Professor Schoon, there were four eras of Native Americans: The Big Game Hunter from 10,000 years ago; the Archaic from

10,000 to 3,000 years ago; the Woodland from 3,000 to 1,100 years ago; and the Mississippian beginning 1,100 years ago. It mentioned thousands of burial mounds. Pottery, weapons, and copper ornaments were sometimes buried along with the dead. Sam wondered if Breyton's workers noticed a mound before they started their desecration.

Sam slammed the book shut. About all she knew for certain was that permanent settlers came to the area after 1833. So the victims at the construction site had to have died prior to 1833.

13

"Forget the pit," T.J. yelled, "and help me out up here." He pulled the scarf from his neck, removed his hat, and dabbed at the dirt and sweat on his face. Two wheelbarrows sat near the pile of dirt. Framed screens had been placed over the wheelbarrows as dirt from the pile had been sifted in search of any remnants of bone or artifacts.

"What about the pit?" Greg asked as he flipped the dark lenses up on his wire-rimmed glasses. "The grid has already been set up."

"This will go much quicker with three of us working. We are down to the last couple feet. At least we know these items haven't been touched." He stole an accusing glare at the two men standing outside the orange fencing. One or two Natives had been arriving each day to watch from a distance. "And why the hell do they have to keep glaring at us? They are the thieves, not us."

"Maybe if you treated them and their property with respect they wouldn't treat you as though you were the culprit," Greg suggested.

"Your heart is bleeding all over my site. Just get to work."

Greg flipped the dark lenses down and turned his back on T.J.

Angel moved alongside Greg and whispered, "Don't let him get to you."

"He doesn't. He's an arrogant ass but he's good at what he does. Just the experience working on a dig with him is worth the aggravation."

"Just wish Inga were here. She has a way of putting him in his place." Her face was shaded under the baseball cap as she bent over the screen. Her skin smelled of sunscreen. Greg couldn't help staring at her legs. The sun had turned her hair the whitest blonde and her skin a dark bronze, equal to the skin color of their observers. The Natives weren't that much of an interference but T.J. had the police move them to an area outside the second barrier claiming some Illinois statute which prevented contamination of an excavation project.

Greg and Angel worked in tandem. With any luck they should be able to finish the pile by tomorrow afternoon. Behind the dark shades Greg watched T.J. closely. The professor's main interest was the pit because any find of value enabled him to write an article for *National Geographic* or *Archeology Today* magazines. It would mean speaking engagements and slide presentations.

T.J. moved like a man on a mission, climbing down into the pit, then back up to his truck, eventually ending up by the wheelbarrows, hands on his hips. "Before the close of the day, I'd like to set up a tent over the pit. They are expecting rain in a couple days." T.J. returned to his truck and unlocked the back hatch.

Angel studied the pit then looked at the bronzed faces watching their every move. "Once T.J. erects the tent, they won't be able to see what's happening."

Greg straightened and followed her gaze. "Maybe that's T.J.'s objective."

An inky darkness seeps across the sky. Night sounds are varied yet distinguishable. There is a buzzing of insects and chattering of small rodents. The faint sound of crunching could be attributed to animals eating or stones underfoot.

Off in the distance two moons glow like tiny pinpricks, increasing in size until they shine like two beacons. Sam picks up speed as she runs. She turns abruptly and brings her arms up to shield her face as the two moons plunge from the sky. And then she hears an ear-piercing scream.

Sam woke with a start and jolted to a sitting position. Her heart pounded and her legs twitched as though she had just completed a marathon. She looked over to see if she had awakened Jake. He was sleeping soundly, the sheet pulled up to his waist. The clock on the headboard said it was a little before four in the morning. She cocked her head and stared at the baby monitor. Was it her dream that woke her or did the baby stir? Silently she slipped out of bed and padded down the hall to the nursery.

Dillon was sleeping as soundly as his father. Sam grabbed a diaper and carefully unfastened the snaps on his sleeper. He was due to awaken any minute since it was close to feeding time. She made a quick diaper change, tossing the soiled one in the disposal next to the changing table. He stirred once, eyes opening to slits. Tiny stars in the ceiling displayed winter constellations. There wasn't a need for a night light. Dillon stirred again, eyes snapping wide open. He stared briefly at the fascinating lights before starting his hunger whimper. Sam had it down to a science, which whimper meant hunger, which meant his diaper was wet or that he was bored or over-tired.

She gathered up the crying bundle while opening her robe. He nursed noisily while she rocked him in the cushioned glider. "Hey, slow it down, buddy." She picked a piece of blanket fuzz from his hair.

A narrow, picket fence traveled the wall. It was Alex's handiwork that put the finishing touches on the nursery, along with the animals Abby had stenciled on the wall shown peering from behind the fence. She had also stenciled a large tree in the corner behind the crib. Floral vines climbed the walls and magnets in the shape of insects clung to nail heads.

Insects. The thought brought Sam back to her dream. Insect noises meant she was right that the victims had died during the summer. But there was something too familiar about the two moons, how they had grown rapidly in size. And the sound of gravel crunching. It seemed to her the sound was louder than just feet crunching along rock. She closed her eyes and continued rocking, thinking back to the morning in the garage when she had held the skull and the splintered tibia.

Sam lifted Dillon onto her shoulder and rubbed his back. Her mind felt conflicted with too many thoughts trying to be deciphered at the same time. Her dream had shown the two moons rising in the night sky, at the same speed and the same height. *How could that be?* Sam stopped her rocking. *Unless...*

She held Dillon close while she grabbed the phone off of the dresser. What she wanted to do was rush over to Benny's lab but it was four in the morning. She pressed a speed dial number and walked to the window. Dillon's steady breathing told her he was asleep.

"Come on, pick up." Her suspicions felt so far-fetched she was too embarrassed to wake up Jake to share them.

A voice grumbled in her ear. "This better be important."

Jake and Frank were buzzed into the lab by Benny. Captain Robinson lumbered behind cradling a mini keg-sized thermos mug. Benny hovered over one of the table of bones, a magnifying glass in one hand.

"What's up, Benny?" Jake asked.

Benny held up one finger.

"Must be important to demand my ass over here," Robinson growled.

"It is," Benny said to the magnifying glass. "I had my doubts when Sam called me at four this morning."

Jake's eyebrows crawled toward his hairline. "Sam called?"

Benny glared at him over the top of his glasses. "Thought you two lived together." He walked over to Table Three and gestured with a sweeping motion. "Not one nick or cut on these bones to indicate she was shot with an arrow like the other three. Sam's phone call to me this morning followed another one of her dreams of two moons."

"Dreams," Frank said.

"Two moons." Robinson gulped his coffee.

"Dreams, visions, whatever you want to call them. Either way," Benny continued, "Sam has a distinct impression those moons were headlights."

"Headlights." Now it was Jake's turn to parrot Benny's words.

With the tip of a pen Benny pointed from one long bone to another. "At first I thought these injuries were from the backhoe but they aren't new."

"Maybe a horse fell on her," Robinson suggested.

"Except they aren't old. I'm ninety-nine percent sure these are compression wedges. I've seen these countless times in victims of automobile-pedestrian accidents. We call them bumper fractures."

"Hit and run horse and buggy?" Frank said.

Jake wandered over to a light box on the wall where an X-ray of a skull was mounted. "How do you know who this skull belongs to?"

"Age," Benny said. "The victim with the bumper fractures is closer to thirty. The other three victims are in their late teens."

"Could be your thirty-year-old killed the other three with a bow and arrow and then someone killed her or something fell on her." Robinson took another long sip of coffee. "I haven't seen anything yet to convince me this is a current death."

"Really." Benny joined Jake at the light box. He tapped a pen against the screen. "How about dental implants?"

14

"Implants." Robinson twirled the empty thermos on Benny's desktop. "Well, unless some alien came down with new technology in the eighteen hundreds, we've got a homicide on our hands. But what the hell was she doing in a burial pit with three Natives and artifacts?"

"You saw the size of that backhoe," Frank said. "It mangled centuries of history in a few swell swoops. If there was any evidence in that pit, it's gone now."

"I have seen just about everything that came out of that dig site." Benny tossed his clipboard on the desk. It clattered to a halt just inches from Robinson's thermos. "I didn't see anything that looked like evidence of a homicide. My office could take over the entire…"

"No," Robinson bellowed with a shake of his head. "People will get suspicious. No one out of this office, not the press, not the archeologists, is to be told about Jane Doe until we have her identified. Let the bone people keep digging, tell them you want to see all non-artifact items."

"Well, then, let me contact a forensic dentist I have worked with in the past. Maybe Jake and Frank can pay him a visit and ask him to come take a look at the remains," Benny offered.

Jake asked, "Can you tell how long she's been dead, Benny?"

"I can have a chemical analysis of the nitrogen levels in the bones done but your guys can probably find out quicker."

"How's that?" Robinson asked.

"Find a name. Can't be that many people missing from this area, not with two dental implants."

* * *

"Dr. Les Payne." Frank chuckled as they entered a conference room on the third floor of the Professional Dental Associates building. "Clever on his part to create a fictitious name that's memorable. Wonder if he has a brother named Moe."

The three-story building was located on the opposite side of town, close to the expressway. It had conference rooms on the top floor, surgical rooms on the second floor, and the X-ray lab and examination rooms on the first floor. This was also a teaching facility with new graduates working side by side with experienced dentists.

Jake walked the length of the wall studying framed pictures. There were photos of Dr. Payne with local and state politicians, with an entire high school tennis team along with their trophy, the same familiar face in a South American country, and another with a caption of Bosnia – 1995. The last photo showed a cluster of people standing around a plane crash. Fit and trim, the only change in the doctor over the years appeared to be in the addition of gray hair.

"Quite a busy guy," Jake said. "Look at these certificates. He's a maxilo-facial surgeon, pedodontist, oral surgeon, orthodontist, and forensic dentist."

"Sorry to keep you waiting." The figure at the door stood ramrod straight with a crew cut so close to the scalp it was hard to tell Payne's true hair color. He was dressed casual in a golf shirt and cotton pants.

"Detective Frank Travis." Frank reached a hand out to him. "And Detective Sergeant Jake Mitchell."

After the handshaking, Payne motioned them to the chairs. "Dr. Lau forewarned me you would be paying me a visit." He poured three glasses of water and sat down. "Now, how can I help you?"

Frank explained that they were trying to identify the body of a woman who had two dental implants, without revealing that it had anything to do with the recent discovery at the construction site.

"Sounds like an interesting case." Dr. Payne opened a cabinet behind him and retrieved what looked like a plaster upper and lower jaw. They listened intently as the doctor proceeded to give a show-and-tell version of implants, explaining the process in a lecture mode.

Jake picked up the plaster mold of the upper jaw. He studied the placement of the implant. "I know they put some type of identification on dentures. Is the same done for implants?"

"Unfortunately, no. The posts are made of NI-TI, nickel titanium. The tooth is porcelain fused to base metal or high noble gold to prevent plaque build up. What materials are used is strictly up to the dentist. But as far as placing the patient's name or some identifying code number, that hasn't been done…yet."

Frank asked, "Is it possible to tell if the two implants on the deceased were done at the same time?"

Dr. Payne returned the plastic molds to the cabinet. "To be honest, I have yet in all my years had the opportunity to look at an implant post-mortem. But I'll give it a try."

"How can you just lay there? Aren't you bored? Don't you want to get out of here?" Quince paced like an angry caged lion.

Alex was lying on his back, hat covering his face. His sigh was long and drawn out. How impatient young ones were these days. He lifted the hat from his face and stared at the youth. His hair was worn straight, touching his shoulders. But that was the only thing traditional about the teen. Alex flung his hat off and shoved himself to a sitting position. He ran his eyes down the length of the lanky youth, shook his head in disgust at the slacks that hung low on the teen's hips. The dark, sleeveless tee shirt clung to a torso that was starting to fill out.

"*Wanka wan!*"

"Huh? What are you saying, old man? The pretty lady isn't here to interpret for you." Quince's lips curled in a snarl. He was a boy looking for a street corner.

"Look at that, the way you dress," Alex said.

"Well, you do speak English. About time."

"You should be ashamed, walking around with your pants around your *unze*. And what do you call that kind of shirt?"

"It's a wife beater shirt. Frees up your arms so you can punch and slap without tearing your shirt." He said it with a smile.

No wonder Quince's grandfather was having such a rough time with him. "You have no respect for women or your elders. You have been influenced by the white man's school and the hop-hop music."

"It's hip-hop. It's good music. Better than that rattle hopping rain dance your ancestors did."

"Hip-hop." Alex pushed at the air with his hand. "Your grandfather and I fought the influence of the white man's school in our day. They wanted us to lose our traditions, our customs, our way of life."

"That's wonderful advice, old man. You want me to quit school? Maybe hang out on the street corners?"

"No. *Nuhcan*. You have deaf ears. An education is the only way you will get ahead in this world. You helped to hide the artifacts and bones. Why?"

"I was able to get out of school for the day." He smiled broadly, showing a mouth of stark white teeth. "It was fun."

"*Aksaka*. Too bad. You do not see importance of your heritage. You have no idea what has been done to our ancestors' remains in the past."

"Dead is dead." Quince wrapped his fingers around the bars and yanked repeatedly. "I want out of here. You are letting the white man keep me caged."

"No," Alex said softly. "YOU are keeping yourself caged."

"I know my rights. I haven't even seen a lawyer. My parents would never leave me in here."

Alex smiled. How naïve this young man was. How blind to

what was happening around him. "The police can hold you for forty-eight hours. And it is your parents and grandfather who want you in here and refuse to visit until you straighten out."

"You lie." He paced with more fury this time, pounding the bars with each pivot.

"This is the middle of your summer vacation," Alex said. "Your grandfather wants you to go to Eagle Ridge with him for a week. That's all he asks. Visit the reservation and learn from the elders. He and I had already been on a vision quest by your age."

"Fairy tales." He scowled at Alex with dark eyes that burned with an intense fury.

Alex recognized that fury. At Quince's age and even through his thirties, Alex saw that same fury whenever he looked in the mirror.

"Did you ever hear the story of the fight between two wolves?"

"Great," Quince muttered. "Another old lady's tale." He crossed his legs at the ankles and plopped down on the floor, back against the bars. Lockup was empty today. The drunks had been released and the weather had thieves soaking up the sun and resting for the weekend.

Alex ignored his comment. "It is a story about life, as told by an elderly Cherokee to his grandchildren. He told them that a fight was going on inside of him, a horrible fight between two wolves. One wolf represented anger, fear, envy, greed, arrogance, self-pity, guilt, resentment, and pride. The other wolf represented joy, peace, hope, love, humility, kindness, friendship, truth, and compassion. The old Cherokee tells his grandchildren that this same fight is going on inside each and every one of them. The grandchildren thought for a moment. Then one child asked the grandfather, 'Which wolf will win?' You know what the elderly man said?" Alex waited for Quince to reply but the youth kept staring at the ceiling. "The elderly man replied, 'The one I feed.'"

Quince appeared to roll the words around in his head. Then his upper lip curled in a snarl as he asked, "Which wolf do you feed, old man?"

Alex's eyes fired with anger for several seconds. Then he threw back his head and laughed.

"What's so funny, old man?"

Alex clenched the sides of the bunk, head shaking as he continued to laugh. Wiping his eyes, he said, "That's the same thing I said to my grandfather when he told me that story."

"Nice to see you again." Benny shook Dr. Payne's hand and led him into the room.

Payne hadn't changed out of the golf shirt and pants they had seen him in earlier. The detectives stepped aside to allow Payne to see the full scope of the room.

"It has been awhile." Payne took several minutes to study the bones lying on the examination tables. "These aren't the bones from the recent discovery, are they?"

"Yes," Jake replied. "Three of the remains are of interest to our archeologists. But the fourth," he said with a nod toward Table Three "is of interest to our Homicide Department."

Benny left the room and returned several seconds later with the skull. He placed it on another table, then slid the X-rays into the light box.

Dr. Payne stepped closer to the screen. He remained quiet and his only acknowledgement was a slight nodding of his head. He retrieved the skull from the table and brought it back to the screen, again remaining silent except for a few grunts as he tilted the skull to examine the teeth.

"There is a good chance these were done at the same time. I'd say this lady was of considerable means. Few insurance companies will pay for implants."

"So we are looking for a rich woman around thirty who has been missing for…" Frank looked at Benny.

"Five years is my best guess," Benny replied. "Nitrogen levels were high but temperature and moisture can affect those results so it isn't exact."

"She may not be from this area, though," Jake reminded him.

Payne handed the skull back to Benny. "We have a national databank. There are about ten years worth of records including X-rays we can access."

"I had a chance to go to Peru," Greg said. He tipped back the bottle and took a long swallow of water. "Would have been a lot more interesting than digging up a few bones and arrowheads." He watched T.J. slap the dust from his hat and toss it on the front seat of his truck. The professor studied his reflection in the truck's side mirror, smoothed stray hairs back with his fingers. "Look at him," Greg said. "You'd think photographers from National Geographic were here to take his picture."

"Green is not your color, Greg." Angel rummaged through the cooler for a bottle of water.

"He doesn't even like to get dirty. He'll spend the rest of the day filling his clipboard of notes."

"He's done his share."

"Right," Greg hissed. "Wonder why it's only his female students who praise him to the heavens."

"And I wonder why only the guys find fault in everything he does."

On other digs it hadn't bothered Greg that women gravitated toward T.J. Greg just wanted the experience of working with one of the best. Why the change? His only answer could be Angel. Greg's voice softened and he reached out to brush dirt from Angel's face. "I can't believe how he treats you, though. He's supposed to be the ladies man yet he appears to detest you."

She turned her face away and stared at T.J. There was a wistfulness there that Greg couldn't decipher. Finally she turned back to him and said, "Guess not every woman is his type." She turned to leave but Greg touched her arm.

"Did you want to be?"

15

The Irish setter kept pace with Sam as she power-walked the asphalt path that led to Alex's house in the back acres of the property. Poco slowed as they approached the house, then halted and sat at the bottom of the stairs. A whine erupted from her throat and she looked at Sam with the saddest eyes. It broke Sam's heart.

"He'll be home soon, Poco. How about I see what kind of treats he has for you?" Sam patted Poco's head then bounded up the stairs and across the porch. Alex never locked his door so Sam easily gained access to the two-bedroom, one-story house. A breeze filtered through the open windows while a ceiling fan droned slowly overhead. The house was tidy with Navaho-designed area rugs scattered over oak floors. It could use a few paintings or basically a good woman's touch but it was Alex's domain and neither Abby nor Sam interfered.

Sam found the treats in a canister on the counter. She set two dog biscuits aside, then filled up a glass of ice water and returned to the porch.

"Here you go." Sam tossed one biscuit to Poco, then sat on the top stair and watched the pup flop on the grass to enjoy the treat. Several yards away was a timber structure covered with blankets. The *inipi* was used to cleanse and purify the body. One hundred yards beyond the timber structure was a thirty-foot tall tipi constructed by Alex where he would sometimes sleep and eat. He said he felt closer to the spirits there. The acres beyond the tipi were left untouched, the wild flowers and brush growing natural. Ivy grew wild around tree trunks and fencing.

She took a long swallow of the cold water and closed her eyes briefly to savor the warm sun. When she opened her eyes it wasn't daytime.

Sam is standing next to a small green two-door sports car. It's nighttime and the car is jacked up, a tire lying in the grass. Without street lights it's difficult to tell what's on either side of the road. The moon plays tag with wisps of clouds and now Sam sees that she is standing on the shoulder of an expressway. The buzzing of cicadas fills the air yet the only trees she sees are off in the distance.

The trunk of the sports car is open, hazard lights flashing. Sam looks down at the jean cutoffs and scuffed sneakers she is wearing. How did her mother ever let her out of the house dressed like this? An ankle bracelet with palm trees and pineapples are wrapped around her right ankle. Sam rakes a hand through her hair and is surprised to find it is straight and barely touches her shoulder. What happened to her long curly hair?

Lights erupt over the hill and the throaty cough of a truck brings hope that some good Samaritan will offer to change her tire. Sam shield's her eyes from the bright lights as the driver pulls the truck behind the sports car. The driver's side door opens and a man steps out. He's husky and wearing a dark uniform of some type, a baseball cap and sunglasses. He walks around to the passenger side, opens the door and steps aside. She doesn't need to tell him anything. He just grabs tools from the back of his truck and sets out to replace her tire.

Sam hesitates, not sure if she should watch him work and make small talk or sit in the truck. He obviously left the passenger side door open as an offer for her to sit inside, away from the impending storm. Off in the distance, thunder rumbles. The truck isn't a semi. It's more a delivery truck of some type. She can't make out the name on the side. The letters are weathered.

She hikes up her dress and climbs into the truck. Dress? She wasn't wearing a dress a minute ago. The driver offers her a bottle of water and then tends to her car. By the time he is done changing the tire she is feeling sleepy. Matter of fact, she is downright tripping. She sees two men now, big, broad and flat faced like boxers. They are blending together then pulling apart.

Before she realizes there is something in the water, his hands are around her neck and he has her down on the front seat of the truck. With one knee on her chest he tightens his grip. She can't breathe. With what little strength she has left, Sam tries to raise her arms to fight but they lay uselessly at her side. Drugged and paralyzed, she can't fight back. The whine from the cicadas gets louder, filling the air, filling her head.

She feels bones crushing in her throat and the life seeping from her body.

Poco's barking snaps Sam back into daylight. The Irish setter whines and nuzzles Sam's arm.

"I'm okay. Just went away for a little bit." Sam gulped the water.

The puppy cocked its head and stared at her. Tiny pinpricks traveled up Sam's back. This had never happened before. How much time had elapsed? Her hands went instinctively to her throat which felt raw and bruised.

Instead of witnessing an event as though watching a movie, she actually was in it. This was puzzling. What happened to the chase through the woods? What happened to the arrow? Why would the spirits choose now to show Sam another murder? It didn't seem as though answers were coming anytime soon. And this was one incident she couldn't share with her skeptical husband.

There was a knock on Jake's office door and the two baby dicks walked in. Andy Brainard and Maury Jackson were fresh-faced and spit-shined. Although identical in dress, from tailored suits and flashy ties, they were complete opposites on the DNA scale. Andy was red-haired and freckled and of Irish descent. Maury was Jamaican black and adorned in gold bracelets, necklaces, and one gold earring. They clicked so well together they were known to sometimes finish each other's sentences.

"Anything else we can do…?" Andy started.

"Like narrow the search down further?" Maury added.

They each had relatives high on the food chain which also helped to fast-track them. But they had more than proven themselves over the past year.

Jake's massive dark wood desk took up most of the space in his office. It seemed a waste since the desktop held just *In* and *Out* boxes, a calendar, pens, an FBI coffee mug, and whatever file he was working on at the moment. Family pictures or certificates would not be found hanging on the walls. One wall had windows halfway to the ceiling.

Jake rubbed the fatigue from his eyes. "What about Dr. Payne's database? Has he dropped it off yet?"

Frank crossed in front of the windows waving an envelope in his fingers.

"Finally," Jake said. "Thanks for the help," he told the baby dicks. After they left, Jake took the disk from Frank and loaded it into the computer.

Frank grabbed the listing the baby dicks had compiled and sat down. "Looks like they included the entire Midwest. Females aged fifteen to forty."

"What does it look like?" Jake tapped a few keys and Dr. Payne's listing appeared on the screen.

Frank thumbed through to the end of the stack. "Looks like they found around four hundred. They includee the dates reported missing, too."

Janet appeared in the doorway. "Looks like someone needs coffee." Deep dimples appeared when Janet smiled. She grabbed both of their cups and returned a couple minutes later.

They smiled their thanks. Frank said, "You are going to make someone a great …"

Janet pushed at the air with one hand. "Don't want to hear it. You two and the captain are the only ones I get coffee for. You know you're my favorites."

"And such a flirt, too," Frank added. "Listen, have you ever thought of what you want done with your remains?"

Jake leaned back and rolled his eyes toward the ceiling. "Remains?"

"Yeah. You ever think about it? I can't decide on whether to be buried, cremated, put in a drawer, a vase, a crypt, made into a diamond, buried in a squad car."

"Of course I've thought about it." Janet flashed a coy smile, eliciting just one of the dimples. "I don't plan on dying."

Frank blinked several times as if her response needed serious consideration. "Well, there you go," he said. "That's my answer. I don't plan on dying."

"Later," Janet said, and closed the door behind her.

Jake took a sip of the fresh brewed coffee and wished he could mainline it. It wasn't the fresh ground beans Abby prepared for him but he wasn't complaining.

"How did Dr. Payne compile his report?" Frank asked, one hand wrapped around his coffee mug, the other holding the first page of the baby dicks' report.

Jake scrolled down the listing. "Looks alphabetical. He has a column for the date of the implant and additional columns with dates of subsequent implants." He scrolled back to the top and was just ready to start reading the names off to Frank when his finger hovered over the keyboard.

"What's wrong?"

Jake clasped his hands behind his head and whooshed out a long breath. "I think we just identified our victim."

Bored with the dig site, Greg joined Inga at Benny's lab where she was attempting to organize the artifacts.

"Oh good," Inga said. "You're here."

"Where do you want me to start?"

"Start with the bones. That will give me time to put these additional artifacts in order." Inga carefully moved the pottery to one area. "I'm surprised the workmen didn't break more of these pieces." She held up a beaded pouch and admired the handiwork. "What kind of trouble is T.J. making?"

"The usual. He's really trying my patience."

She carried the pouch to a table reserved for adornments. "He does throw his weight around from time to time."

"He throws more than his weight around. It's hard to get picked for one of his digs. I'm just glad you were in charge of the crew this time. Whenever Professor Logan picks a crew, it's mainly all female and they are all attractive. They play up to him, too, wearing tight shorts and low-cut tops. I've seen different girls popping in and out of his tent at all hours."

Inga abandoned her work and walked over to Greg. "Those are some serious charges. Are you sure this isn't just sour grapes?"

"Now you're sounding like Angel. She thinks I'm just jealous."

"Well, maybe there is a little bit of that. T.J.'s very charismatic and you are very cerebral. Smart women will see through him pretty quick."

She stood for a few minutes and watched as Greg snapped

pictures of the remains on the first table. "At least it looks like we retrieved the majority of the bones," Greg said.

"Most, but not all. Dr. Lau found marks from an arrow on three of the Natives. He said they were shot in the back. Could be the women were trying to escape. Sam seems to think it was prior to 1833. We will just have to narrow it down a bit more in order to know which tribes were involved."

He could feel Inga's eyes on him as he changed the batteries in the camera.

"You and Angel seem to work well together."

Greg could feel his face flush. He continued to snap pictures and tried to sound casual.

"She's nice."

"Ummmm." Inga smiled at him. "She thinks you're nice, too."

"She said that?" Maybe this project wouldn't be a waste of time after all.

16

"I certainly hope you are telling me I can finally start construction again." Breyton unbuttoned his suit jacket and took a seat at the conference table. The detectives sat across from him. Captain Robinson remained standing against the wall. If the wall could talk, it would probably emit a painful groan. Breyton's attorney had a habit of being late, something Breyton had little patience for. He checked his watch, then pulled out his cell phone.

Attorney Stephen Weber rushed into the room and slammed a briefcase on the table. "I have to be in court in one hour. I hope this is important."

Robinson shoved away from the wall saying, "You may need to reschedule." He walked over to the table and motioned for the attorney to take a seat.

Weber was spit-shined and dressed in designer threads. His high forehead glistened under the harsh ceiling lights. Robinson introduced the detectives to Weber.

"Mr. Breyton," Robinson started. "Have you spoken to your wife recently?" Robinson asked.

Breyton snorted. "Like she gives a damn. She took off with some young stud three years ago. What the hell does that have to do with anything?"

Jake opened a file folder. He took his time placing pictures of the victim from Table Three. Jake saved the dental X-rays for last.

"What are we looking at here, gentlemen?" Weber asked.

Robinson placed the palms of his hands on the table and stared at Breyton for a few seconds before saying, "Your wife."

"WHAT?" A gray hue settled over Breyton's face. "That can't be. Where did you find these?"

Robinson walked back over to the wall. "She was one of the victims found at your construction site."

"She had two dental implants," Jake said, "and the X-rays are a match to those on file in her dentist's office."

"That's it?" Weber said. "That's all you have to go on?"

"She left a note in her own writing," Breyton protested.

"You received no follow-up letters or phone calls from your wife?" Frank asked. "No calls to taunt you or ask for money?"

"I told her she was on her own. If she thought that new boyfriend was all she needed, then fine. She wasn't getting anything from me." Breyton wagged a finger at Jake. "This is a trick. You'll try anything to keep me from making my construction deadline just to please your mother-in-law and your wife. Don't think I don't know what's going on. It's a conflict of interest if you ask me."

Frank said, "You married Amanda when she was nineteen. A bit of a trophy wife, I'd say. Did she love you or your money?"

"Wait a minute." Breyton raised up. Weber placed a hand on his arm. Breyton sank back down.

"They were married for eight years," Weber said. "Of course they had a happy marriage."

Robinson chuckled. "But did she love him?"

"Obviously not since she found someone else to love." Frank cocked his head to catch Breyton's attention. "Viagra didn't work for you?"

"Fuck you," Breyton breathed. "I worked sixty-hour weeks to keep that whore in diamonds. And look how she repaid me."

"Whoa." Frank held up his hands. "Little anger there, brother. Did you get mad enough to run your wife down with your Cadillac?"

"Or maybe pay someone to do it?" Robinson added.

Even Weber's hand didn't hold Breyton down. He lunged from his chair. "I DID NOT KILL MY WIFE."

"Wait a minute." Weber held the X-ray in his hand. "You're saying she was murdered?"

Robinson dug another X-ray from the file folder. "According to our medical examiner, it shows what he calls bumper fractures which is evident in automobile-pedestrian accidents."

"I want copies of everything," Weber said. "I'll get a second opinion not only on the injuries but also on the identification. Until you have positive proof that my client is responsible, then I assume he is free to go."

"For now." Robinson handed the file folder back to Jake. "In the meantime, this information doesn't go out of this room, unless you want to see your client's face on the five o'clock news. Give us a chance to pound the pavement."

"We have DNA," Breyton offered. "Amanda convinced me to take part in that *National Genographic* research data bank several years ago to trace our geneology."

Jake shoved a pad of paper across the table and told Breyton, "Write down every detail about the last day you saw your wife. Who did you talk to? Who might she have talked to? Who can vouch for your whereabouts the entire twenty-four hours?"

"That's ridiculous." Breyton shoved it back across the table.

Weber said, "I think we need answers, Elton." His face was hard to read but his words weren't. Weber may be a good corporate lawyer, but Jake doubted he ever tried a murder case.

Robinson added, "We also need a list of any friends or acquaintances who might have spoken to Amanda before she disappeared."

"What about her family?" Jake asked.

"She was an orphan. Lived in a foster home in Pennsylvania somewhere. Hasn't talked to them in years," Breyton replied.

They left the two men in the interrogation room and walked back to Captain Robinson's office.

"What a mess." Robinson sat down with a hiss of leather and squeak of wheels. "We have no way of knowing how far down Amanda Breyton's body was in relation to the Native American remains."

Jake leaned against the doorjamb. Frank preferred to perch on the edge of the credenza. The outer office was a buzz of activity as phones rang and people drifted down the hall from the break room to the elevator and stairway.

Frank said, "Amanda definitely wasn't killed there because clothes have not been found, unless she wasn't wearing any when she was killed."

"The archeologists are still working the area. We'll have to close the site down which isn't going to make Professor Logan happy," Jake reminded them.

Robinson rocked back and forth, eyes narrowed in thought. He propped one elbow on the armrest and jammed a beefy fist under his chin. The clock above the doorway ticked off the minutes.

"We're really jammed in the corner on this one," Robinson said. "When the press learns about Amanda Breyton, they'll be all over that pit so we have to make sure it's locked up tight as a drum. We probably have about all we can get out of it. Maybe the pile of dirt next to the dig site might produce some clues but I seriously doubt it. Let's not dismiss the archeologists just yet. Soon as our crime techs give the go ahead, the bone people can get back in there. Agreed?"

The detectives nodded.

"Shall we cut Breyton loose?" Frank asked.

"Nothing to hold him on...yet," Robinson replied. "Get the list of acquaintances and talk to everyone and anyone who knew Breyton and his wife. There must be a disgruntled ex-wife somewhere, too. Get the baby dicks to help you out."

As the detectives rose to leave, Robinson barked out, "Sit." With a glare meant only for Jake he said, "Now what the hell did your wife take out of this department?"

17

It didn't take long for the press to hear about Amanda Breyton. Although Captain Robinson tried to keep the discovery quiet for as long as possible, it was Chief Dennis Murphy who had held a press conference after lunch to stress to the public that all men are innocent until proven guilty. And it was Breyton himself who made a public statement that he had loved his wife, was innocent of any wrongdoing, and needed time to grieve before answering any questions from the press.

After making copies of the list of known friends, relatives, and associates, and splitting up the contacts with the baby dicks, Jake and Frank drove to the condos by the Three Oaks Golf Course for their first interview.

"You can't be here for my son so I must be a prime suspect in something." Carmen Valukis held open the door for the detectives. They had met several months ago when working on another case. Her son had been a person of interest in a homicide. When Jake saw Carmen's name listed as one of the acquaintances of the late Amanda Breyton, he decided to start with her. Carmen missed her calling. She should have been a gossip columnist.

"Where did Danny go?" Frank asked. "If he's in prison again, we didn't put him there."

Carmen barked out a laugh. "He decided he was going to be another Hemingway and moved to the Florida Keys. Naturally, I gave him a few bucks but he prefers to live on the street and sleep on the beach while he finds himself."

Jake wanted to tell her she should move and not leave a forwarding address but he kept his mouth shut. They shielded their eyes from the bright colors in the living room. Carmen hadn't changed her décor. Her condo still looked like the inside of a roll of Lifesavers. Now Jake regretted not offering to meet her at a restaurant or at Headquarters.

They refused her offer for something to drink, hoping to make it brief and give their retinas a rest. Jake picked the lemon-colored barrel chair; Frank settled into the lime-colored one. Staring at Carmen didn't make it any easier. Although the couch she decided to drape herself on was white, she was dressed in a painter's palette of chiffon.

"Okay, what can I do for you boys." She shoved a cigarette in her mouth and waited for Jake to light it.

Frank started the questioning. "We understand you worked on a number of committees with Amanda Breyton."

"A blast from the past." Plumes of smoke drifted from Carmen's mouth. "What a piece of work. I wouldn't say we worked on committees. All she did was show up a few times and that was it. Never did any work. Was always rushing off to a hair or manicure appointment."

Jake fired up his own cigarette. "Did she talk about her husband?"

"Loved his money, hated him. You see it all the time. Rich old fart thinks he can get any woman in the world as long as he tosses enough money her way. Then he's shocked that she doesn't have undying love for him. He was what? Twenty-five years older than her? Jeez, Louise." She waved the smoke from the air, as though making room for her next exhale. "She played dutiful wife for all of about six months."

"Did she have undying love for *anyone*?" Frank waved his hand at the clouds of smoke drifting his way.

"Anyone? How about everyone?" She barked out another laugh. "The masseur at the country club, her golf instructor, the landscaper, the pool boy." Her laughter sent another plume of smoke drifting across the coffee table." She pulled out a second cigarette and lit it from the tip of the one in her mouth.

"So she had a string of boyfriends." Jake asked, "Any idea

which one she left town with?"

"None of them. But, like I said, she got her name on the committee member lists but didn't show up often. I'd see her more at the country club, the spa, or shopping center. She gave up all those other guys. Had fallen hopelessly in love, she told me. But I couldn't drag details out of her to save my soul. She had changed. Started volunteering at the hospital in the children's AIDs wing and even taking classes at the local college."

Jake started forming a picture in his mind of Amanda Breyton. It was a different picture than the staged wedding photos. Amanda was young, beautiful, fun loving. More likely to be in a *Girls Gone Wild* video than *Volunteer of the Month*. Elton described her as a money-grubbing wench. Would Amanda Breyton give up all that money for love?

Jake asked, "Did Amanda mention if she and Breyton had a prenuptial agreement?"

"He'd be a fool not to. If she stayed with him less than ten years, she received nothing more than a hundred grand."

"Wow," Frank said with a shake of his head. "She must have really fallen hard for someone to give up all that money."

"What about his will?" Jake wasn't about ready to give up on the money angle. "What if Breyton died while they were still married?"

"Oh, why she'd get everything, of course."

"So, what do you think?" Frank asked as they climbed into the unmarked car.

"Lots." Jake rolled down the window and lit another cigarette. "Amanda and the new boyfriend could have planned to kill Breyton but he found out about it."

"Yeah. I can see those bruiser bodyguards of his killing a defenseless woman."

"But then, where's the boyfriend's body?" Jake asked. "It

wasn't in the pit."

"That would have been too obvious. Better to scatter the bodies. Put cement shoes on one and toss him in Lake Michigan. I swear, if global warming becomes a reality and Lake Michigan dries up, we're going to find a lot of missing bodies."

"That doesn't work," Jake said. "Breyton is too smart to dig where his wife's body is buried. And how lucky could someone be to pick a spot where Indians are buried?"

"It's his property. He might have discovered the other bones years ago when he first bought the property. Then it came in handy when he was looking for a place to bury his wife. Figured no one would question the fourth body not being a couple hundred years old."

Jake blew smoke out of the window as he watched golfers tee off at the golf course adjacent to Carmen's building. Golf was one sport he loved but had little time for. Other than the annual golf outing, he did little other than chip balls in the backyard which sent Alex into cardiac arrest at the divots in the grass.

"If Amanda was planning to run off with this guy, where's her suitcase?" Jake asked. "Where are her clothes? I can't see her leaving her diamonds behind."

"You forget. The lady was head over heels, willing to give up hubby's fortune and probably not want anything Breyton had given her. Unless" Frank added, "she demanded a price to stay and Breyton wouldn't pay it. We do like the money angle."

Thunder rolled, growing in intensity, bringing with it flashes of light. Sam is walking along a concrete path being pushed and shoved by forces unseen. It is humid and crowded and the people surrounding her are void of features. She can't see their faces, much less bodies. All she can feel is their presence.

They push and bob along like buoys in a lake. Sam feels as though she is carrying a huge weight. Her hands drop to her stomach where a noticeable bump swells. She is pregnant. Pregnant? The lights along the wall of this concrete tunnel flicker off and on as thunder shakes the solid ground under her feet. She feels the crowd without features again, their shoulders jarring her from side to side. Up ahead the ground appears to drop off. A stairway. The crowd moves like a swarm down into the abyss. And then she feels a hand against her back and a forceful, vicious shove catapults her over the faceless, unseen crowd. Down, down. Her feet not touching the ground, her hands unable to grip a handrail or a passerby. The faceless crowd there, but not there. They are just wisps of energy, nothing solid to grab onto.

In those last few seconds, her arms instinctively surround her stomach, attempting to shield her child. She lays crumpled at the bottom of the stairs as a bolt of lightning illuminates the surrounding area.

Sam's eyes snapped opened. She blinked several times, then slowly sat up in bed as thunder rumbled overhead and rain pounded the outside balcony.

The clock radio on the headboard said it was after one in the morning. Jake's side of the bed was empty. Sam shook the residuals of her bizarre dream from her head and stumbled to the opened patio door. The roof's overhang did little to prevent the wind from blowing the rain against the glass. She inhaled the fresh air as she tried to clear her head. Rain had a cleansing effect. It washed the trees and brought a new earth smell to the air.

She padded down the hallway to the nursery. The ceiling stars sprayed a soft glow through the room. Dillon was lying on his back, lips wrapped around a pacifier. She placed her fingers under his left hand and marveled at the perfection of this little creation. Ten fingers, ten toes, his father's build, and, thank God, his father's hair. Sam slid the pacifier from his mouth and set it on the dressing table. She watched him sleep for several minutes and thought back to the dream. Just before giving birth she'd had a number of dreams where she had gone into labor. Upon waking, she would touch her stomach to see if it were true. Was the nine months over with and the labor part just a dream? This was the first time after Dillon was born that she had a dream that she was still pregnant. Bizarre.

She slid onto the window seat and watched as lightning streaked across the sky and rain fell in sheets. Winds tugged petals off the daylilies and blew water from the birdbath below. The next flash of lightning zapped the outside lights, fooling the solar powered system. The wind whipped, blowing rain against the window. Beads of water trailed slowly, meandering in a haphazard fashion. She paid little attention until a shape materialized on the window pane. It was brief, freezing in place as though waiting for the image to bore a hole in Sam's memory. Then it vanished just as quickly, disintegrating into numerous water trails. Sam chalked it up to lack of sleep or her over-active imagination. But she could swear she had seen a skull.

18

After a late breakfast, the detectives decided to follow up with more of the names Carmen had given them. They started with the women's shelter where Amanda had volunteered.

They stood in the doorway while chaos reigned around them. Toddlers in diapers charged around the coffee table. Infants who hadn't quite acquired the fine art of standing crawled around the floor doing what babies do best—tasting every crumb and dust ball on the rug. Three women lounging on upholstered chairs appeared oblivious to the racket as they engaged in conversations. They looked tired and beaten, literally. Bruises were fading and swollen lips were slowly healing.

The director who had left the detectives standing at the door, probably for their own safety, held up a finger to let them know she would be one more minute on her phone call.

"We should have waited outside," Frank whispered. He winced as another unknown substance made its way into the mouth of one of the baby vacuum cleaners.

"I think I'm beginning to pine for Carmen's bright décor." Jake pulled off his sunglasses and shoved them in his shirt pocket. He felt his partner's eyes on him. "What?"

"Is Sam grounded?"

"Yeah, right. The one who should be grounded is Ed Scofield. He's always had a soft spot for Sam."

"At least we know Robinson is more bark than bite. You are like the sacred cow of The Sixth."

"The captain is more worried about Murphy. The chief would welcome any excuse to fire my ass."

The director finally ended her call and maneuvered around the obstacles in the living room as she made her way to the door. "I am so sorry for the wait." She held out her hand. "Sarah Whitcomb. I'm Pastor Whitcomb's wife." She shook hands with both of them, then motioned to the door on their left. "It will be quieter in here."

And it was. The conference room was small but tidy. A wall of windows looked out onto a playground where older children were swinging on swings and climbing stairs to a slide.

Sarah's position as a pastor's wife was broadcast by the way she dressed and spoke. Her blouse fit snug around her neck. Her skirt hung mid-calf revealing little of the shape of her legs although it was evident there were curves under the plain white blouse and gray skirt. Her shoes were selected for comfort, not style, and were more befitting a nun. Sarah's face was void of makeup but there was a natural beauty even without the makeup. Her blonde hair was pulled back, twisted, and held in place by a large barrette.

"We understand Amanda Breyton volunteered at your shelter," Jake said as he opened his notepad and wrote Mrs. Whitcomb's name at the top.

"Yes. She was here quite often. Lovely woman." As an afterthought, Sarah squeaked out a, "was." Sarah's hands were clasped on the table and she sat as though a ruler were placed on her head. And she waited. And waited.

It was obvious Jake would have to pull information out of her. "Did she ever talk about her husband or home life? Maybe working for the shelter was helping her to cope with any marital problems she might have been having."

"Not at all. She loved her life and felt so fortunate. It's wonderful that she wanted to give back to the community." Sarah's smile never wavered. It was permanently drawn on, or practiced.

Frank asked, "Did she ever talk about her personal life? It isn't too much of a secret that Amanda had a lot of male friends."

"Everyone loved Amanda. What wasn't there to like? She was beautiful, had a wonderful sense of style, easy to talk to. What she was really good at was helping the women here to learn to dress, walk, apply makeup. She helped them build self-esteem. We all know men have a way of robbing women of their self-esteem."

Stepford wife, Frank wrote on his notepad.

Jake had a feeling he would get better feedback talking to the women in the shelter. "Was there anyone here at the shelter that Amanda might have bonded with?"

"That was several years ago, Sergeant. We have turn-over just about every six months. Other than helping with the makeup and hair, Amanda didn't get much closer to the women." She stood abruptly. Jake thought maybe she had to go back to the factory for new batteries. "I'm sorry I can't be of more help, detectives." She walked to the door signaling the end of their meeting. "I have to be at the rectory in a few minutes to watch the phones. Please forgive me."

Sam considered it multi-tasking. Jake would consider it suicide and grounds for divorce. She was talking on the phone and composing a list as she drove. At least she didn't have Dillon in the back seat. The president of the Horticulture Society was the first name on her list. Sam had told the receptionist that she wanted to interview the president and was given the address for the Nettles Greenhouse.

She was still shocked that Captain Robinson had requested her assistance. Robinson had stressed she keep a low profile. Jake was so good at perceiving opportunities. Sam had wanted to blurt it to the newspapers how Chief Murphy had sat on the evidence that exonerated her from any wrongdoing in the murder of a fellow cop. Instead, Jake had said to use it to her advantage. Now Murphy had to play nice and the chief didn't like it one bit that Sam had something on him.

Amanda Breyton. Sam wasn't sure how or why she was seeing two different ways Amanda died…either by strangulation or victim of a hit and run. Could have been both, though. Perhaps she was able to get away from the man trying to strangle her and when she tried to escape he ran her down with his car…or truck. Made sense to her.

She stepped out of the Jeep and noticed in the distance acres of cocoon-shaped buildings shielded in weathered plastic. Besides flowers, Nettles Greenhouse also sold trees, shrubs, groundcover, all types of perennials and annuals, and an array of backyard décor such as gazing balls, birdbaths, and handcrafted bird feeders.

The shop was a maze of human worker bees. A cashier pointed Sam to the back of the shop which opened out into an immense yard of shoppers and a buzz of activity. Sam followed a decorative brick path to an area shielded by a ceiling of netting to shade a makeshift classroom.

A woman in a straw hat and bib apron addressing a group of fifteen shoppers wore the name tag of *Rose*. She was creating a planter of annuals and instructing the class on proper depth, potting soil, use of fertilizer, and pruning. The shoppers were engrossed and some were even taking notes. Rose was surrounded by what looked like a variety of planter and hanging basket creations.

Two of Rose's assistants were carbon copies, probably sisters. Their name tags read Iris and Camelia. Fat chance those were their real names.

Rose added ivy to a hanging basket. She worked barehanded and her apron gave meaning to getting down and dirty. After a fifteen-minute question and answer period, the crowd started to disperse. Iris and Camelia brought out brooms to clean the lecture area.

Sam shoved the notepad and pen back in her purse and approached Rose. "That was very informative." The woman's face lit up as though it were the first time anyone had ever given her a compliment. Rose had the pale eyes and blonde hair of Swedish genes. Creases at the corners of her eyes were the only signs of middle age. "Are those your real names?" Sam asked with a nod toward the two sweepers.

"Yes," said Rose with a smile. "And our mother's name was April. Mom and her sisters were named after the months. We were named after flowers."

Sam's fingers hesitated over the geranium petals. "I seem to kill everything I touch. Do you think there is something in my skin?" Rose laughed, all but dismissing that idea. "Your office at the Horticulture Society told me where to find you," Sam started. She explained she was a private detective trying to find anyone who might have known Amanda Breyton. Sam kept her fingers busy playing with the ivy and flower petals while Rose talked.

"Amanda had an artistic flair. She could whip up a centerpiece in no time flat. I told her she should take a course in floral design."

"Did Amanda come to the meetings by herself or with anyone in particular?"

"By herself. We were basically a garden party, meeting once a month for lunch and inviting a speaker on a variety of subjects. There were committees, like planting the flowers at the Veterans' Memorial or designing the flower planters along the meridians by the mall but she never volunteered for those tasks. She was just filling her day."

Sam hoped Jake was learning as little from his investigation as she was. She was just glad she took the time to do a dossier on the old fart, Breyton. "What was your impression of Amanda, woman to woman?" *Get as catty as you want, sweetheart.* Sam could swear the pupils in Rose's eyes narrowed like a feral beast.

Rose scanned the immediate area to make sure they weren't going to be overheard. "About the only thing she had going for her were her looks. Think of a cheerleader who sets her sights on, not the star quarterback, but the coach. Think of a young singer who ignores a band member in favor of the owner of the record company. She was wined and dined by a very rich man old enough to be her father. The only dumb thing she did was find a man in good health. Breyton's former wife was devastated. Out with the old, in with the new."

"Did you know Nora Breyton?"

"She was my best friend."

"Was?"

Rose shrugged. "What can I say? I knew Breyton was cheating on her but I didn't want to hurt her so I kept quiet. Breyton and my husband golfed together at the country club which is how I found out. Nora thought I should have told her. She has never forgiven me."

"Does she still live in town?"

"Sure. She got the mansion in the settlement which is why Breyton demanded a prenup with Amanda. Said he didn't want to get screwed again."

"Other than Breyton's cheating, how did he and his first wife get along?"

"He wasn't a wife beater, if that's what you're asking. Breyton started out building houses. Nora sold them through her real estate agency. She made a lot of money in real estate. Squirreled a chunk of it away that his lawyers never found during the divorce. He paid her off with a lump sum settlement and the house just so he could be free to rob the cradle."

"So there were no hard feelings on her part?"

Rose's smile said *what planet were you raised on*? "The word revenge was created with women in mind."

19

"Look at you. You are so cute." Sam nibbled on Dillon's cheek, much to his delight as he squealed and squirmed.

"Sam, you are going to leave a hickey on his face," Jake said.

She ran her fingers across Dillon's cheek. "Just marking my territory, much like I do to his father." She flashed Jake an air kiss. Dillon grabbed at her feathered earring. Sam grabbed his fingers and kissed them. "That's mine."

Abby set out four plates and an extra cup, then brought out the cake saver. One-half of a chocolate cake oozing with thick frosting could be seen through the glass lid.

"Was the database updated with the information the Korwin's gave me?" Sam asked.

Jake served her a dose of his cold stare.

"I'll make it up to you," she said, serving him a dose of coyness.

"Their glowing letter of praise they sent to Robinson certainly saved your cute ass."

"Even you would have crumbled if you had seen their look of hopelessness." She pulled the sugar bowl off the counter and grabbed the pint of half-and-half from the refrigerator. "How's the investigation going? Has anyone spoken to Nora Breyton, the ex-wife?"

"We've been playing telephone tag with her office for far too long," Jake admitted. "We've left business cards all over town, messages on her voicemail, even had a squad car parked in front of her house but the officer was told she had a meeting in Chicago and was staying overnight."

Sam retrieved the napkin holder from the cabinet and carried it to the dining room. She returned, grabbed the cake and again disappeared into the dining room.

Jake appeared mystified by the number of plates Sam had brought out. "Expecting company?"

"We didn't tell you?" With that the doorbell rang. "That's our guest."

Abby took her piece of cake and coffee to the study and left Sam to escort Nora Breyton to the dining room. It had been a small fib. Sam had used Abby's name to schedule an appointment with the real estate agent on the pretense that she wanted to sell her four-thousand-square-foot home. Sam was expecting a dowdy woman, a housewife stuck in the seventies as far as fashion sense. Instead, she was staring at an aging movie star who wore her makeup well, who wasn't embarrassed by the smile lines around her eyes. It was obvious the former Mrs. Breyton took time to attend a gym or had an exercise instructor at her disposal. Her suit was a designer label, Sam was sure; and her hair, honey-colored with a hint of frosting, had to have been styled by a Chicago hairdresser. A hairdo blunt cut to her chin, pulled behind her ears, with a fluff of bangs, had been designed with her face in mind. Manicure, pedicure…this woman had attended a spa in Chicago, not a meeting, as Jake had been told.

"This house is magnificent," Nora gushed, her gaze drifting past the door to the study, taking in her surroundings, the décor, the fireplaces in both the study and living room. "I have to come back in the daytime to see the exterior before I can give you the fair market value."

Sam motioned to one of the high back chairs. She retrieved Dillon from the kitchen and set the carrier on the table close to their guest. His eyelids were at half-mast. Sam had an ulterior motive in mind. People had a tendency to lower their voices when they saw a sleeping baby. Once Nora discovered the real reason she had been called out to the house, Sam wanted to make sure her guest stayed calm and reasonable.

Jake had been more accepting of her tactics. He had done his usual eye roll but had to admit he and Frank had been unable to persuade Nora Breyton to give them five minutes of her time.

Nora gushed almost as much at Dillon. "He is just adorable. How old is he?"

"Three months." As Sam had anticipated, Nora spoke in hushed tones. "We just got him to sleep. He doesn't sleep well." Another slight fib which was acknowledged by a glare from Jake. Dillon slept like a rock and had only been getting up once in the middle of the night.

"I remember Bryce when he was that age," Nora said. "They just kind of lie there and sleep all the time. Can't wait until they start to walk and do cute things. Then you miss the days when all they did was lie there and sleep." Her face appeared to cave in on itself, indicating to Sam that Nora had more regrets than just children growing up. Was she regretting the divorce? The happy family life? Did Bryce not measure up to what she had expected?

Sam plied Nora with cake and coffee first before admitting the ruse to get her to the house.

Nora set her fork down. "So your house isn't for sale?"

"No." Jake pushed his business card across the table.

"Well." She gave a brief shrug and said, "This will call for a second piece of cake. If it wasn't so good I would have been out of here. Amanda Breyton isn't my favorite subject."

Sam caught Jake's eye. Neither said anything but the fact that Jake was sipping coffee and shoveling cake into his mouth told her he was handing the reins to her. "She was quite a few years younger than Elton. How did the two meet?"

"The country club. She was a waitress, not that anything is wrong with waitressing. I did my share in my youth. Not sure how she got hired since her family isn't a member but I'm sure if you had seen her you would have hired her on the spot."

"Did you suspect an attraction between the two?"

"E Three is an outrageous flirt. I was used to that. And he has a sort of charming character. Looks a bit like William Shatner in his younger, thinner days."

E Three? Elton Breyton the Third. How clever. "But he didn't marry any of them." *Well, that was a little brash*, Jake's raised eyebrow told her.

"That's true." Nora scraped the icing from her plate, then looked eagerly at the cake saver for her second helping. Jake grabbed the knife and did the honors. "But none of the other women were as brazen as Amanda. She literally threw herself at him, leaning down and brushing against him with those big…" She glanced quickly at Jake as though just realizing they were in mixed company. "Let's just say she had an extremely attractive body, face, the whole package. She could have had just about any good looking, attractive young man in town but she goes after a man twenty-four years her senior." Nora dove into her second piece of cake.

Jake finally found his voice. "Men her age didn't have Elton's financial portfolio."

"That would be true if there hadn't been a prenup," Nora corrected him. "No, E Three claimed to be in love for the very first time in his life, as though twelve years of marriage to me and one son was just an infatuation."

"Did that make you angry?" Jake asked.

Now who sounds tacky? Sam watched Nora closely. Her fork never halted but a smile had formed on her lips.

"If you want to know if I was angry enough to kill her, yes," Nora said matter of factly. "At the time," she clarified, her smile broadening. "What wife wouldn't have been? I ran the gamut of hurt, denial, anger, begging to change whatever I was doing wrong, promising anything to keep the family together. Our son was ten years old at the time and he took it pretty hard. But rather than getting even, I took him for all his lawyers would allow. I didn't want the construction company but I did want that house and a sizeable child support payment." She gave a brief shrug of her designer clad shoulder as if to say, "What's a woman to do?"

Sam watched Jake cut himself another piece of cake. That was unusual for him. He supposedly didn't have a sweet tooth until he was introduced to Abby's baking. Or was he just keeping his mouth busy?

Sam took the clue. "Did your son get along with his father after the divorce?"

"E Three spoiled that boy silly. Built a tree house next to the house. It had a wooden bridge connecting the tree house to his bedroom so he could go out there any time he wanted. Said he was giving Bryce his own space."

"I take it Bryce didn't like Amanda," Sam commented.

"He was a young boy who wanted his father to himself. Even when we were married, Bryce and E Three had their father-son excursions—baseball games, dune buggy rides, golf, you name it. I just loved the fact that they were so close."

"Kids always have stories to tell after spending time with their parent and the new spouse," Sam prompted. "Bryce have anything to tell you after visiting?"

"Kids," Nora said, as though that answered everything. "All you get out of them is an 'okay,' 'guess so,' 'I don't know.' I never wanted to be the type of ex-wife who grilled their kids to learn all the dirt. And I didn't play that *I love you best* game."

Sam wondered when Jake was going to jump back in. She was sure he had a mental list of questions. "How were Amanda and Breyton getting along before her disappearance?"

Nora scraped the last of the frosting from the plate and sat back with a satisfied moan. Abby's cakes had that effect on people. "That is one thing E Three never shared with me. He would never admit he made a mistake. He would never confide in me so, unfortunately, I can't help you there."

"But rumor has it she left town with another man."

"That's the story and I wouldn't be surprised. Although E Three was an outrageous flirt, Amanda could attract men like the proverbial bee to honey. When she dressed she left little to the imagination and I will admit, she was drop dead gorgeous."

"Breyton was okay with that?" Jake's comment made Sam smile. How like Jake to jump in with a traditionalist viewpoint.

"Of course. He loved showing her off. She was the trophy wife, what all men in the country club admire and envy about another man."

"Did they pass her around?"

Scratch that traditionalist opinion, Sam thought. Jake was sounding all male now.

Jake's comment made Nora laugh. "E Three did not share anything," she admitted but then frowned when she realized her implication.

Jake picked up on it immediately. "So if Amanda had found someone else, Elton would have been angry?"

"Angry enough to kill?" Sam added.

20

Sam missed Jake's exit the next morning. They exchanged goodbyes in the steaming shower they had shared. She breezed into the kitchen where Abby was cooing to her grandson. Dillon was all smiles and jerks.

"Good morning, Mom." Sam gave Abby a peck on the cheek, then leaned over to peck Dillon on his forehead. The recognition in his eyes when he saw her filled Sam with an overwhelming warmth. Just as quickly, though, he turned his attention to the colorful toys attached to the front of the infant carrier. Sam's hair was damp from the shower and would take hours to dry. She hoped the tons of conditioner she had used would keep it under control in the summer's humidity.

"Dillon is fed. There's half of an omelet on the counter." Abby pulled the carafe of coffee from the coffeemaker and filled a cup.

Sam noticed a notepad on the kitchen table. "Was Jake sitting here?" When Abby said he had been, Sam grabbed a pencil and sat down. Carefully, she ran the pencil across the paper.

"Don't waste your time, Samantha. Jacob was careful to rip off the three pages underneath the page where he wrote his notes." Sam's pencil stopped in mid-stroke. "Your husband knows you too well."

"Did he throw the pages in the garbage?"

"Of course not."

"Damn," Sam huffed under her breath. "He's hell-bent on making me work for every smidgen of a clue." Her eyes shifted to Abby. "You didn't happen to look over his shoulder when he was writing, did you?" Sam knew Jake would have made a list of suspects. She was curious if his list matched the one in her head.

"How old is Mrs. Breyton's son?" Abby asked.

Sam slowly smiled. Abby would never be that unethical to purposely look over Jake's shoulder, and if she happened to have seen what Jake was writing, she would never purposely mention them. No, instead Sam's mother would casually mention in conversation a name she just might have seen or heard.

"I'm not sure. If he was ten when the Breytons were divorced and E-Three was married to the new wife for eight years and she has been missing for three years, that puts him at about twenty-one or twenty-two." Sam jumped from the table. "Nexus-Lexus. I bet Jake did a search on the Internet." She made a move to the study.

"He deleted his files," Abby announced, much to Sam's disappointment. She returned to the table. "Sit." Abby placed a cup of coffee and the heated omelet in front of Sam. "Eat." Two commands Sam was eager to obey. Abby moved Dillon to the kitchen table where he could see them. "Now tell me who you have on your list."

"Breyton for one," she said as she generously sprinkled the omelet with salt and pepper. "Bryce might be a suspect but I don't know enough about him, yet." She took a bite of the omelet, which was filled with turkey, vegetables, and cheese. "Good." She washed it down with coffee before continuing. "I have to add Nora Breyton, the ex-wife to the list."

"You said she was a very nice lady."

"I thought the same of Judge Wise's wife and look where that got me." Eleanor Wise had seemed the epitome of class and integrity but had actually murdered her husband's teenage lover seventeen years earlier, stabbed her over twenty times in a fit of rage, all the while faking the disability that had kept her in a wheelchair. "I refuse to make that mistake again. And I'm sure Jake has Nora on his list."

"Ummm."

Abby didn't exactly say 'yes,' but Sam knew what her mother's 'ummms' meant. "Then there are faceless suspects," Sam continued. "The boyfriend Amanda was going to run away with, any other jilted boyfriends, enemies of Elton Breyton, wives or girlfriends of men Amanda Breyton might have slept with. And there is the off-chance it was a simple hit and run and the killer buried her in a panic."

"But her remains were down to bones, according to the paper. If she had been buried immediately, that wouldn't have been the case."

"You've been watching *CSI*, haven't you?"

Abby flashed a smile of her own. "Guilty. And I might have eavesdropped a little on conversations you and Jacob have had."

Thoughts formulated in Sam's head as she carried the dish to the sink and let hot water run over it before placing it in the dishwasher. Amanda's bones had looked almost bleached, as though her remains had been left out in the sun. Did that mean someone knew a little bit about forensics? She grabbed the carafe and filled both of their cups. Her mother's love of tea didn't prohibit her from enjoying a cup or two of coffee every now and then.

"Someone knew enough about the breakdown of the human body in the summer to know how long it would take to reduce remains to just bones," Sam said. She set the carafe down and returned to her chair.

"Someone also knew enough about the area to place the body where it might be mistaken for a two hundred-year-old death," Abby offered.

"Or they were pretty lucky." *Or good planning.* "The backhoe destroyed the site completely. We have no way of knowing where Amanda's remains were in relation to the Natives." Sam sipped her coffee and thought about that coincidence. She didn't believe in coincidences. Neither did Jake.

"Kill another plant?" Rose asked. The bleeding heart hanging basket Rose was pruning was full and lush.

"Not today," Sam replied. "Usually if I give the sick plants to my mother in time, she can resuscitate them."

Rose handed the hanging basket off to Camelia. "What can I do for you today?"

"Bryce Breyton. What can you tell me about him?" Since Bryce was an only child, Sam felt he could have been worried about being cut out of the will. Bryce would have been eighteen at the time of Amanda's death and certainly capable of driving a car into his stepmother.

Rose's smile tightened into what resembled a grimace. "Typical kid for my circle of friends." When Sam remained silent, indicating it was a circle Sam was unfamiliar with, Rose explained further. "He was doted on by his mother, given everything he wanted by his father, and still wasn't satisfied. He dabbled in everything, overindulged in the wrong things, and was your basic spoiled brat. Was almost kicked out of the most prestigious school until Breyton made a sizeable donation. Spent some time in rehab which was nothing more than another place to be doted on." Rose slipped into a pair of garden gloves and proceeded to fill another basket with potting soil. Her hands moved with the ease of an expert who could probably plant and pot in her sleep.

"Any idea where I might find him?" That was one question neither she nor Jake had asked Nora Breyton last night. Sam assumed Jake already knew where the kid went to college, spent his summers, partied at night. Unfortunately, Sam didn't have Jake's network of contacts.

"He uses an artist's retreat as a self-induced rehab. The Sanctuary I believe it's called. It's somewhere near Lake Michigan by Michigan City. Bryce didn't care to work for his father's company. Elton believed in the kid working his way up the ladder. Bryce wanted to be a vice president and work at his leisure." Rose pushed the dirt aside, creating a symmetrical hole Sam wouldn't have been able to accomplish with a ruler and plumb line.

Sam asked, "Did he resent his new stepmother?" If Bryce was eager to pull down a V.P. salary without working, he would probably be willing to own the company and just delegate the work. But how would he feel if Amanda ended up owning the company should Elton die?

Rose set the azalea basket aside and started on a large white cistern. "As far as Bryce's attitude toward his stepmother, all I can give you is gossip . You will remember that Nora shunned me after she discovered I knew about Elton's indiscretion."

"I can deal with gossip. Somewhere buried underneath is always a kernel of truth."

"Several women I lunch with at the country club had lent a shoulder or two to Nora after the divorce. Bryce was ten at the time and sided with his mother." Iris approached pushing a flat cart with all the plants Rose needed. Once Iris left, Rose continued. "Bryce was disrespectful to the new wife, moody, threw tantrums, ran away, you name it. Secretly, I think Nora enjoyed it. Elton was furious. Thought Nora was coaching the kid." Rose poured potting soil into the cistern, then sifted her hands through the dirt as though she were tossing a salad. "When he hit fifteen, he was at all night drinking parties, took Elton's car for a spin without a license. Wrecked it. He's just lucky he didn't kill himself."

"When did the drugs start?"

"Ohhhh," Rose looked up at the shade netting overhead as though the answer were written there. "I think when he was seventeen. Yes, because he was a senior in high school and Nora was afraid he wasn't going to graduate and would screw up his chances for college."

"I take it he wasn't a stellar student. No scholarships?"

"Actually, he was on the dean's list every year. Was supposed to start college in the fall, I think at Notre Dame. Instead, he ended up in rehab two, maybe even three times." She moved the dirt aside to make room for a geranium.

"Do you recall if that was before or after Amanda disappeared?"

"I'm not sure." Rose made quick placement of the ivy and

spikes, then pulled off her gloves, her brows scrunched in thought. "I don't recall the exact month Amanda ran off with the other guy."

"Was there any gossip as to what other love interest Amanda had? Maybe someone else at the country club? Maybe a close friend of Elton's?"

Rose shook her head. "Took all the women by surprise. They prided themselves on being able to sniff out a rumor but there wasn't one man in particular that Amanda showed more interest in than the others. She appeared to do a three-sixty, I'm told. Changed the way she dressed, her attitude, started volunteering at the hospital. Someone joked that it was as though she joined a convent."

"Did Bryce have any close friends?"

"Sure." Rose grabbed a broom and started to sweep up the clippings. "Just about every guy working the country club for the summer knew Bryce. They played tennis, golf, and caddied together until Bryce hit fifteen." She swept the debris into a small pile and then into a long-handled dust pan. "At that age he couldn't take the ribbing about his stepmother, the way she dressed, the way she flirted. She loved to wear low cut tops and watch the teenage boys sniff after her like dogs in heat. After a while Bryce just stopped coming to the club. He's probably closer to his fellow Sanctuary residents."

As Sam walked back to her Jeep, she wondered if taking a woman's life would turn a young man to drugs.

"Kind of macabre, isn't it?" Greg said to no one in particular. He was back in the lab snapping more pictures of the artifacts. Inga and T.J. stood vigil at the empty spot where Table Three used to be. Benny's assistants had moved the table to the morgue once it had been confirmed the deceased was Amanda Breyton.

"Yes," Inga said. "It's a first for me, finding remains that aren't over one hundred years old. Angel couldn't bring herself to come to the lab today, thinking the bones would still be here. Poor kid." She watched T.J. pry his gaze from the empty space and move toward the table of artifacts. "What about you, T.J.?" She could swear his skin had turned pasty. "T.J.?"

"What?" He dragged his attention back to her. "Uh, no. It certainly feels different when the bones have a name attached to them." He studied the artifacts, picking up the index cards and reading Inga's descriptions as he moved along the tables. "It certainly complicates things."

"How so?" Greg asked. He moved around T.J. to get an unobstructed picture of a large knife.

"Our work has come to a bloody halt while their crime scene people scour through our dig."

"I spoke to Captain Robinson earlier," Inga announced. "He only wants what we have sifted through so far and after today he will let us continue the sifting as long as one of their techs oversees our work. Just in case we come across any evidence."

"Evidence?" T.J. asked.

"Sure." Greg pressed the focus button and took another picture. "That's what they look for when there is a murder."

Inga never thought there was a hue lighter than pasty but T.J.'s face had just displayed it.

21

"He's the young man on the beach," Clarice St. John told the detectives as she motioned toward the shoreline where a young man sat in a director's chair, a tablet in his lap. "I was starting to worry about him. This is the first day Bryce has come out of his room in three days."

Three days ago the newspapers had announced that the body of Amanda Breyton had been found. The significance wasn't lost on Jake or Frank.

Clarice stood erect, toes out, in what could only be from years of ballet instructions. It was hard to tell her age. Her hair was bottle platinum or naturally white. Jake wasn't up on his hair colors. Her face had few lines but looked pulled tight, as though she had suffered through a number of face lifts. The brochure stated that Clarice had acted on Broadway, was a skilled painter, poet, as well as a dancer. Her acting could have been in Vaudeville as far as Jake could tell. Clarice had founded the retreat twenty years ago for writers and artists to hone their skills in a natural setting, away from the normal day-to-day distractions. Rooms were rented on a two-week basis with those financially capable spending as much time as they wanted. Bryce's residency had extended well beyond the limit.

Jake thought The Sanctuary looked more like a nature center, landscaped with every plant imaginable, with infinity ponds for maximum effect. Some residents in flowing gowns were demonstrating Tai Chi near one of the ponds. The building itself looked like a French chalet crafted of flagstone with verandas off what Jake would guess to be suites rather than dormitory rooms. The prices in the brochure screamed elitism but the fine print said donations from various foundations offset the cost for the truly gifted but financially strapped students.

"We'd like to take a look around his room," Frank said.

"I'm sorry. Without a search warrant, I can't let you invade the privacy of our residents."

The two detectives did their silent communication. *No problem. We'll just insist that Bryce talk to us in his room.*

"I'll be in the atrium if you need anything else, detectives." Clarice turned and walked back to the building.

"Nice place," Frank said.

"Good place to have your ashes spread."

They crossed the lawn where three women sat in yoga fashion, eyes closed, faces lifted skyward, thumbs and forefingers touching.

"I'll pass. Bet they have a vegetarian menu or nibble bark off the trees."

The lawn ended a good one hundred feet from shore, either chewed off by high tides or storms. A white picket fence with a gate had several Private Property signs affixed. Other than sail boats and tankers in the distance, there wasn't much to inspire an artist. Even the Chicago skyline wasn't that clear and distinct to attract an artist's eye.

"Bryce Breyton?" Jake announced.

"Who wants to know?" Bryce's right hand moved in quick sweeps. He was working with a charcoal pencil on a sketch pad. He gave a passing glance to the shields Jake and Frank displayed. Bryce was barefoot and dressed in cut-offs and a white poet's shirt left unbuttoned. His hair was sun-bleached blonde and collar length.

If the detectives had expected a sketch of the skyline or sand dunes, they were sorely mistaken. Bryce was sketching a seagull picking at the flesh of a female corpse. One eye was missing, the woman's mouth open in a silent scream, the body naked and covered in jagged cuts.

Frank worked a toothpick around in his mouth. "Hope they

have a shrink on staff."

Bryce smirked. "Art is in the eye of the beholder. Pull up a piece of sand, detectives. It's free." Bryce drew a tendon and extended it to the seagull's beak. "Should really do this in colored pencils. Makes it more dramatic."

Jake walked around the chair to face Bryce. He wanted to look into this guy's eyes. Bryce's chest was tanned and beach buff, muscular but not in a frenzied body builder way. Bryce wouldn't look at him.

"You're blocking my sunlight, detective."

Jake pulled the tablet from Bryce's hands and handed it to Frank. "We have several questions about Amanda Breyton. It would be better if we talk in your room."

"Out here is fine." Bryce finally raised his eyes. Jake had expected dark and soulless eyes. What he saw were soft baby blues, clear, not dilated. "She was married to my father. Go ask him."

Frank fanned through the sketch pad. "Whoa. For such a surfer-looking guy, you've got some weird fantasies." Frank turned the pad around to show Jake a picture of a woman being strangled, eyes bulging, blouse torn, breast exposed. "He has nice landscapes in the front but some pretty weird stuff in the back."

"It's nothing different from any graphic detective magazine you find on a newsstand."

Jake asked, "What can you tell us about your stepmother? Any idea who the other man was in her life?"

"How many men are in Chasen Heights?" Bryce replied with a disinterested shrug.

Frank's eyes widened at another picture which he showed to Jake. A woman was being attacked from behind, her assailant wadding her hair in his fist, a knife pressed to the woman's neck. If it was one thing Bryce had down pat it was the fear in the women's eyes. The assailant was faceless.

"Do you think your father is capable of murder?" Jake asked.

"He'd never get his hands dirty. He might make a killing in a land deal but anything physical or messy he'd run like a sissy."

Frank closed the sketch pad. "What about your mother?"

Bryce's cocky smile faded and his eyes turned cold. "Leave my mother out of this. She's suffered enough."

"Was she angry enough to kill?" Frank pressured.

Bryce jumped from his chair. Jake straight-armed him away from Frank. "Don't do something you are going to regret." Bryce glared at Frank then appeared to take a deep, cleansing breath before returning to the chair.

"Mom was hurt for a long time but she got over it."

"Doesn't sound like you got over it." Jake took the sketch pad from Frank and thumbed through the pages. Bryce had one hell of an imagination.

"I was in rehab when she disappeared. But if you want to charge me, charge me. It will make the value of my sketches go up."

Sam watched the encounter through the large window in the lobby of The Santuary. Jake and Frank were a little quicker at locating Bryce than she had hoped. Her chances of talking to Elton's son had just dwindled. And the halls were always filled so she couldn't even pick the lock on Bryce's room which she discovered was on the second floor. She didn't want Jake to see her there so she would have to come back. She needed a plan.

An easel with a poster near the front desk announced that the next afternoon's art class featured a nude drawing. All artists interested could draw or paint a nude model. It had to take a certain type person to expose herself for hours on end while men oogled her, Sam thought.

A woman duck-walked to the front desk. She had white hair styled like a Gibson girl but stark black eyebrows that could have been drawn by one of the artists. Sam strolled a bit closer. The woman's name was Clarice St. John and her badge said she was the administrator.

"What are we going to do for a model?" Clarice moaned. "It's such short notice."

The young woman behind the desk was thumbing through a rolodex. "Maybe if we up the payment to one thousand dollars."

"It's one day's notice, Monique. I don't care what we pay, just get me someone. And don't use that agency any more. They aren't reliable."

Sam approached the desk. "I couldn't help but overhear. I'm actually here about the modeling job."

Clarice stepped back and did a quick assessment of Sam. "Yes, you just might work."

Sam stammered out, "I wouldn't be the model. I'm an agent for my friend. I only stopped by to get a brochure and contact information so I don't have any of her stock photos with me, but I can assure you…"

"She's hired," Clarice said with a resigned sigh. "Have her here at noon tomorrow."

That was pretty easy, Sam thought as she rushed to her Jeep. *Now all I have to do is convince Jackie.*

"You want me to do what?" Jackie's eyes lit up like charcoal beacons. "Stand naked for hours on end in front of a bunch of men and women I don't know?"

"You'll be paid a thousand dollars," Sam countered.

"Do I look like I need the money?" Gold bracelets jangled on Jackie's wrist. She walked to the closet in her bedroom and rifled through a side rack.

"It's the only way I can get into Bryce's room. Everyone will be at the … uhh exposure." Jackie shot her a look of scorn that made her take a step back. "You know what I mean," Sam said. "It will give me time to search his room. Clarice said the students are given two hours to sketch so it isn't like you'll have to lay naked for six or eight hours. Besides, you won't be completely naked.

Clarice said you can wear whatever you want as long as part of you is exposed."

"What do I tell Lamon?"

"Tell him it's for charity. Donate the money to that women's shelter."

Jackie opened another door which had racks of shoes. She pulled out a pair of four-inch high, white ankle wrap heels and tossed them on the floor. "You really stretch our friendship, you know?"

Sam winced. She had never seen Jackie so mad. But she had to admit—in the past she had talked Jackie into doing some of the most outrageous things.

Jackie pulled out a stool to reach something on a top shelf. "Remember that grand opening where I had my girls model negligees and underwear ala Victoria's Secret with the white angel wings?" Jackie pulled down a pair of white angel wings and tossed them on the bed. Then she opened a dresser drawer, pulled out a pair of white satin thong panties and tossed them on the bed. "How's that for a costume?" Jackie slowly smiled, and then cackled with laughter.

"You aren't mad?" Sam asked.

"Sugar, I swear you live vicariously through me. I just like to see you sweat."

22

The next day Sam and Jackie showed up early at The Sanctuary to set up Jackie's props. "What are you going to do with this?" Sam helped Jackie drag a white wooden archway across the floor of the art studio. More than fifteen easels and chairs were scattered throughout the floor. An octagon-shaped stage was set up at the front of the room. It was three feet high with stairs on each side.

Jackie said, "I called that Clarice lady and asked what she had for props. She said I could go through the storeroom and pick what I wanted. I looked for anything white."

"Did she tell you what to bring?"

"Just said I needed to show one animate and one inanimate object and a contrast in color."

Sam studied the white wings and the archway which was also white. "Where's the contrast of color?"

Jackie looked toward the double doors leading to the hallway. "Looks like it's here." The double doors opened and two men in blue uniforms carried a bulky garland of red roses as though it were a struggling python. The flower heads were the size of a man's fist.

"You ordered the flowers?" *You nut*, the tall man's unspoken comment said with a flick of his caterpillar eyebrows.

Sam had a feeling the florist hadn't cut the thorns off the flowers. The man bringing up the rear was wincing with each step. His fingers had obviously found some of the thorns. He was a head shorter and half the girth of the man in front which was why he was practically hidden as he trailed.

"I need the garland draped over the archway," Jackie said.

"What?" *Fat chance, lady*, was what the tall man's snort and chuckle said.

Jackie smiled and slowly slipped out of her white suit jacket to reveal a bronze-colored chiffon camisole and a barely there low cut matching bra underneath. Her skirt was also white but short enough to also be called barely there. Jackie flicked her hair back with one hand, aware that the quick movement made her heavy breasts sway.

Sam had to turn away from the men whose fingers were losing their grip on the garland.

"Joe," Shorty said, "I think we've got time to help da lady."

"Sure, sure."

They gently placed the garland across the deep wooden countertop which ran the width of the back wall. After dragging two folding chairs on either side of the archway, they picked up the garland, climbed onto the chairs, and filled the archway with the fragrant flowers.

"Anything else we can do for you?" Joe sucked on the tip of his bleeding thumb.

Jackie reached into her wallet and pulled out two bills. "Thank you so much." She pressed a twenty into each of their palms.

Sam watched the men as they stole glances over their shoulders on their way to the door. "You sure have a way." Sam said. She knew Jackie would take a slow stroll down the main hallway in search of Clarice knowing she was teaching a class, knowing there would be a number of opened doors, all in a well-planned tactic to garner as many attendees as possible for Jackie's appearance.

They entered a side room which Clarice had said Jackie could use as a dressing room. Jackie hung up her clothes, opened a cosmetics bag, then set about touching up her makeup.

"What if Bryce locked his door?" Jackie stood in front of a full length mirror, a palette of eye shadows in her hand. Sam's expression in the mirror erased any doubt her friend might have of Sam's ability to get in and out of locked rooms. "Sorry. Forgot who I was dealing with."

* * *

The Sanctuary was an old building, tastefully decorated but with outdated door locks. A simple credit card helped Sam gain access to Bryce's room on the second floor. She closed and locked the door behind her, slipping the card back into her purse. The room was very male—clothes draped over the chair and couch, shoes dropped on the floor as though Bryce had stepped out of them on the way to the bathroom. Her eye caught a calendar on a bulletin board over the desk. Tomorrow was maid service day. Guess at these rates, they better provide a cleaning service.

Beyond the wall of windows was a fantastic view of the gardens and Lake Michigan. Bryce probably had one of the largest suites. There were only two other rooms with this view on the second floor. She stood in the doorway to a massive bedroom with a four poster bed. Sam was surprised to find that Bryce had made the bed.

She crossed the living room to the opposite side of the suite. A room just as large as the bedroom appeared to be a studio. A work table, several easels, and a couch with a pillow told Sam that Bryce slept in this room, perhaps waking in the middle of the night with a spark of artistic creativity. Just like the bedroom, this room also had doors which led onto the balcony.

Each of the easels had a canvas in different phases of completion. All were landscape scenes of the beach, Lake Michigan, sailboats. Sam didn't feel there was anything that special about his work. Bryce appeared to work in charcoal or black pencil. She wasn't up on her art methods. A sketchpad was lying open on the couch. She fanned through it only to find sketches of children at play, an elderly woman waiting at a bus stop, a man sleeping under a tree at the park. These images showed more of Bryce's talent. She tossed the sketchpad back on the couch and walked over to a closet. More easels and supplies were stacked neatly against the back wall and on the shelves. How young was Bryce when he started drawing? If he started at an early age, Nora Breyton probably conducted public displays of her young Picasso.

She grabbed several of the sketchpads from the closet and carried them to the living room. She found an upholstered settee next to the desk. Checking her watch, Sam made sure she kept track of her two-hour time limit.

She settled back, opened the first sketchpad and was equally bored with images of fruit, animals, country scenes during what appeared to be winter, all drawn with a skilled hand. A lot was missing, though, when a picture was void of color. Black and white didn't do much for her. She fanned through several blank pages. Why would Bryce hide certain sketchpads in a closet? Sam fanned past additional blank pages, then froze. Bryce had graduated from inanimate objects to women. Here was a sketch of a woman nude and nailed to a cross. Her eyes were skyward in a replication of the Crucifixion.

"I hope this was just a phase you were going through." She wondered how old Bryce was when he graduated from fruit to women. Proceeding pages were just as explicit. There were sketches of women in bondage, tied to front bumpers of cars, on a railroad track.

How far did Bryce go with his dark obsession? Did he act out on these strange impulses? Out of force of habit, Sam reached over and touched a pencil on the desk, the computer, a shirt draped over the desk chair, trying to pick up some inkling of darkness to this young man's persona. He obviously didn't have an evil streak deep enough to conjure up any aura for Sam to feel.

She returned to the sketchpads. Bryce appeared to tame down the torture in some pictures and focus mainly on women being subjected to assault, but was there really much difference? One woman had a knife to her throat. Another was being choked, her eyes bulging. Bryce's women were either totally nude, or barely clothed, or their clothes were tattered as though someone had ripped them off of their bodies.

Sam studied the room again, feeling she had missed some telltale sign that Bryce was a good candidate for a serial killer or rapist. She hadn't found a wall of female faces used for darts or a photo of Mom with scissors through her eyes.

There was something too familiar about the women in the drawings. Sam went back to the first sketchpad and studied the women, then the second and third. Sam was sure every woman had the face of Bryce's stepmother. There was enough resentment toward Amanda in these pages to make Bryce a number one suspect.

A key was shoved in the door. Sam's heart quickened but there wasn't time to hide so she kept her head down and her attention focused on the pages. The door closed and a figure slowly approached.

"I take it these pictures aren't of your biological mother," Sam said. She kept her eyes on the sketches, her fingers slowly turning the pages.

"I KNOW I locked my door."

Bryce's voice wasn't slurred, not that Sam had expected Bryce to still have a drug problem. Clarice had made it clear that they had strict rules regarding drug use. Matter of fact, the voice was sensual and she expected bedroom eyes to go with that voice.

"Can't trust old buildings. Cheap locks, warped wood." Sam turned the page and was suddenly staring at what could be a centerfold. She had to rotate the sketchpad to view the full image of a woman, nude, stretched out at the bow of a ship, arms stretched over her head and tied at the wrists. "Is there a reason why all of these women resemble Amanda Breyton?"

The chair in front of the desk was pulled back several feet. As Bryce sat down, Sam finally lifted her face to view the son of Nora and Elton Breyton. And he did have bedroom eyes. They were a soft blue and turned down at the corners. He had a lifeguard's body and sun-bleached hair. He didn't smile. Just grabbed a sketchpad and pencil. She felt a chill as his gaze slowly swept down her face and body like some human scanner storing her vital statistics.

Sam suddenly wished she had worn a blouse that buttoned to her neck rather than one whose top buttons refused to stay fastened. The slit of her peasant skirt ran up her thigh exposing her right leg which was crossed at the knees. His eyes literally undressed her and she had to will herself not to button up or give the impression she was uncomfortable. Instead, she reached into her purse for a business card, then flung it several feet onto the bed, within Bryce's reach. He gave it a passing glance, then shrugged.

"Who hired you? Mom or Dad?"

"Does it matter?"

His hand moved swiftly across the page. Just like a writer supposedly always writes, Sam figured an artist was always drawing. It would make it hard for her to tell if he were lying.

"By now," Sam said, "you have heard that Amanda's body has been found."

The pencil barely stopped, scratching across the pad, his face intense. "So I've heard."

"According to your mother, you were ten at the time of the divorce. How did you get along with your stepmother?"

His hand continued with expert strokes. It reminded Sam of a cartoonist her father used to work with at the *Post Tribune* who could draw a cartoon in less than a minute.

"From the looks of these pictures," Sam prodded, "it doesn't appear that you cared too much for your stepmother. If I were a cop, I'd start to question your whereabouts the night Amanda disappeared."

Bryce appeared disinterested as he glanced at her before returning his interest to the sketchpad. "You have beautiful eyes. Nice breasts."

"It's called lactation," Sam replied, not hiding her irritation that he wasn't staying on subject.

At least that got Bryce smiling. "Lucky baby."

"Have you always been this obsessed with the female body?"

"Artists have always been obsessed with the female body. It is far more interesting naked than the male's, wouldn't you say?" His eyes licked over her once again. At times it appeared as though his hand was moving of its own accord, with Bryce barely glancing at the sketchpad.

Although the pictures Sam was thumbing through left her with the impression they were drawn by some perverse, sexually depraved person, when Bryce looked at her his stare wasn't lewd or psychotic. He could have just as easily been studying the latest sports car at the auto show or sizing up a piece of antique furniture at an auction. There was an appreciation in his eyes but also a cool detachment.

"A picture of a woman partially clad or nude and being brutalized hardly shows respect and admiration for the female body."

"Anyone can draw what he sees," Bryce replied. "It's a true sign of creativity when one uses his imagination to see what isn't there." His gaze dropped to the sketchpad again. His brow furrowed as though in intense concentration.

Sam wasn't sure where this guy's buttons were. "According to Clarice, most artists stay just two months. You've been here for three years. Are you hiding out?"

"It's a rather relaxing atmosphere without the distractions of..."

"Home life?"

A smile barely creased one side of his mouth. "Parental constraints. I want to draw, Mom wants me to go to college. Dad wants me to learn the construction business."

"With your talent you could probably do architectural drawings." This comment awarded Sam with a full smile.

"Exactly what he said. But people don't hang pictures of buildings on their walls."

Sam studied the furnishings, deep pile carpeting, art equipment in the adjoining room she was sure wasn't cheap. "If you thumbed your nose at your father's offer, I would assume he cut off your trust fund."

Another smile. "Dad isn't the only one with purse strings. Mom prepaid my room here for three years and she sends me monthly checks."

"Bet you've never forgiven your father for the divorce."

"Nope."

"You never answered my question. How did you get along with your stepmother?"

"Not as well as my father."

"Your mother told me you were in rehab at the time of Amanda's disappearance. But I checked. You were released two days before she disappeared. Where did you go?"

He moved the pad slightly to stare fully at her exposed leg. Sam wanted to reposition her skirt, to cover every exposed inch of skin.

"Not sure. That was a long time ago." His pencil paused and with a shake of his head he sighed out a, "Damn, you've got nice legs." He made an obvious glance at her left hand.

"Something tells me you don't forget a thing. You must remember if you stopped by to see either of your parents."

"Nope."

Sam wasn't getting anywhere. She might have to sic Jake on the kid again. "Your mother tells me you hated the weekend visits you had with your father. He even built you a tree house to escape." Sam turned a page on the sketchpad. Although she hadn't seen Elton's house or the location of the tree house, she was formulating a scenario from the picture. In it, a woman who looked amazingly like Amanda was standing in front of a window nude, arms tied to something on either side of the window, probably the drapery rod, breasts pressed against the window, the glass broken, breasts bleeding. She turned the sketchpad around to show Bryce. "Your tree house didn't happen to be right outside your father's bedroom window did it?"

If Sam wasn't mistaken, Bryce's blue eyes hardened, but he blinked away the cold reaction and remained silent. Sam was starting to understand a little of Bryce's psyche.

"Every face in these sketches is Amanda's. You didn't respect her for what she was and what she did to your family."

"And what was she?"

"In your mind, a whore, a gold digger, someone who used her body to get what she wanted. She loved to tease, flirt, and in your eyes, on the pages of these sketches, you were giving her exactly what you felt she deserved. She deserved to be punished."

Bryce walked over to the desk, opened a drawer, and retrieved a brown envelope.

"What kind of car did you drive back then, Bryce?"

"Didn't own one."

Sam laughed at that. "Please. I have the Department of Motor Vehicles on speed dial. Your father bought you a Ferrari to try to soften you up."

"He sold it when I went into rehab."

"So he told you. Instead, Amanda was cruising around town with it."

His eyes hardened again. Sam didn't think any of this was news to him. She had a feeling Nora Breyton filled her son in on every little trinket her ex-husband purchased for his young wife.

Bryce ripped the drawing from the sketchpad and slipped it into the brown envelope. He handed the envelope to Sam saying, "A gift for your husband."

Sam grabbed the envelope and carefully pulled the sketch partway from the envelope, exposing her head and neck. She had expected to see Amanda's face but it wasn't. It was an excellent likeness.

"I suppose you want payment." She let the drawing drop into the brown envelope, then fastened the clasp.

"This one's on me."

23

"I'm sorry I missed his bath." Sam checked the clock above the sink. She not only missed Dillon's bath, she had missed tucking him in.

"No problem," Abby replied. "Jake and I handled it."
Sam checked the cloud forming over Jake's head. She had told him very little in the phone message she left other than to say she and Jackie had gone to The Sanctuary. He was none too happy that the two were again going off on their own to do what he was sure was illegal, unethical, and dangerous.

Jake was leaning against the sink, arms folded, face hard to read. "Tell me again what Jackie was doing?"

Sam rambled through her story of how she had met Clarice yesterday and arranged for Jackie to model today for the art class. She watched for telltale signs of irritation on Jake's face but he had too good of a poker face.

"A thousand dollars to model?" Abby said.

"Naked." Jake rolled his eyes and re-folded his arms. Folding them once was bad enough.

"This gave me a chance to check out Bryce's room because I knew he would be busy drawing for two hours."

"Please tell me his room was unlocked." Jake washed his hands over his face.

"Yes…of course. After I used a…credit card." When he opened his mouth to, she was sure, spout off a list of laws she had broken, Sam hurried on. "You have to hear what I found."

Abby skirted around her to the stove to turn the water on under the tea kettle. Sam knew this move by heart. Abby was already anticipating an early retreat to her room.

"Bryce has pads filled with nude sketches of Amanda Breyton."

Sam saw Jake blink. This was a good sign. It was Jake's way of showing he was paying attention. "But the most bizarre thing is that each of the pictures shows her being brutalized, tortured, or threatened in some way." She remembered the envelope she had in her hand. "He sketched me as we talked."

Jake unfastened the flap of the envelope. "We know his alibi for the night Amanda was killed didn't hold up." Jake pulled the sketch from the envelope. The envelope fell from his hands as his jaw clenched.

Abby stepped back from the stove to view the sketch. Her eyes widened and a look of disbelief spread across her face. It reminded Sam of the time she was out past midnight with a boy on the reservation. They hadn't done anything wrong but Sam was an hour past curfew with a boy Abby explicitly asked her not to see.

"What's wrong? I thought he did a good job." Sam walked over to Jake and pulled the sketch from his hands. A scream caught in her throat. Bryce had drawn her with her blouse torn in strips and barely hanging on her shoulders, breasts fully exposed, wrists tied to each of the settees' arm rests. There were two slits to the skirt which was torn to her waist exposing the full length of both legs. "I didn't pose like this," Sam argued. "When he gave me the envelope, I only pulled the sketch out far enough to see my face, to see if he had drawn Amanda's face." Sam felt her skin flush. Her fingers instinctively flew to the buttons on her blouse that refused to remain fastened. "THAT LITTLE TWIRP!"

Abby grabbed a tea bag, a hot cup of water and announced, "I think I'll check on Dillon."

Sam waited for Abby to leave, then made a move to rip up the sketch but Jake stopped her.

"Oh no you don't. This is evidence."

"Evidence?" Sam's eyes grew with the horror that the sketch would be passed around the precinct. "You can't. You wouldn't."

Jake shoved the sketch back in the envelope, a twinkle lighting up his eyes. "Bryce appears to have an excellent attention to detail but I noticed he didn't draw the mole on your left breast. So he obviously didn't see you naked."

"Maybe I asked him to leave it out." She playfully finger-walked the buttons on his shirt.

"I can't even get you to strip for me so I know you didn't strip for this kid. Now sit and start at the beginning."

While Jake grabbed a beer for himself and a glass of iced tea for Sam, she filled him in on the sketches, Bryce's lack of cooperation at responding to her questions about whether either of his parents were capable of murder or why he was hiding out at The Sanctuary for three years or how he really felt about his stepmother.

"He was coy, dodged every question but I have to tell you, I didn't pick up one dangerous vibe in his room."

"That doesn't mean anything. The pictures are disturbing enough to tell you something isn't quite right with that guy." Jake told her about the picture of the seagull Bryce had been drawing on the beach. "I already asked for a search warrant for his room. Clarice refused to authorize a search without a warrant and no matter how many times Frank and I suggested he might be more comfortable answering our questions in his room, he refused. He probably knew what we would find."

Sam stared at the brown envelope lying on the island counter. "You aren't going to take that to work, are you?"

Jake reached across the table and grabbed her hands. "I don't like it when you and Jackie go off on your own. I need to know what you are doing when it involves a case I'm working on."

"I know the boundaries, Jake. I won't compromise your case."

"If Breyton's lawyer finds out I obtained the sketchpads the day after you showed up and just happened to let yourself in and that you are my wife, the judge would have good reason to toss out the evidence. Not to mention Murphy's reaction."

"Jackie and I are always careful."

"And how many sketches of Jackie are going to float around town or find themselves on the Internet? How will Robinson feel about that?"

"Lamon is proud of Jackie. He'd laugh it off."

"You think so?"

Sam carried her empty glass and Jake's empty beer can to the sink. "Sometimes I think you are more of a prude than I am." She reached for the envelope but Jake was quicker.

"I'm keeping it in a safe place."

"Right. Some place where Dillon stumbles onto it when he's ten years old?"

"That won't happen."

Sam was pretty sure Jake would not take the sketch to the precinct. The last thing he would want would be for her sketch to be tacked to the corkboard in the break room.

"Are you coming up?" Sam asked.

"In a minute."

After Sam left, Jake pulled the sketch from the envelope and placed it on the counter. Bryce had captured every fine detail of Sam's mouth, her eyes, even the way wisps of hair wrapped around the third earring of beads and feathers. Sam had only questioned Bryce for twenty minutes and in that short amount of time he had completed a fully detailed drawing.

The rope around her wrists was tight and Bryce gave the impression she had struggled against them because he had drawn the skin raw and bleeding. Jake thought back to the one picture Sam had mentioned of Amanda in front of a window. What if the son was only drawing what he saw?

Jake slipped the sketch back into the envelope and carried it to the study. After retrieving a book from the top shelf, he slipped the envelope in the inside cover. The title of the book he randomly chose made him chuckle—*Wonders of the World*.

After turning off the lights and setting the alarm, he climbed the stairs. Thoughts of how he might get Elton Breyton to drop the charges against Alex rolled around in his head. Just maybe, Elton might be more concerned with the fate of his son than the charges against Alex. He would have to check with Sam first on how Alex might react.

Jake stepped into the room and closed the door behind him. The light above the headboard was dimmed. A slight smile crossed his lips. He could clearly see Sam sitting on the upholstered chaise lounge in front of the patio windows, her blouse unbuttoned and barely hanging on her shoulders, her breasts fully exposed. The skirt was hiked up and pooled around her waist. Scarves were tied around her wrists and she held her hands out as though they were tied to the chaise.

Maybe he would wait until morning to talk.

24

The next day Bryce was left stewing in the interrogation room. Jake and Frank worked their way through two file boxes of sketchpads which they had obtained with the use of a search warrant. Although they had offered the use of the phone to make calls, the young man had declined.

The detectives stepped into the room with only one of the file boxes. Their entrance brought a smug smile to Bryce's face. Jake dropped one of the file boxes onto a chair. Frank pulled out the adjacent chair and sat down.

"About time," the young man said. "I do have more important things to do." His attention was drawn to Frank's muscles which were barely contained in the bright yellow tee shirt. "You've been doing some major body building. You know all of that is going to turn to fat when you get older."

Frank flexed his muscles. "Looks good, huh? Hour a day in the gym, four days a week. You should try it."

Jake dug through the box, flipped open one of the sketchpads and slapped it on the table. "Where do you get your subjects?"

"Wow, right down to business." Bryce turned to Frank. "Is he always this serious?"

"This is his humorous mood."

"You seemed a lot friendlier yesterday."

Jake flipped the page. "Why so much hostility?" He flipped another page. "And why do they all look like your deceased stepmother?"

Bryce pulled the sketchpad closer, as though trying to refresh his memory of what his stepmother looked like. "Well, what do you know." He gave a disinterested shrug and sank back in his seat.

Jake drilled the youth with a glare that was meant to unsettle him. All Bryce did was glare back with a grin of amusement. *Good. Let him be overconfident.* Jake closed the sketchpad, emptied the box and stacked the sketchpads in the middle of the table.

The door to the interrogation room burst open and Stephen Weber stormed in followed by Elton and Nora Breyton.

"Don't say another word, Bryce," the attorney ordered.

"I'll sue this city," Breyton piped up.

Bryce sank back in his chair and groaned. "I didn't call for a lawyer, and even if I had, it wouldn't have been you."

Nora wormed her way around the men. "Bryce, if you don't want Stephen, I can get you a good lawyer." Stephen's eyebrows popped together as he realized he had just been insulted. Nora ignored him and turned to the detectives. "Why has Bryce been arrested? What is he charged with?"

Jake replied, "He hasn't been arrested and we haven't charged him with anything."

"I want him out of here, both of them," Bryce said, pointing at the attorney and his father. "I don't want anything from you." The last comment was directed at Breyton.

"Fuck you, you little snot. Who the hell do you think pays for that artsy fartsy retreat you are staying at?"

"Mom pays. I don't need you or your money."

"Who the hell do you think gives her the money?"

"Oh, Breyton, shut up," Nora snapped. "The money comes out of my account."

Weber already had his briefcase shut and was glancing at his watch. He obviously was aware he wasn't going to make any money standing around here.

"I had to sell the house in the Caribbean as part of the divorce settlement, you witch. Instead of monthly child support payments, you put the proceeds in a trust fund. He's been sucking the trust fund tit ever since."

Nora's voice raised several decibels. "I had to. Amanda was

spending your money faster than you could make it."

Stephen hefted his briefcase off the table and checked his watch again. "Am I representing him or not?"

"*Him* has a name," Bryce sneered.

"Excuse me." Captain Robinson's voice boomed from the doorway. A hush settled over the room. "Can you tone it down or take it somewhere else?" He settled his gaze on Bryce. "Do you want this man to represent you?"

"I've been saying *no* for the past ten minutes."

"You have the right to have an attorney present," Robinson reminded him.

"Son, never talk to the police without an attorney." Breyton was almost coddling the youth.

"Now I'm a son," Bryce mumbled under his breath.

"He has nothing to hide." Nora placed her hands on Bryce's shoulders. "If he doesn't want an attorney, he doesn't want one. I'll just stay with him."

Bryce rolled his eyes. "Mom, will you please leave. All of you."

"You heard the gentleman." Robinson stood against the opened door and waited for the intruders to leave.

Jake knew Robinson would offer to have Bryce's parents witness the interrogation from the room on the opposite side of the one-way mirror. He doubted either would refuse, which is why Jake was saving the best for last.

After the door closed, Frank picked through the stack of sketch pads and randomly selected one. "This looks like a good one." He handed the sketchpad to Jake who walked behind Frank's chair and held up the drawing for the benefit of the audience behind the one-way mirror. The sketch showed Amanda naked and standing in front of a patio window.

"Want to explain this picture?" Jake said. "According to the date, you were just fifteen years old when you drew it."

Bruce sat a little straighter and smiled. Jake read pride in that smile and wondered how the parents were reacting on the other side of the mirror.

"Probably my first drawing of Amanda. She knew the bedroom window faced my tree house. She always left the drapes open after showering and would walk around the bedroom naked. Maybe she thought I was too far away to see but I had binoculars and the tree house walls were slatted. If you ask me, she knew damn well I was watching."

Without turning around to see the picture, Frank asked, "And who trussed her up like that? It may be a black and white drawing but I detect some blood on her face and across her torso."

Bryce flashed his cocky smile again. "An artist controls the canvas."

Jake slowly leafed through the pages of the sketchpad, keeping it held up for the viewers. He was sure Robinson was getting an earful, especially since he probably locked the door and wouldn't let either of the parents out. He could imagine Nora was appalled and blaming Elton. Elton was embarrassed and furious at a dead woman.

"And all these pictures, too?" Jake asked. "Bondage, torture, tied to train tracks, the front of a car. You started the scrapbooks of your stepmother pretty early on. Lot of pent-up rage over the woman."

"As I told you before, I was in rehab the night Amanda disappeared."

"Nope. Doesn't jive." Frank turned to a page of notes. "According to the nurse on duty, you checked yourself out two days prior to Amanda's disappearance."

"Where did you go?" Jake asked.

A scuffle and pounding could be heard from the next room. It sounded like a hand or foot had made contact with a wall.

Bryce's smile stretched across his face. "Here, there, and everywhere," he sang in a rendition of a Beatles song.

If Jake wasn't mistaken, the punk's reaction appeared more of amusement. If he wasn't mistaken, he would think Bryce knew his father was watching everything from the next room.

Elton stormed out of the room. "You were holding us against our will," he yelled. "I'll have my lawyer on you."

"Your lawyer had better things to do," Robinson replied, since Stephen Weber hadn't cared to stick around.

Nora trailed behind, face flush, a hankie dabbing at her eyes. "I should have never let the courts give you weekend visitation rights. No wonder our son's head is filled with such horrible…" Nora couldn't seem to find the right words.

"If his head is screwed on wrong it's from your constant coddling."

Jake guarded the door to the interrogation room, leaving Frank to baby-sit. The door was locked and he had no intention of letting either of the parents near Bryce. Captain Robinson sidled up to him, out of earshot of the parents.

"We can hold the kid for forty-eight hours," Robinson said. "He looks like a pretty good suspect to me."

That was something Jake would like to use for leverage as another plan percolated in his head. "I'd like to try something else."

"How do you want to play it?" Robinson rarely had a problem with Jake's hunches.

"Make it sound like we are targeting Bryce as our main suspect."

"We aren't?" Robinson was puzzled by Jake's sudden reluctance to hold the kid over. But he shrugged his bulky shoulders and said, "Go for it." The captain motioned to the distraught parents. "Let's have a seat in my office." He maneuvered the couple away from the interrogation room.

Nora sank into a chair in front of the desk and cradled her purse like a life vest. She kept her eyes averted from her ex-husband.

Jake remained standing, leaning against the same credenza Chief Murphy liked to use.

Robinson hefted his bulk behind the desk. He clasped his hands under his chin and studied the couple for an agonizing full minute. "I have to honestly say it doesn't look good for Bryce."

"He couldn't hurt anyone," Nora said. "No matter how much he resented her." Even Nora sounded unconvinced, though, her words catching in her throat. A dash of boldness seemed to course through her as she said, "He never brought those sketchpads home. I saw all of his work in his teens. He drew children and sunsets, floral arrangements, for godsake. He had to have kept those sketchpads at your house." She jabbed a finger in Elton's direction. "You're going to tell me you never saw them?"

"Maybe he did," Jake said. "Maybe that caused a deeper rift between you and your son. Is that it, Mr. Breyton?"

Robinson and Nora appeared to catch on at the same time. Robinson pushed slightly away from his desk as though the close proximity to the warring parents wasn't safe. Nora's eyes widened with suspicion. Jake's words confirmed what they were all thinking.

The lull in the room was filled only by the ticking clock on the credenza until Jake said, "Maybe Bryce was the other man in Amanda's life."

"NO!" Elton shook his head back and forth and kept repeating 'no' like a mantra. Nora started sobbing into her handkerchief. "He was just a kid. Amanda wouldn't have done that."

Robinson picked up on the thread. "According to several sources, Amanda played up to a lot of men. Besides, you've got teachers these days getting it on with thirteen-year-old boys. Don't say it isn't possible."

"YOU WORM!" Nora struck out, hitting Elton on the shoulder. "I told you she was nothing but trouble. And you, being as jealous as you were, how do we know you didn't run her over?"

"Me jealous?" Elton face was a shade of scarlet. "What about you? You once said you could have killed her with your bare hands."

"That's enough." Jake took a slow stroll behind the couple as he laid out the charges. "The way I see it, all three of you had motive. However, for now, Bryce is the only one without an alibi for the night Amanda disappeared. If that man wasn't Bryce, then how do we know Bryce didn't follow Amanda to find out exactly whom she was meeting? Maybe Bryce killed the boyfriend, too. We just haven't found the body yet. The sketches tell us the degree of Bryce's rage. Unless either of you are going to confess to Amanda's murder, I have no choice but to hold Bryce for forty-eight hours while we piece together his movements the night Amanda died."

"No. You can't lock him up like some animal."

Spoken like a true mother. That's what Jake was hoping for.

"Bryce may be a pain in the ass but he's not a killer," Elton said in a sober voice. "Besides, I can't have the Breyton name dragged through the mud."

Nora's fingers reached for the ceiling. "Your name? That's all you are worried about?"

"It's your name, too," Elton countered. "Who's going to buy a house from someone whose son is on trial for murder?"

Nora gave up on Elton and looked to Robinson. "Please. Bryce won't be able to take being confined. He has a very delicate psyche."

Elton rolled his eyes.

Jake returned to perching on the credenza. He had to wait for Elton or Nora to make the offer first.

"Is there anything I can do?" Elton almost made a move to his wallet but stopped himself.

"I guess there is one thing," Jake replied. The parents sat up, two hungry birds waiting for any kind of handout. "You can drop the charges against Alex Red Cloud."

"WHAT?"

"Do it." Nora's voice was a command.

"He tried to kill me. Do you think I'm nuts?"

Robinson's eyes asked Jake if he knew what he was doing.

"The way I see it, you made a threat to Abby Two Eagles, a representative of the Bureau of Indian Affairs. That is a government agency," Jake said.

"I never touched the woman." Elton looked at Nora's withering glare. "I didn't. Never had a chance. The guy was all over me. No." He made it sound like his final answer. "That's blackmail," he sputtered. He turned his attention to Captain Robinson. "Can he do this?"

"Make it public knowledge that your son is being held as a suspect? Yes. Share those sketches with the press? Absolutely."

Elton rubbed beefy hands up and down his face. "Damn," he mumbled between his fingers.

Nora sat back with a satisfied smile, as though Elton's comeuppance was long overdue. "Looks like the only option you have, E-Three. I want my son out of jail."

"That means you'll quit looking at my son as a suspect?" Elton asked.

"Didn't say that," Jake said. As far as he was concerned, all three of them were still viable suspects. "Make sure he doesn't leave town or we will arrest him. Matter of fact, all three of you should remain in town until we sort things out."

Nora heaved out a long sigh. "Agree already, Elton. Drop the charges."

"All right already."

25

Greg rushed down the hall to the examination room. He looked through the plate glass window but didn't see the medical examiner or any of his assistants. T.J. and Inga were at the dig site and would be busy for hours. He swiped Inga's access card and pushed through the doors. Inga's reference books were on the counter, exactly where he hoped they would be. Good. Now he wouldn't have to try to retrieve them from her room without telling her why. How soon until she realized what he suspected? It was only because of his internship at the Buffalo Bill Historical Center in Wyoming last summer that he became captivated by the history of the Northwest Coast tribes.

He studied the knife with the handle of inlaid abalone shell. Next to it was a beaded sheath. On another table he found the beaded pouch in the shape of a turtle. It served as a sacred fetish… Sioux 1880 to 1890. Greg had a photographic memory for details. But what about the other items? He was sure he had seen the round coins before, but were they coins? They were made of bone with detailed faces carved on one side. Inga had only found four when sifting through the dirt but Greg was sure there had to be six. His heart quickened. He needed to find a more current reference book. Perhaps the library or one of the large book stores in the mall.

"Greg?"

Greg spun around to find Angel standing in the doorway. He willed his heart to slow and hoped his face wasn't as red as his hair. "Just admiring our findings." He forced out a laugh. "This is great." He couldn't contain himself. If he didn't tell someone soon, he was sure he would burst. First, he needed proof. "That bastard, Logan. Thinks he's the expert here. We'll see." He grabbed a startled Angel in a bear hug. "We'll celebrate." He held her at arms length, admired her face, her sparkling eyes. Then he kissed her. He released her before she could protest. "Gotta go. Love you." And he was out the door wondering why he had added the *love you*. Maybe he did love her and maybe, when he proved what he suspected, she'd love him, too.

Sam set a wine glass in front of Alex. He was seated at the dining room table, a sour look frozen on his face. She couldn't stand the silence any more, and obviously Dillon couldn't either as he cocked his head to find a friendly face.

"Hi, sweetheart. Did you forget what Uncle Alex looked like?" Sam placed a hand on Alex's shoulder and smiled at the tiny bundle sitting in the infant carrier. "He doesn't always look this angry, Dillon." She tightened her grip on Alex's shoulder. "Do you, Uncle Alex?"

Alex forced a smile, the first one Sam had seen since Abby brought him home.

"You would think he would be happy to be out of that jail cell." Abby set a covered basket on the table. A warm, yeast smell filtered through the cloth. "He should be happy Jacob was able to get those charges dropped." She shook her head in frustration and returned to the kitchen.

Alex finally found his voice. "Your husband wouldn't let me see the artifacts."

Abby returned with a bottle of wine and a cork screw and handed it to Alex. "*Your husband* has a name," she reminded him. "And you should be grateful he used some pull to get you released."

Sam leaned over the infant carrier and wiggled Dillon's foot until she got him to giggle. "Uncle Alex is just angry because he couldn't get the entire Eagle Ridge Reservation residents to come to town to picket the police station or to get the big Chicago newspaper to send a reporter down here."

"We are the only ones who care, Sam," Alex said, anger still hardening the edges of his words. Dillon shifted his attention to Alex and emitted a whimper.

"Everyone who counts cares, including Jake." She wiggled Dillon's foot again to get his attention. "There are procedures to follow. Everything will work out, you'll see."

"Hrmppf," Alex snorted. "Your husband couldn't even keep me out of jail."

Abby returned in time to nail him with her eyes. "Can't keep someone out of jail who wants to be in jail. You can do more out than in, Alex."

Alex wouldn't let up. "Your husband…"

Jake appeared in the doorway, having silently slipped through the back door, and even placed his gun in the wall safe before materializing in his usual stealth way. "*Your husband,*" he mimicked, tossing a packet on the table in front of Alex, "brought pictures of the artifacts for you to examine."

Dillon's arms and legs pumped at the sound of his father's voice. Jake walked around the table, planted a kiss on Sam's lips, then lifted the squirming baby from the carrier.

"Let's eat first," Abby told Alex, "then we can look at the pictures." She placed a hand on Jake's arm. "Thank you, Jacob. He has been impossible since I picked him up."

Sam lit the candles while Abby brought in the serving dish of roast and potatoes. Dillon, having been fed and content to be in Jake's lap, remained surprisingly quiet. His tiny fingers were clenching a wad of Jake's shirt as though unwilling to let him go.

Sam set a beer in front of Jake. "Do you still suspect Bryce?"

"He's just one of a growing list. You were right about those sketches. They show more than a little hostility."

Alex had disregarded Abby's suggestion that he wait until after dinner to look at the photos. He was slowly sifting through the pile as he ate. Every now and then a grunt would burst from his throat.

"I hope those aren't the only photos Inga has," Sam said. "Alex is mutilating the corners."

"Alex, please," Abby cautioned.

"Those are copies." Jake pointed his fork in Alex's direction. "But don't tell anyone I gave them to you."

"Something puzzling about these." Alex turned one photo at an angle and shook his head. "But I don't know exactly what, yet."

Abby sighed. "After dinner, Alex. Now, I want to hear more about Quince. Did you convince him to visit Eagle Ridge with his grandfather?"

"Yes. They will leave next week. And the berry root paste worked on his rash."

Jake pushed his empty plate away from Dillon's curious fingers. As usual, he was the first one finished. "Hope you let Quince take it home. His brother had a pretty bad rash, too."

Alex shoved the photos back into the packet and stood.

"Where are you going?" Sam asked.

A look of confusion settled over Alex's face. "I need to look through the files back at my house."

Thunder rumbles through the dark sky. Sam is running along an asphalt path, the light drizzle morphing into a heavy downpour. She sees the truck ahead, its taillights flashing. This stretch of road looks vaguely familiar. Drenched and out of breath, she gladly climbs into the cab of the truck. The driver, a large man with a baseball cap and sunglasses, offers her a bottle of water. The good Samaritan exits the truck and dons a rain suit before trotting back to her car to fix her flat. Lightning flares and streaks across the sky, illuminating billowing clouds that are racing east. The fast-moving clouds are being chased by gathering storms in the distance. Nature's sky show reveals puddles of rain gathering across the expressway.

Why aren't there any other cars on the road? Sam wonders. Staring out of the side window, Sam sees a cobblestone walkway. In the distance she can see the outline of a house, its windows dark. There isn't even a light above the door.

Sam takes another sip of water and then grimaces. It has a strange aftertaste. She holds up the bottle and studies it. Why is she feeling dizzy? A moment of panic propels her out of the truck. Her feet land in four inches of water soaking her gym shoes. She tears across the cobblestones, her arms and legs moving as though someone else were controlling them. It's too dark to see but she keeps running, hearing splashing footsteps in pursuit. The ground is slippery, branches whip across her face. Her legs feel like rubber and the house appears to move away from her. She takes big gulps of air hoping to clear her head but it isn't helping. Is she dodging the trees or are they dodging her?

If only she could reach the house, get some help, call 911. Where is her cell phone? Why doesn't she have it on her? She tries to yell for help but the word is frozen in the back of her throat. Why isn't she any closer to the house?

Suddenly a sharp pain slams her to the ground and she feels the bones in her face crunch on impact. The scent of wet leaves and pine needles assault her. Then she hears the laugh. He isn't running anymore. His footsteps are slow and deliberate, squishing through the soggy ground. The laugh is low and maniacal. She claws the earth, trying to get to her feet but the pain in her back is excruciating. And then he's standing over her.

Sam bolted to a sitting position and arched her back to relieve the sensation. The clock radio behind her was flashing midnight. The storm had obviously knocked out the lights. The tiny lights that ran along the baseboard in the hallway were on so the electricity had been restored, but now all the clocks had to be reset.

Jake was sleeping soundly next to her. He could fall into the deepest sleep that not even a roaring thunderstorm could shake him from, but just let him hear the click of a gun and his eyes would snap open.

She climbed out of bed and limped to the patio doors. The wind and torrential rains were getting to be a royal pain and she wondered if Alex had been doing more than just chanting while in jail.

The visions were too confusing, especially when she couldn't readily interpret them. There wasn't anything she could do for the three Natives who had been killed centuries ago, so why keep showing a victim being shot with a bow and arrow? And what does an expressway and a truck driver have to do with anything? What wasn't she grasping? Maybe all of the murders were mingling. That's what she gets for touching all the bones.

Across town at the dig site, the rains had chased the watchers to safety. Breyton's security guard had left at the first drop of rain. He was now sitting at the bar in Flanagans having a beer. The cop on duty was sitting in his car, a can of soda in his hand. The rain pounded the roof of the squad car. It was a steady rhythm that was lulling the older cop to sleep. It was after midnight and he wouldn't be relieved until six in the morning.

From the curb only the top of the field tent could be seen. T.J. had made sure sandbags had been placed three high around the outer perimeter of the tent to prevent water from destroying the dig site.

The rain flowed down the dirt ramp and gathered in a makeshift trench. Like a tiny creek on a mission it veered off and traveled left, diluting the stained ground. Lightning flashed like nightclub strobes revealing the red color of the water which pooled around the body lying face down in the mud, an arrow protruding from his back.

26

Jake stood at the crest of the pit. Below him Benny was going over the body of Greg Stiles. From the amount of blood, Jake was sure the arrow had penetrated the heart.

"A patrol car is picking up Breyton's two guards," Frank said. "Officer Bracken said he didn't see anyone else in the area."

Jake studied the ashen face of Officer Bracken. He had taken one last look around the property before his shift ended and was the first to find the body. The cop in Jake said he should look first toward the Native American community. One or two Natives had been showing up during the day to watch but always disappeared in the evening. Both Alex and Quince had been released from jail. Jake had called Sam after arriving at the scene to ask her to find out if Alex stayed home last night. He hated the implication in his voice but the question had to be asked. Abby had confirmed that she and Alex were up until one in the morning going through files at Alex's house, using candlelight when they lost electricity. But it still didn't look good.

"Inga and her crew should probably hear it from us, don't you think?" Frank asked.

Jake checked his watch. It was seven in the morning. Inga wouldn't have heard it on the news yet. Ever since the police started communicating with Dispatch via their in-car computers, police scanners no longer gave reporters a heads up on crime. Reporters had to rely on phone tips.

"We'll go as soon as we finish up with Benny."

Benny climbed the ramp trailed by two assistants carrying the body, the arrow jutting from the partially zipped black bag. He ripped off his gloves and approached the detectives. "Victim died less than twelve hours ago. I'd say even eight hours. Lividity isn't completely set. Killer was outside the pit because the arrow penetrated in a downward motion."

The detectives studied the dig site, the portion concealed by the tent, the exposed section surrounding the tent, the street south of the site where the bank and other businesses were located.

"Officer Bracken was sitting in his car right at the curb. He didn't see or hear anyone," Frank said. "Although he did confess he might have dozed off."

"Storm started around ten last night." Benny looked behind him at the bank, then turned back to check the buildings on the opposite side. "Victim would have had to enter the area after everyone fled to their cars."

"According to Bracken," Jake said, "he didn't see anyone arrive on foot or by vehicle. It's hard to think someone would have walked in a downpour, though." He shielded his eyes from the sun bursting over the roof of a building a block away. The rain had washed away any footprints or evidence they had hoped to retrieve. "No matter what sidewalk or street the killer stood on, Bracken would have seen him. Someone would have seen him."

"Arrows are silent. A gun shot would have awakened our napping officer." Benny looked at the officer who was leaning against the front of the backhoe, his skin still pasty.

Jake gave Frank a nudge. "Let's go break the news to Inga."

Inga was seated on the couch in her hotel room, dabbing her eyes with tissue. "I can't believe this," she kept repeating. "We had workers bitten by snakes before but no one has ever been murdered."

Angel sat curled up on a side chair, sobbing silently. She looked as though she had been tugged from bed and thrown into a sweat suit. Her fingers made a poor substitute for a comb.

"I need to ask you two what you did last night. When was the last time you saw Greg?" Frank started.

"Yesterday, around five, I believe," Inga offered. "Angel and I were going to clean up before dinner. I suggested we meet at the hotel restaurant around six-thirty."

"All of you?" Frank asked.

"Except T.J.," Inga replied, giving her nose a final blow. Her eyes were red but the tears had finally stopped. "He said he wasn't hungry, had work to do. Then Greg called and said not to wait for him. He had to do something first."

"Any idea what that was?"

Inga shook her head no. Angel pressed her lips together.

"What time did you and Angel leave the restaurant?" Jake watched as Angel grabbed another tissue. She was letting Inga do all the talking.

"About eight-thirty," Inga sniffed. "We had about a thirty-minute wait for a table."

Jake watched Angel twist and untwist the tissue, mangling the fragile paper until it was unusable. She tossed it in the garbage and grabbed another.

Frank asked, "So Greg was at the dig site with you?"

Inga again was the only one to offer a response. "Not all day. When we broke for lunch, I had to make several calls to bureaucrats from my room. I saw Greg in the hotel lobby. He was headed to the library or a book store, he said. I didn't see him the rest of the day."

Jake decided to wait it out with Angel. He and Frank both settled quiet stares at her.

She looked nervously at the detectives while bits of tissue floated to the carpet. "I saw him later in the day," she said in a voice deemed more appropriate in a confessional. "I stopped by the morgue to see the artifacts. He was taking pictures."

"How did he seem to you?" asked Jake.

"He was upset. Something wasn't right, he claimed. He said..." Angel's voice trailed off and she focused her attention on the mangled tissue.

"Said what?" Frank prodded.

"He said he needed to check something out."

"That's not all he said, is it, Angel?" Jake took note of the nervous fingers that curled and uncurled the tissue, the eyes that looked everywhere but at him. She buried her face in the tissue and sobbed.

Inga moved to Angel's side and wrapped an arm around the young woman. "Angel, don't hold back on anything that might help the detectives."

Angel sniffed and dabbed at her red eyes. It took her several seconds to regain her composure before replying. "Whatever was bothering him about the artifacts, all Greg said was, 'That bastard, Logan.'"

Twin girls climbed the stairs to the top of the slide, trailed by a boy whose face and hands were smudged with dirt. A stocky woman with a staff badge clipped to her collar stood in the middle of the yard, eyes robotic as she appeared to gather in all the sights and sounds around her, spitting out orders for one boy to stop throwing rocks, a girl to not push the swing too high, the twin girls to not go down the slide in tandem. Her eyes and attention were everywhere and Sam had a feeling the woman was either a former school teacher or the mother of ten kids herself.

The back door to the shelter opened and a woman hurried over to join Sam. "I'm so sorry to keep you waiting."

Sam turned to find everything Jake had described about Sarah Whitcomb. That squeaky clean, plain Jane smiling at Sam almost had a hint of embarrassment in her eyes. Sam immediately sized up the woman as someone who walked two paces behind her husband.

"I'm not sure what more I can tell you about Amanda." Sarah took a seat in a lawn chair across from Sam. "I told the detectives everything I know." She studied Sam's business card before slipping it in her pocket but didn't ask who had hired Sam.

They were seated in the shade of one of the numerous maple trees. Sam had to keep her mind occupied after hearing about Greg. How similar his death was to the dream she'd had last night were still puzzling. Since Jake and Frank were going to have their hands full with Greg's murder, Sam figured she'd keep working on Amanda's. Although she wasn't sure yet how Sarah could help, the pastor's wife was one of the few people Amanda had considered a friend.

Sam held up Bryce's picture. "Do you know this man?"

Sarah's eyes appeared to dilate. "I don't believe so. Should I?" She clasped her fingers tightly in her lap, one nail scraping on another.

"He is...was...Amanda's stepson. Did she ever talk about Bryce?"

"Oh." Sarah gave a nervous laugh, her eyes dancing around the yard. "Of course. Just didn't recognize him all grown up, is all." The nail of one index finger scraped and picked at a thumbnail.

The scraping drew Sam's attention to Sarah's hands. Jake had mentioned Amanda's involvement with the women at the shelter, how she had helped them with hair and makeup to build their esteem. If Sam wasn't mistaken, the pastor's dowdy wife was attempting to scrape nail polish off of her thumb.

"Does your husband come to the shelter often?"

Sarah scraped harder. "Rarely ever. He travels two weeks out of the month, helping to organize churches in other cities and build homes."

"You don't travel with him?"

"No, never." Scrape, scrape. "He needs me to keep things running smoothly here."

"Is he out of town now?"

"Yes," Sarah answered quickly. "Why?"

"I just thought Amanda might have consulted with him."

"About what?" Sarah looked down at her hands and breathed a

short sigh of relief. The polish had been completely removed.

"I don't know. A confession maybe. Or trouble she was having at home with either her husband or her stepson."

Sarah's eyes renewed their dance around the playground. A nervous laugh escaped from her throat. "I wouldn't know about any confession. Those are between Reverend Whitcomb and the parishioner."

"Was Amanda one of his parishioners?"

Sarah's hand flew to her neckline, as though making sure her blouse was buttoned to her throat. Sam was playing a hunch that Amanda might have been tempted by a teenage Bryce and sought guidance from a pastor. Then again, maybe Amanda had been one to enjoy the attention from a teen.

"Could you tell me if Bryce ever consulted with your husband?"

Now both hands flew to Sarah's neckline. "My goodness, what for? His parents weren't even parishioners." Tears squeaked from the corners of Sarah's eyes. She quickly blinked them away.

The self-consciousness, Sarah's reaction to Bryce's picture, her haste to remove the nail polish, were all starting to come together in Sam's mind. "Oh my God," she said in a hushed tone. "Bryce drew your picture, didn't he?"

Sarah's face flushed red. Sam imagined this plain Jane in a whole new light. "Amanda didn't help just the women at the shelter with hair and makeup. She also helped you with yours." If Sam placed a mirror in front of Sarah's mouth, she didn't think this woman would show a breath. She was as still as a statue, unblinking. "Don't feel bad. He drew mine while I was interviewing him. Said it was a gift for my husband. So I took it home."

Sarah gasped. "What did your husband say?"

Sam shrugged. "He knew I wouldn't pose like that. He said he can't even get me to strip for him so he knows I wouldn't strip for a stranger."

This brought a brief smile to Sarah's face.

The stocky woman was ushering the children back into the house. Sarah flashed a quick wave. "You had fun today, didn't you?" Sarah's smile was forced and she kept the tears in check until after all the children were in the house and the door closed.

Sarah stared at the ground, either willing the grass to grow or aching to pull up some dirt and crawl inside. Sam waited her out, letting her imagination see Sarah without her hair in a tight French braid, maybe a wild, curly carefree style. She could see Sarah perhaps dressed in Amanda's clothes, her face and nails painted. They appeared to be the same size. Had Amanda taken her to some hot spots outside of town to show her how the other half lives? She wouldn't have taken her any place local where people might recognize the pastor's wife. Would Amanda have taken her home? Not if Elton was in town. Elton wouldn't have known the pastor or his wife. After Amanda's disappearance, did Sarah continue to experiment with makeup and nail polish when her husband was out of town?

Sarah's voice was a whisper. Sam had to lean forward to hear her. "The picture arrived in the mail two days after I spent the night at Amanda's house. We had gone out that night, to that casino boat in Michigan City. No one would have ever recognized me. Heck, I didn't even recognize myself. Even wore one of Amanda's dresses. We looked like Hollywood starlets."

Sarah smiled and Sam could see the natural beauty coming through. "You liked it, didn't you? I mean, what woman wouldn't?" Sam clarified. "Getting admiring stares from men and women. Why wouldn't you want to dress that way for your husband?"

"Oh, my, no. He doesn't believe women should have their faces all painted."

"What did you do with the picture?"

"Ripped it up. I thought someone at the casino boat drew it and was going to blackmail me. I was sick waiting by the phone for a call or running to the mailbox in case additional pictures or a blackmail note showed up. I didn't know that David had already opened the mail before I got to it. He resealed the envelope and waited to see my reaction."

"Bryce never said why he mailed it?"

Sarah seemed startled that Sam would suggest that. "It was Amanda. She called and asked if I got a special present in the mail."

Wait. "Amanda knew Bryce was drawing nude pictures?"

"Oh, sure. As soon as he turned fifteen, the boy's eyes were glued to Amanda. Even searched his room when he would leave after a weekend visit. Found his sketchpads. She told me she never walked around the house nude no matter what the pictures showed but she was flattered."

"Do you think Amanda and Bryce had a relationship?" Sam had expected Sarah to gasp but she didn't. She appeared to give it some serious thought.

"I don't think so. But there was someone else in her life. She changed after she started taking some college courses."

Somehow Sam had a hard time envisioning Amanda in a classroom. How could any of the male students concentrate? "Which school?"

"Cal-Sag College. But I know what you're thinking. When I say Amanda changed, I mean she really changed. She spoke different. Not those lusty, sexual innuendos. She dressed down, casual, no makeup. Amanda without makeup, though, and me without makeup are two different things. She looked like a college kid but you could still see she was an absolute beauty."

"You think she might have fallen in love with another student? She had left her husband a note that she was leaving him."

"I definitely think it was someone she met at school. Amanda didn't share any information with me, which was another change in her."

"You know," Sam added, "these women don't have Amanda anymore to teach them about makeup and hair. I bet Amanda taught you enough to share and help them out. And I bet if you slowly made changes, your husband wouldn't even notice."

Sarah appeared to consider her suggestion but something else clouded her thoughts. "If you've looked at all of Bryce's drawings, you didn't see any more of me, did you?"

Sam shook her head. "Matter of fact, Bryce's drawings of Amanda changed. He showed a lot of anger and resentment toward her. It was like he was drawing all the different ways to kill her."

That hard look crossed Sarah's face again. "Amanda thought it was funny, addressing the envelope to my husband. She liked to do that, get a rise out of people. She thought nothing of flirting with another woman's husband in public, in front of the wife even. I was furious with her."

Enough to kill? Sam thought.

27

After letting T.J. stew, the detectives finally entered *The Box* to find the professor napping. Frank slammed the door to the interrogation room hard enough to jar the man awake. He carried two bottles of water and a protein bar. Jake carried a bottle of water.

"Professor," Frank said in a friendly greeting. "So sorry to keep you waiting." He set the water and protein bar in front of T.J. "The vending machine didn't have tree bark but this is close."

T.J. straightened and stretched. "Thanks. I'm trying to cut down on my tree bark anyway."

"Archeology. Interesting occupation." Frank cocked his head and studied the professor with renewed interest. "I read somewhere that bodies found out in a hot, dry desert, are perfectly mummified." He pulled out a chair and sat down.

Jake slapped his notepad on the table, knowing exactly where this conversation was going. "Are you looking at mummification as another option?"

Frank explained to the professor how his wife wanted him to make a decision on his final arrangements.

"It's not the worst way to go," T.J. offered.

"Don't know about that. The skin looks all hard and papery. Eyeballs sunken in. And if my voodoo relatives get ahold of me, they'll make me into a zombie. You see the way them guys dress? Clothes all dirty and tattered, draggin' one leg behind them. Ain't no way for a good lookin' black man to dress and walk."

T.J. edged slightly away from the table, a stunned look on his face. "I trust you aren't disrupting my day to help you make a decision."

Jake said, "We are trying to re-trace Greg's steps yesterday. When is the last time you saw him?"

T.J. pushed himself to a sitting position and reached for the bottled water. "Never had a death on a dig site before. Had someone with asthma once. One hundred and five degrees in the shade and the idiot never told me he was asthmatic. Had a tough time getting a helicopter in to get him the hell out of there. Set me back a month because it was impossible to get a replacement at such a late date."

"Did you have breakfast with Greg yesterday?" Jake asked.

T.J. shook his head no. "I always get to the dig site early, seven in the morning. Try to get a feel for what needs to be done, what our priorities should be. Coffee and a bagel and I'm good to go. I don't socialize too much with the help. For lunch," T.J. continued with a bored sigh, "I got a sandwich from the Subway down the street. I was gone for maybe forty-five minutes. When I returned to the dig, Inga and Angel were there. All Inga said was that Greg was doing some research."

"Did you see him at dinner?" Frank asked.

"I went to Gibson's in our hotel. Didn't get there until eight o'clock. I like to eat late, get in as much work as possible while there's still daylight. Unfortunately, not everyone shares my work ethics."

Jake studied T.J., let the silence drag on. Then said, "The bartender claims you and Greg got into it in the bar."

T.J. sank back against the chair, hands washing over his face. "Greg found me in the hotel bar. Our voices might have gotten a little loud but I wouldn't say we were arguing."

"What were you talking about?"

"I don't remember."

Jake folded his arms and glared at him. The professor dropped his gaze to the table. The only sound in the room was from Frank's pen, making lazy circles on a pad of paper.

"He wanted to work the dig at night and I overruled him, that's all."

"I don't believe you." Jake thought for a bright guy, Logan

could have come up with a better excuse.

"That's your problem, not mine. But it's the truth."

Frank paused his pen from the dizzying circles. "You've got security guards and a cop and Greg thought no one would see?"

"That's what I told him. But he said there was a storm coming. He counted on everyone running for cover. The tent is a pretty good shelter, doesn't let out light, no one would notice anyone was working there. I told him he was nuts. He said I was spending too much time in the bar. That was the argument. If your witness heard anything different, let him or her tell me to my face."

"Were you with anyone after you left the bar? Anyone to verify your whereabouts between nine o'clock and midnight?"

"No. I went to my room, watched a little television, read over research papers. And yes, I went to bed alone so I don't have anyone to collaborate my whereabouts the night Greg was murdered."

T.J. was hiding something. "What about the Natives that sometimes came out to watch during the day? Did Greg have run-ins with any of them to your knowledge?"

"Now there's a cerebral explosion. Finally, the cops are looking at the people with the bows and arrows." He slowly slid back to his slouched position.

If Jake didn't know better, he would think T.J. was nursing a guilty conscience about something. "Greg didn't have heated exchanges with the Natives?" Jake watched Frank's circles expand, filling the notepad. There wasn't one usable word on the page.

"I wasn't there all the time, and when I was, I was busy. I don't have time to notice who was watching, how many Natives came to bang on their damn drums nor did I see the changing of the guard every night. All you have to do is check out the entire Native community. Your killer has to be among them."

"What do you think?" Frank studied the arrows in the showcase on the second floor of the Cultural Center.

Jake unfolded a picture from Benny and laid it flat on the glass. "The arrows are similar but not identical."

"Back again, Sergeant."

Bill Lighthorse appeared behind Jake as silently as his mother-in-law sometimes materialized at home. He studied the moccasins Bill wore and vowed to purchase a pair just to make things even. Cody, Bill's grandson, poked a head from behind Bill's leg. The rash around the child's mouth had not improved. If anything, it had gotten worse. Bill's attention was drawn to the photo. "Ahhh, the murder at the dig site. The red man's weapon of choice."

"Does it look familiar?" Jake handed the photo to Bill who gave it a cursory examination and handed it back.

"I can point you to a number of books where anyone can purchase the crafts necessary to make their own arrows."

"So it is homemade, nothing you'd buy off of a store shelf?" asked Frank.

"I didn't say that." Bill's smile of amusement contradicted the dark suspicion in his eyes. He turned to Cody and said, "Go ask your *Unci* for a snack." The six-year-old took off, pounding down the stairs to the first floor. Bill turned back to the detectives. "I take it you want to know where Quince was after he was released from jail."

"For starters." Jake nodded in the direction of the first floor. "I noticed posters downstairs advertising a workshop on how to make your own bow and arrow."

Bill led the detectives down the hall to a large room with conference tables and chairs. He opened a closet door and pulled out several boxes, setting them on one of the tables. From the boxes he set out bows, arrows, fibers, feathers, and other materials.

"As you can see, these are obvious replicas of the real thing. Artificial feathers, nylon string to replicate the animal tendons used for reinforcement, plastic arrowheads instead of stone or knife tips. We are teaching the children the old ways but we don't use the same materials used by our ancestors. As for Quince, he has never handled a bow and arrow and probably couldn't shoot straight even if someone held the bow for him." As he placed the items back in the boxes, a wry smile formed on his face. "Don't tell either of my grandsons, but I wouldn't know an authentic bow and arrow if it bit me."

"I'm sure you must know someone in your community who is a master archer," Jake said. He didn't think anyone unfamiliar with archery could have aimed at Greg from a distance and hit him so accurately.

"I may know someone with the skills, but not someone who would kill. You want an expert on archery, talk to Alex."

Alex trailed behind Jake as they entered the forbidden lab. Benny stood over one of the table of bones, a perplexed expression on his face. He looked up, then motioned the two to a metal table against the wall where the arrow pulled from Greg Stiles' body lay.

"According to Bill Lighthorse, you are the expert on these," Jake told Alex.

"Can I touch it?" Alex asked. Benny nodded. Alex carefully lifted the arrow at the center and held it with the tip pointing toward the ceiling. "Length is about two feet." Alex touched the three feathers at the end of the shaft. "These are called fletchings, the flight feathers from a hawk. They have been dyed. Someone went through a lot of trouble to replicate the original." The feathers were in shades of blue, green, and red. He gave a close inspection of the arrowhead. "Looks like flint. Hoof glue and sinew are holding it in place."

"Tendons from what?" Benny asked. "You can't buy sinew from a craft catalog."

Jake said, "The Indian Pow Wow takes place in Chicago each year. A collector would have these on display, wouldn't he?"

Alex gave a slight nod and a lift of his shoulder in a silent response of "maybe" but his eyes puzzled over something that escaped Jake. He gave a sniff of the arrow's shaft. "Not certain of the wood used but it sure looks like reed."

Jake pointed at three grooves cut into the length of the shaft. "Any idea what these are?"

Alex didn't have an answer but instead looked around the room as though expecting to see the victim. "Was it a direct hit?"

Benny nodded. "Right through the heart from back to front."

"Hmmmm."

If Jake didn't know better, he would think Alex was impressed by the killer's skills. "Anyone in the Native community capable of such a shot?"

"Other than me?" Alex placed the arrow back on the table. "No one local if that is the tree you are barking up. But then, I don't get into Chicago that often to be familiar with everyone's specific..." He paused as though searching for the right word. "Talent," was the one word he settled on. "Now back at the rez, there are several people but to my knowledge, no one has paid a visit to Chasen Heights."

Alex was drawn to the tables of artifacts. He gave a backwards glance at Jake, whether to see if anyone were watching him or to see if anyone would stop him. Jake knew it was useless to toss Alex out of the room.

"May I?" Alex finally asked. Benny and Jake joined him in front of the first table. Alex examined one of the button-sized artifacts. A face was carved on the front. He turned it over, rubbed the back with his finger. His brows furrowed with confusion. "I remember seeing the pictures but had to see these up close. I think they are earrings."

"Really?" Benny walked back to a counter and retrieved a plastic bag. He returned and handed it to Alex. "We found one in Greg's pocket. Now we know why he went back to the dig site. Somehow he knew there were more of these out there."

Jake had watched Alex numerous times mulling over problems, whether planting a bush or deciding on the location of a birdbath.

This seemed different. Alex wasn't just puzzled, he was worried, troubled, even a bit incensed. But to get him to open up was asking too much.

Angel remained on the sidewalk, watching T.J. from a safe distance. He had his hands shoved in the pockets of his khaki shorts. The outback hat was tilted back off of his forehead. Yellow crime scene tape still cordoned off the area. How long would T.J. stick around without a dig site to work?

She approached silently and sidled up to him. His shower soap wafted in the air, or was it bug spray? It was sometimes hard to tell since bug spray these days had such a pleasant odor.

"Where did they find the body?" Angel asked.

"Just outside the tent, from what I understand."

Angel chewed on her bottom lip, not sure how to make her offer. What if he turned her down. "Do they have any suspects?"

T.J. laughed at that comment, but the smile faded quickly. "Just me."

"You?" Angel shook her head. "How could they possibly believe you had anything to do with Greg's death."

"Probably because someone in the bar saw me arguing with Greg a couple hours before he was murdered."

"Surely you had an alibi for the rest of the night."

T.J. gave a shrug and a look of helplessness that tore at her heart. "Unfortunately, no. But I'm sure there could be other suspects if the cops opened their eyes. Just about every Native who had thrown himself into the pit the day the artifacts were found could be a suspect. But do you think they are looking at them? No. It's bias if you ask me, especially when the lead detective is married into a Native American family."

Angel took a deep breath, her teeth gouging at her bottom lip. *How to say it, how to say it. Just spit it out.* "You could tell the police you were with me all night."

His bark of a laugh made her face redden.

Stupid, stupid, stupid. "I mean, we could have sat up talking all night, about the dig. It doesn't have to sound like some tawdry affair."

He turned his attention to her. He didn't inventory her entire body, even though she had caught him on several occasions checking out her legs. "How you ever got a degree in anything is beyond me. I already told the police I was alone. How would it sound if I suddenly changed my story? And do you really look like someone I would share anything with?"

He choked up a chuckle and with a shake of his head turned and walked away.

Angel's eyes bore a hole at his back. Arrogant, belligerent, callous, deceitful, egotistical—she could probably run through the alphabet with words to describe him.

28

"I was so sorry to hear about your co-worker." Sam dragged a bowl of peanuts from the end of the table and set it in front of Angel. By the looks of the young woman's eyes and smudged mascara, she had been crying and drinking her way through lunch. Inga was seated next to Angel, trying to entice her with chicken fingers.

The hotel bar was sparsely occupied with partakers of liquid lunches. Sam had plied the women with a round of Bloody Marys, including one for herself, in hopes of loosening a few lips.

"I don't see T.J. around." Sam fished an olive from her glass and slid it into her mouth, noticing a shrug of disgust from the younger woman.

"He's more aggravated that the dig site was closed down." Inga removed her arm from Angel's shoulder and started lunching on the celery stick from her glass. "T.J. is all brain and no heart. Even left me to gather all of Greg's belongings for his parents to pick up."

"I take it the police went through Greg's hotel room?"

"With a fine tooth comb," Inga replied. She smiled then, a sign of female camaraderie. "I take it your husband isn't sharing information with you."

Sam smiled back and gave a helpless shrug in return, a sign of a fellow sister in dire need of assistance. "He does a little, but with Abby and Alex involved, Jake can't risk the case being compromised in the press. The chief wanted to remove him from the case but Captain Robinson promised that Jake would keep me under control." Her smile widened. *Fat chance.*

Inga understood completely and she couldn't move fast enough to help a fellow sister in need. She slid the plate of chicken fingers closer to Angel who had remained silently staring at the table.

"Try to eat something, Angel. We'll be right back." Inga led Sam away from the table. When Sam looked back, she saw Angel drag both of their unfinished drinks in front of her.

"Who was the last one to see Greg?" Sam asked as they road the lobby elevator.

"Angel said she saw him at the medical examiner's office taking pictures of some of the artifacts."

"Does Greg usually do that?"

"Sure. We each keep a scrapbook of some type. Each dig is unique."

The elevator opened onto the sixth floor. Greg's room was near the ice machine. As they approached the door, Inga reached into a pouch at her waist and pulled out a key card.

"I have the extra room key to both Greg's and Angel's rooms. Comes in handy if I need supplies or equipment," Inga explained. A privacy sign was hanging from the doorknob.

Sam trailed Inga into what looked like an executive suite with separate living and sleeping quarters. "Nice room."

"I hold the purse strings on this project," Inga said.

Sam found her way to the bedroom. Dresser drawers were partially open, the bed unmade, and clothes draped across one chair. "No computer?"

Inga checked the closet. "Police must have taken it. Greg usually keeps it on the desk."

They returned to the living room. A digital camera was sitting on the desk. Sam turned it on and studied the dials and buttons.

"Let me. I'm more familiar with his camera." Inga turned a dial and pressed a button. "Nothing there. Must have downloaded them to his computer. He likes to get them to a color printer immediately before anything happens to the camera. Can't tell you how many cameras I have lost in rivers and off cliffs."

Sam flipped open her cell phone, then stopped. "I wonder if you could do me a favor." Jake would recognize Sam's cell phone number. "Could you call Jake from the phone on the desk?" Inga agreed and waited for Sam to dial the number.

"Sergeant Mitchell?" Inga took a seat at the desk and explained how the Historical Preservation Society would need any pictures Greg had taken. She also asked if the police finished their examination of Greg's computer. "Really?" Inga shrugged at Sam with her palm raised to indicate nothing. "Just his reports, no pictures? That is so unlike him…yes…I see." Inga's brows furrowed as she listened to something else Jake was telling her. "I don't understand. Greg would never do that." Inga shifted her gaze to Sam and shook her head. "Of course, Sergeant. Thank you." Inga hung up and pushed away from the desk.

"What did he say?"

"Dr. Lau found one of the artifacts in Greg's pocket."

Sam left the hotel and headed to the medical examiner's office. "Hi, Benny, good friend of mine. Hungry?" She dangled the bag by her fingertips.

Benny snatched the bag from her hand as though wanting to eat the offerings before they were held up for ransom. "I promised Jake you would be kept behind the glass walls unless he or Frank were here to baby-sit you."

"You can be my babysitter." Sam fussed over the collar of Benny's Hawaiian shirt. "That's better."

"Even if you offer to straighten my desk and sweep the floors, I can't let you in the lab."

"That's okay." Sam smiled sweetly as she opened the bottom drawer of the file cabinet. "I'll just set out a plate and napkin and make you a cup of tea. You go find what I need."

"What you need," Benny parroted with a shake of his head. "I trust you need a gardener when I lose my job." He picked up a pad and pencil.

"You won't need that." Sam flipped the red lever on the water cooler to fill up a cup with hot water. "Greg was in the lab yesterday taking pictures. Those pictures weren't on his camera nor his computer so I have a hunch he uploaded them to the computer in the lab. Could you check that computer and see if any pictures were uploaded yesterday and then print them out for me?"

"That's it?"

"That's it."

"Simple enough. Shouldn't lose my job. I'll just be demoted to morgue attendant."

Sam watched through the plate glass window as Benny made his way to the computer. If her hunch was right, Greg had more than a passing interest in the artifacts, especially the earrings. Now the question was…why the earrings? She dipped the tea bag several times, then placed the cup on the desk.

Benny returned to the office empty-handed. "No luck?" Sam said. The printer on Benny's back credenza started humming.

"They are coming out as we speak, your highness. There were three pictures of each of the artifacts but at least ten of the earrings."

Sam grabbed the first picture while the printer continued to hum. "This is the earring Greg had on him?"

"Hmmmm. And who told you that?"

"Jake told Inga and Inga told me."

"Huh." Benny didn't sound too convinced. "Somehow I have images of your foot on Inga's throat demanding the information."

"Not true. Inga was more than happy to help a fellow oppressed female."

Benny barked out a laugh as he took a seat at his desk. "You, oppressed. Right." He squeezed the tea bag and tossed it into the garbage.

"Why would he go to the dig site in the middle of the night, during a storm, no less? Why not wait til day light?"

"Obviously didn't want someone to know what he was doing."

"But why? He was part of a team and they always worked in

teams. Why would he risk his reputation?"

Sam laid out all three color pictures on the desk. Greg had focused on a group picture of all four earrings, both front and back. He had then placed one earring face up and another face down and taken one picture.

"Inga said they always take pictures of the artifacts but Greg had a particular interest in the earrings. Wonder why." Sam stacked the photos and shoved them in her purse.

"I'm not sure I should let you leave with those pictures, Sam."

"Pictures? What pictures? I wasn't here. You never saw me."

Jake checked the clock behind the bar. It was midnight and he was sitting on the couch, a file folder in his lap, papers scattered on either side of him. He had told Sam one hour ago that he was coming up to bed. If there was one thing he was thankful for it was that he wasn't married to Claudia. Depending on her mood, Claudia could give Frank the cold shoulder for a week if he spent time at home rethinking a case, especially if he missed a family function, like a birthday, anniversary, or spending time with her or their son, Justin. Claudia felt the job should be left at the precinct.

Having been a cop, Sam understood how a case sometimes took over every brain cell. She was a good sounding board and often interjected her own advice and theories, whether he wanted them or not. Her way of getting at the truth was a bit too peculiar for his logical brain but she had been right too many times for him to dismiss her tactics entirely.

The folder Jake was going through was the same one Abby asked him to read after the artifacts had been found. It contained various articles on the Native American Graves Protection and Repatriation Act. There was something concerning the case that kept drawing him back to this file folder. It wasn't in the pages of legislation Abby had included in her file. It had to be in the newspaper clippings on dig sites and there were more clippings than he recalled.

He was also curious about the file folders Alex and Abby had spent so much time going over and exactly how they tied in with the case or Greg's death. Neither of them was too forthcoming. All they would say was that they would let him know when they had confirmed their suspicions. Suspicions of what?

His fingers gravitated to an article from the local papers on a dig at what was called Hoxie Farm at the Wampum Lake Forest Preserve in nearby Thornton back in 2002. If he wasn't mistaken, the archeologist in the foreground was T.J. He wasn't identified but the person did wear T.J.'s signature outback hat.

Most of the articles were on the Kennewick man. Because the debate between T.J. and Abby had been on this subject, Jake had focused his attention primarily on those articles. But somewhere in the file something else had caught his attention. Maybe he should sleep on it.

Jake was just about to gather up the papers and stick them back in the folder, when a headline caught his eye—*Artifacts returned to tribes may pose health risk.* Jake skimmed the article which reported how artifacts were treated with arsenic to prevent damage from insects. In this specific incident, the artifacts were masks which spiritual leaders decided to wear. Their faces broke out in a rash from the arsenic that had been used. *Rash!*

Jake placed the articles back in the folder with the one article about the health risk on top. He left it on the kitchen counter with a note to Abby asking her to join him tomorrow on a trip back to Chicago to talk to Bill Lighthorse's two grandsons.

29

"Abby, it's an honor." Bill Lighthorse sandwiched Abby's hand between his. They stood in front of the guard's desk in the lobby of the Cultural Center.

Abby slowly slid her hands from his.

Jake noticed Abby either avoided shaking hands or pulled away quickly with a quick pat on the person's arm. Sam had once told him that Abby's powers were with the living, that she could touch them and sometimes intuit their darkest secrets. The logical side of his brain told him this was impossible. The skeptical side of his brain questioned why, when he had first met her, Abby seemed to touch him and hold onto his hand far longer than she had anyone else's. Had it been an attempt to learn everything she could about her daughter's new partner? But what was there to learn? After all, according to Sam, Abby had seen him in a dream months before she had ever met him. Jake shook the thoughts from his aching head.

"Are Quince and Cody around?" Jake asked Bill.

Bill led them toward a side door and away from the guard at the front desk. Cody came bounding through the side door with Quince close behind. "Whoa, slow down, Cody." Bill grabbed his grandson's arm. "We have company."

Cody's mouth broke into a fractured smile that looked raw from the rash. It had worsened since the last time Jake had seen him.

Abby bent down to examine Cody's face. She straightened and checked Quince's mouth which had almost healed during his stay in jail but appeared to have the start of a fresh rash. She folded her arms and sighed. "I need whatever you kept from the dig site. It is obviously dirty and you have a bacterial infection."

Bill knelt in front of Cody. "Abby, Nona and I thought they had poison ivy. He keeps crawling around in the woods out back." Bill stood and placed a hand on Quince's chin. "Is it true? Did you keep one of the artifacts?"

Cody hung his head. "The peace pipe. Do I have to give it back?"

"It isn't yours, Cody."

Quince raised his chin in defiance. "If we give it up, you know what will happen."

Jake felt Quince might have spent a little too much time with Alex.

Abby said, "Quince, if we can't be trusted to keep our word, we will never see the artifacts."

"Go get it, Cody. Now." Bill turned Cody around and gave him a gentle push toward the door.

Abby reached into her tote bag and handed Bill a jar. "Just on the off chance that you are running low, I brought another jar of Alex's berry root paste."

Jake asked Quince, "Is the peace pipe the only item you have?"

"It's only an old coin," Quince protested. When his grandfather held his hand out, Quince angrily shoved a hand into his pocket and slammed it into Bill's outstretched hand.

Bill handed it to Abby. It wasn't a coin. It was an earring, identical to the one they had found on Greg's body.

"I-I-'m not sure if Dr. Lau wo-wo-would like this," Troy Meeks said. The young assistant gave his wire-rimmed glasses a shove. Eager to please Dr. Lau, the young intern was always the first one in, making sure everything was clean and finishing up any computer work the medical examiner might have left the night before. Tops in his forensics class, the intern wasn't even old enough to drink. Far advanced for his age, Troy's genius level didn't come without baggage. When nervous, he had the tendency to stutter and stammer. "D-D-Dr. Lau will be back at ten…o-o-clock."

"I'm n-n-not waiting," T.J. mimicked. "So get out of my way. It's my dig site and if I want to examine the artifacts, it's my prerogative." He moved his hand like a whisk broom. "Now shoo. Go practice your consonants." T.J. watched the red-faced youth stumble his way into the hallway. "Idiot."

T.J. stood for several seconds, his expert eyes taking everything in. What had Greg discovered? The punk had been so vague, dropping hints, pushing his buttons. T.J. thought at first Greg had been blowing hot air. Now he wasn't so sure.

He approached the first table of artifacts cautiously, hoping that Greg had been guilty of an overzealous imagination. After all, you've seen one beaded necklace, you've seen them all. What was important was the entire collection.

The Natal Charm was on the first table. It was a medicine bundle in the shape of a turtle. He picked up the stone figure of a man, turned it over, set it down. He proceeded to the next table and picked up the knife with the steel and copper shaft. The inlaid abalone shell should have been the first hint. His heart quickened as he set the knife down. He closed his eyes and took several deep breaths. *This can't be. It has to be wrong.*

T.J.'s attention was drawn to the counter against the wall. His legs felt leaden as he moved to the peace pipe on the counter. The bowl was made of catlinite and cradled in a deer horn. Beads and feathers adorned the shaft. T.J. felt the sweat make a lazy trail down the side of his face. *My God!*

"Professor Logan."

T.J. jumped at the sound of Benny's voice. The irritating intern was standing behind the medical examiner, a smug grin plastered on his face. "You should never sneak up on a man who is surrounded by dead people." He pulled out a hankie and mopped his forehead.

"Since Greg Stiles death, the police have restricted visitors from this area."

"I'm hardly a visitor, Dr. Lau." T.J. motioned to the peace pipe on the counter. "I don't remember seeing the peace pipe before." Now he wondered if it had been found in Greg's hotel room when the police searched it.

"One of the kids who had helped to hide the remaining artifacts had kept it. Sergeant Mitchell was able to retrieve it."

"Could have told you that was where the police should look. Does Inga know?"

"Not yet but I'm sure you will tell her the good news. Did you want to take a picture of it for her?"

"No," T.J. replied. "She'll see it soon enough." He wanted to ask if anything had been found on Greg's body. Had Greg mentioned his suspicions to anyone else? Did the police know more than they were letting on? The medical examiner broke his silence.

"Anything else we can do for you, Professor?"

"Uh." T.J. forced his eyes from the peace pipe and smiled. "Not at all."

30

Robinson's bulk filled the doorway to the examination room. Jake stood vigil by the first table of artifacts. Frank pulled around Robinson like a compact car passing a semi. Alex and Abby, file folders in hand, stood next to Jake.

Robinson strolled in, hands on his hips, and looked to his lead detective. "I have to tell you, Jake, the chief is fuming that we didn't arrest Alex and treat him as our main suspect in Greg's murder."

"He has an alibi," Jake replied. "If Chief Murphy wants to be accused of profiling, I'll gladly let the newspapers know he wants to target only Natives Americans and ignore the fact that there are 600,000 bows sold every year to bow hunters and archery enthusiasts."

"Well, this better be important to drag my ass across town again. So, who's our killer? Which murder did you solve?"

"Abby felt compelled to share some information with us," Jake said in response.

Benny motioned everyone to the first table of artifacts. "Our illustrious professor was here about an hour ago and showed an unusual interest in the artifacts. This might explain why."

Alex opened his folder. Everyone jockeyed for a view of the table while giving Alex and Abby room to make their inspection. Alex was specifically interested in the earrings. He handed one to Abby. She studied the front, then turned it over to examine the back.

A young woman in a lab coat motioned to Benny from the opposite side of the glass wall. He excused himself, unlocked the door, and stepped out of the room.

"What's going on?" Frank whispered. He stood at the head of the table next to Jake. Alex handed a picture to Jake saying,

"These earrings are called ear spools, carved from bone dating back to 1250. They were part of a collection of six being returned four years ago to an Oklahoma tribe." Alex lifted another item which looked carved from bone. "As is this. It's a gorget worn as a pendant from the 1200s."

"What are you saying?" Robinson asked. He turned to Jake for an answer. "Are they saying these aren't new finds?"

Alex and Abby exchanged looks but remained non-committal as they continued their inspection of the artifacts. Alex picked up a color photo and placed it next to the pottery which had a handle shaped like a bird's beak.

Abby said, "The Sikyatki vessel was missing from a shipment six years ago. It was last seen at an exhibit in New York City."

Alex placed a photo next to the medicine bundle shaped like a turtle. Abby reported, "The natal charm was exhibited at the Mount Rushmore Museum and reported missing eight years ago. It's from the late 1800s, Sioux tribe."

Alex motioned with a nod toward the counter against the wall. "As, I believe, is the arrow removed from Mr. Stiles' body."

Robinson's thick brows hunched closer together but he remained silent. Abby and Alex continued for the next twenty minutes. As Alex placed photos by the respective artifacts, Abby explained the dates of disappearance.

"The rest of these items," Alex said, "all came from the Smithsonian. They were returning them to the rightful tribes but never made it."

Benny returned to the examination room with a report in hand. "Tests run this morning confirm that the artifacts have had a preservative applied."

Alex held up another photo. This one showed a peace pipe identical to the one Bill Lighthorse's grandsons had used. "Oglala Sioux, 1800s. Carved from red catlinite and stolen from the home of an unknown collector."

"I'm getting a real good picture here and I'm not liking it,"

Robinson admitted.

With a shrug, Jake said, "I was suspicious of the rashes the kids had and remembered reading about the preservative causing skin rashes in some Natives who had used ancient masks in ceremonial dances. If the peace pipe was from the dig and it had been preserved, I wondered what else in the dig had already been in a museum."

"Well," Captain Robinson slapped his hands together in an *all done* motion, "we recovered stolen artifacts, uncovered a homicide, all we need to do is find Amanda's and Greg's killer."

Jake walked over to one of the three tables of remains. "Not quite," Jake said.

Robinson lumbered over to where Jake stood. "Why?"

Jake studied the bones in front of him, then shifted his gaze to the artifacts. If his suspicious were correct, they have wasted a lot of time. "Where's your UV light, Benny?"

The group assembled around the table. Benny left the room and returned with the light. After flashing an *are you thinking what I'm thinking?* look at Jake, he scanned the femur with the light. The bone glowed blue.

Jake explained to Alex and Abby, "Over time the fluorescence will diminish from the outside in. Fresh bones will glow a pale blue color under ultraviolet light."

With a frown, Benny moved to each of the tables, taking his time to make sure all the bones were scanned. He turned off the light and looked at the detectives.

"Holy shit," Robinson breathed out in a whisper. "We have a dump site."

"We have to sit on this like a hen on her eggs," Robinson barked, glancing at Abby and Alex.

Frank asked, "How did you miss this, Benny?"

"Hey, don't blame Benny," Robinson said. "Professor Logan

restricted this area, remember?"

"I'm not accusing…"

"Maybe we should go." Abby gave a nod toward Alex.

"It's just getting interesting," Alex said.

Abby suppressed a smile. Jake thanked them for their help, then waited for the door to close behind them.

"When Benny discovered Amanda's remains weren't centuries old, he should have checked them all," Frank argued.

"I had no reason to," Benny countered.

"No reason?"

Benny pulled a clipboard off the wall. "I always came into the lab before leaving for the day to check Logan's notes." He handed the clipboard to Frank. "As you can tell, he noted, and I confirmed, that there are markings on the ribs of three of the victims that are identical to the markings from an arrow. Not a knife," Benny stressed, "but an arrow. Logan also kept the items he brought from the construction area in a crate under lock and key until he had a chance to examine them closer."

Benny walked over to the table and picked up one of the skulls. "Logan didn't display the skulls immediately. Then when I did see them I immediately noticed the lack of similarity to Native American features. The skulls should have had very forward projecting cheekbones and a near perfect edge-to-edge bite." He rotated the skull and pointed to the jaw. "As you can tell, this skull has an overbite, quite common in Caucasians. And the teeth of the Natives show a lot of wear on the biting surfaces, quite common in people who eat food that is pounded with stone which puts a lot of grit into the diet. That isn't evident in these remains." He set the skull down. "I dismissed those details because of the cause of death. I know from history that white woman and young girls were kidnapped by hunting tribes and the fact that they were buried together proved that the women had tried to escape together." He directed his gaze only at Frank.

Frank shoved his hands in his pocket and nodded. "Sorry, man.

Didn't mean to go off on you like that."

"It makes sense that Logan wouldn't let you see the skulls too soon," Jake told Benny. "He was so paranoid about having his work confiscated, he just kept everything close to the vest."

Robinson said, "Someone went through a lot of planning to make it look like these were archeological treasures. Question is, was one person responsible or were the killers lucky enough to pick the same dump site?"

"Amanda wasn't killed the same way as the other three victims," Frank reminded them. "They may still not be connected. Greg must have discovered that the artifacts were stolen and someone wanted to shut him up. And, according to Abby, there are some sizeable rewards for the return of the stolen artifacts. Young guy like Greg had dollar signs in his eyes."

Jake washed his face with his hands and moaned. "Sam has been having these visions of being chased in the woods and then shot in the back with an arrow. She thinks the victims are trying to show her how they died."

Frank chuckled. "Why can't she see who's shooting the arrow?"

"I didn't say I believed it. But knowing the victims were killed by an arrow and that Greg was just killed by an arrow proves it's possible it's the same killer."

"My money's still on Breyton," Robinson said. "Besides, it all seems to take place on Breyton's property. Do we know what that stretch of land looked like three years ago?"

Jake said, "It was undeveloped. No businesses, no residences. Breyton did own the property so we are also looking at any enemies he had, maybe someone he pissed off."

"Sounds like that might be a long list, too," Robinson said.

Sam plopped down on the couch next to Jake, a burp cloth in one hand, a pacifier in the other. Other than placing his left hand on her thigh, Jake didn't move his eyes from the television set.

"How was your day?" Jake appeared to mumble to the remote.

"Dillon and I played. Abby and I made pound cake. And I think I added another suspect to your list of killers."

Jake's index finger paused over the channel select button. His head didn't move but Sam saw his eyes snap toward her. His finger clicked the power button and he set the remote down.

"Which victim?"

"Take your pick."

Jake turned his body to face her fully. "I only have so much room in *The Box*, Sam. Who are you adding this time?"

"Pastor Whitcomb and possibly Sarah."

"The pastor's wife?"

Sam winced and smiled meekly. Jake got up and walked to the kitchen. She heard the refrigerator door open and guessed her comment warranted a drink. Jake returned with a can of beer and sat down in the high-backed chair catty corner from her. He took a long swallow and set the can on the coffee table.

"Would be nice if you shared sooner, but let's hear it," he said simply. "You do remember we now have four bodies, five if you count Greg."

"I've been busy checking my facts. And, yes, I know the body count has grown but you still aren't sure if they were all killed by the same person. Let's work one at a time." Sam told him about her suspicions, Sarah and her rush to remove the nail polish from her fingernails, about the sketch and how Amanda mailed it to her hoping it was the pastor that opened the mail. "It was the look in her eyes, Jake, that sent those little nagging jabs up my spine. If looks could kill. I would almost bet you their friendship started to go south after that little fiasco. But then the good reverend intercepted the mail and resealed the envelope just to catch his wife in a lie."

"So Amanda knew about Bryce using his imagination to fill in the unseen details."

"Right but think of the possibilities." Sam draped the burp cloth across her lap and tossed the pacifier on the coffee table. "Amanda strikes me as dangerously playful. What if she let Breyton think she posed for Bryce? How many other friends of hers got the Bryce treatment? Maybe Amanda sent the pictures to their homes. If these were women from the country club who had a stature in the community to uphold, they would have been furious. The husbands would have been more furious."

"Yeah, but the husbands would have killed Bryce, not Amanda."

"Running someone over is a woman's crime. She doesn't get her hands dirty," Sam said.

"But what about the bow and arrow? Who killed the other three women and Greg? Who stole the artifacts?"

Sam was seeing the dilemma in her line of thinking. "Then we are definitely looking at more than one killer. We have three victims shot by a bow and arrow several years ago. Amanda was the victim of a hit and run. Now we have a current murder by bow and arrow and artifacts that could have been buried God knows when. We are back to square one."

Jake mulled over her comments in his head while making the contents of the beer can disappear. She could imagine his mind lining up all the details and trying to put them into logical boxes.

"Do you think Amanda was blackmailing these people? But for what purpose? She had a huge bank account at her disposal. Unless Bryce was doing the blackmailing." He thought about that, then answered his own question. "No. Bryce would be angry someone was using his drawings that way. He would have known Amanda was ripping out the drawings and mailing them. That would make him angry enough to kill. Maybe he was doing the blackmailing and he had to silence all four women."

"But you didn't find archery equipment in his dorm room, did you?"

"I just can't see Sarah Whitcomb killing someone. Bryce makes a compelling suspect. The drawings are a good indication of his attitude toward Amanda. He hated her."

Sam smiled but she also had a look of pity reserved for a husband who didn't quite get it.

"What?" Jake's look of annoyance made her smile even more.

"Some detective you are. Bryce was in love with Amanda."

31

"He was in love with her." Robinson leaned back in his chair, hands folded across his stomach. The chair rocked for a few beats. "What was that book all three of us obviously failed to read? *Men are from Mars-Women are from Venus?* Apparently no one in this room knows what goes on in a woman's mind. How on earth did Sam come to this conclusion?" Although the captain was speaking to both of the detectives, his eyes were riveted on Jake. First thing this morning Jake had delivered a cup of coffee and a bag of fry bread to Robinson, then dropped Sam's suspicion on him.

All Jake did was shake his head. Frank shrugged. Jake said, "Sam thinks he is acting like the victim of unrequited love. Amanda perhaps slept with him for the hell of it but then told him she wanted a man, not a kid."

Robinson pointed a finger at the detectives. "Now that makes sense. Bryce is looking better and better for this. He wants to piss off his father and let him know in a subtle way that he's been sleeping with his wife. Then Amanda maybe changes her mind to run off with the son and the old man kills her. As far as the other three women, maybe they refused to pay blackmail money."

"All that does," Frank added, "is confirm a motive for Breyton. He finds out his wife has been cheating on him with his son and he sets out to follow Amanda to run both of them over."

"Then there's Nora Breyton who finds out that the woman who stole her husband also took advantage of a teen and dumped him like last week's garbage." Robinson peeled back the flaps of the brown bag and inhaled the warm aromas. "Damn, you have one helluva mother-in-law."

"Do you really think either Breyton or Nora would have a reason to kill the other three women or Greg?" Jake asked.

"Greg could be a random killing. Someone used a bow and arrow to try to steer us to the Natives unaware that the three other women were killed with a bow and arrow," Robinson said.

Robinson's phone rang. He pressed the speaker button and said, "Go."

"It's Benny here."

"Yeah, Benny. Frank and Jake are with me. What have you got?"

"Found something interesting when examining the remains of Amanda Breyton more closely. We brushed and washed all of her bones, rinsing them through a fine screen. Under the mass spectrometer I found particles of clay and sand."

"What's unusual about that?" Robinson asked.

"Clay isn't in Breyton's construction site."

"Are you saying her body was moved from another burial site?" Jake asked.

"Exactly. What is mixed with the clay is sand, and something unique. There were various sand spits in the area formed by glaciers. Some of the residue on Amanda's body has been identified as decayed pine spruce."

"Spruce?" Frank said. "I'm sure there are spruce trees in just about every forest preserve."

"Decayed spruce, like buried during the glacier age," Benny clarified.

Jake said, "And I bet pine spruces were only evident in certain sections of town."

"Not Chasen Heights, though," Benny said. "There was one in Two Creeks, Wisconsin. But another one was just south of Interstate Twenty near Michigan City, Indiana."

"Hmmm. Michigan City," Frank said. "Like where Bryce Breyton's little retreat is."

"Is it possible to narrow the search area down?" Robinson asked.

"You'll need a map from the Army Corps of Engineers.

Someone in the building might have one. Matter of fact, I think there is a Calumet region map hanging on the wall in the first floor meeting room."

"How can you tell how long the body was in Michigan City?" Frank asked.

"Well, it had to be an isolated place where the body could be left out in the elements. If it were summer, give it a few weeks in hot weather to be reduced to bone. If the killer didn't have an opportunity to bury it or waited for an opportune time and place…"

"Right," Jake interjected. "If she was killed in Michigan City, the killer either had a reason to bring the body to Chasen Heights or just drove until he found the perfect isolated spot."

"When was *Phase One* of Breyton's project developed?" Robinson asked Jake.

"Breyton finished the first strip mall a couple years ago. Probably started a year before that, putting in water lines and utilities."

"Flip of a coin," Robinson lamented. "We know the day Amanda disappeared. We just don't know if she was killed here and taken to Michigan City or was meeting someone in Michigan City and killed there."

"It gets better," Benny said. "The other three victims have the same residue of decayed spruce."

"What are we looking at?" Jake scanned the area map on the wall. A sea of blue uniforms drifted in and out of the room on the first floor. Jake was on the phone with Santos from the Chasen Heights Building Department. It was just their luck that Santos used to be with the Army Corps of Engineers and pretty much knew the history of the area.

"Just southwest of Michigan City and Beverly Shores you'll see a red dot marking Pine Grove." Santos spoke at a clip. Although

Santos probably had an identical map in his office, Jake wouldn't doubt it if the man had the map memorized.

"Got it." Jake's finger traveled the red line from Beverly Shores.

"This area is filled with spruce trees that are just as old as the ones that were carbon dated in Two Creeks, Wisconsin. The Wisconsin forest was destroyed and buried when glaciers re-entered the area about twelve thousand years ago. Spruce trees do not grow on the lake bottom so the area around Pine Grove was free of the lake water, hence, still standing."

"Is this a well populated area?"

"Some vacation homes, but a year-round population of a little over seven hundred. "

"Can you get me a list of addresses and homeowners for the past ten years?"

"Sure. I know someone in their Building Department. Were you planning on taking a trip?"

"Not just yet. Tell you what, though. Have him narrow that list to just the homes in and around that stretch of spruces. You can probably explain better what area we are interested in. He can either fax the list or send it over the Internet. Then we'll take it from there."

"Doesn't sound like a fun road trip," Frank said after Jake had hung up.

"We need a section isolated enough that a decomposing body doesn't alert the neighbors." They threaded their way through the shift change and made their way up the stairs to the fourth floor.

"Hope Santos trusts this building department employee. If it's a tight knit community, the whole town of Pine Grove will know we're coming."

32

"Tell me again why we are here?" Jackie shoved the sunglasses back on her nose and plopped down on the bench next to Sam.

Dillon was barefoot and napping in the stroller, clad in a blue sun suit and diaper. He was lying in the cool shade of the stroller's visor. The entire area was shaded by tall oak trees. They were on the campus grounds of Cal-Sag College.

"We are hoping to run into some summer school students who might have known Amanda Breyton. I am a terrible mother for using Dillon as bait but what woman can resist stopping to coo at a cute baby?"

"A terrible, devious mother." Jackie flashed a wicked smile. "But smart."

Sam remembered another piece of her bizarre dream. She brought out a notepad and pen and jotted down *cobblestone* and *brown truck*. Brown or black she wasn't sure. It was always dark out. She'll have to pay more attention next time.

Jackie leaned over and read Sam's notes. "That the trip you aren't telling your husband about?"

"Please use the word vision. Trip sounds so psychedelic."

Jackie waved her hand in a *whatever* gesture. "If it walks like a duck... And why again aren't you sharing this with your husband?"

"He can only handle one vision at a time. Until I know more about what this one means, I'm just going to keep it to myself."

The front doors opened and the first group of students drifted out. Their voices were loud, but just as Sam had anticipated, as they approached a sleeping baby, they lowered their voices.

Sam tried to ignore a few stragglers trailing the female students. She doubted the males would be as quick to stop. How wrong she was. They weren't looking at the baby; they were looking at Jackie.

"How's it going, sugar?" Jackie peeled off her sunglasses and set them on the bench next to her. She flapped her hand at her throat and fanned herself. "Sure is a steamy one today." A bead of sweat trickled down her throat and rushed to the safety of her cleavage.

How the hell does she do that?

"Learn anything today?" Jackie drawled. "Although I'm sure you boys could probably teach the class." The three male students couldn't find their voices. They seemed to be burning Jackie's image on their irises.

One straggler sidled up to the three and didn't have a problem finding his voice. He was wearing an Indy 500 tee shirt over blue shorts.

"Yo, mama," Indy gasped, his body gyrating as though hinged at the hips. "Please tell me you are teaching my Humanities class."

The other three finally found their voices but all they could squeak out was a "Wow."

"I don't know. Why don't you tell Jackie what classes you are taking and I'll tell you if I'm teaching them."

Indy slid onto the bench next to Jackie. "How about Sex Education?"

Now the other three were waking from their comatose condition mumbling English Lit and Foreign Affairs.

"How about Domestic Affairs?" Indy added with a syrupy voice.

"How old are you boys? Why on earth would you go after a mature woman when you have so many young women to choose from?"

"Not like you, mama."

"I am not your mama. And if I were…" Now Jackie was doing her own body gyrating and finger wagging. "…I would have knocked you from here to New York disrespecting women this way. You are supposed to be getting an education in these halls of knowledge, not talking this *yo mama* shit."

Sam had to look away before her eyes popped onto the sidewalk. What was Jackie up to?

"However." Jackie's smile returned and she rested one lacquered nail under Indy's chin as her other hand pulled out a photo from her purse. "You can all be forgiven if you can tell me if you have seen this woman before." She held up a picture of Amanda Breyton.

"Yeah," all four of them chimed in together. "Her face was on the news," Indy said.

"No, sugar. Before then. You ever see her here at the college?"

All of these boys looked right out of high school. Sam doubted any of them attended the college three years ago.

Four sets of eyes studied the picture again. Then four heads shook in the negative. Three of the boys drifted away leaving Indy who took the picture from Jackie's grasp.

"You think she went to school here?" Indy asked. His voice had changed. It sounded different, older, professional. He cast a look Sam's way and said, "You're the ex-cop, aren't you? The one who's…" he waggled his fingers back and forth, "psychic or something?"

Sam studied him curiously, then glanced at Jackie who appeared just as confused over the change in Indy. "No. I wouldn't call myself a psychic."

His eyes drifted to the medicine bundle hanging from her neck and the third earring of beads and feathers. "Whatever," was his response. "Tell you what I can do for you." He slapped his hands on his thighs and stood. "If you think she went to school here, I'll bring up her records on the computer and print it out for you."

Now it was Jackie's turn to be struck silent. She finally found her voice and said, "I don't mean to sound ungrateful or suspicious, but what's going on here?"

Indy leaned in close and said, "I'm undercover narcotics

working the college. I'm twenty-six but look nineteen. What can I say? I help out the Admissions Office with their computer programming besides drifting in and out of classes. Helps me keep tabs on a growing drug business here at the college. Admissions is closed until tomorrow, though." As an afterthought he smiled at Jackie and said, "Don't mean no disrespect, ma'am, and I certainly don't want to get on the bad side of Captain Robinson." He gave her a wink, then slid back into his Indy jive act. "Yo, mama. You got some place private where we can hook up?"

Jackie handed him a business card with the address and phone number for Jackie's Boutique. They watched him pimp-walk down the sidewalk toward the parking lot.

"I'm going to have to tell Lamon to put that boy in for a raise."

Dillon stirred and stretched, blinked a couple times, and promptly went back to sleep. Sam said, "I have a marketing suggestion for your store."

Jackie's right eyebrow jerked up. "I'm afraid to ask. Honey, you are so squeaky clean you'll probably have me dressing the mannequins in robes." As if to prove her point, Jackie's eyes swept the length of Sam's broom skirt."

"What? I've worn shorts before. And the dress I wore when I visited Bryce had slits up to the nether regions."

"Still." Jackie waited her out. "Okay. Let's hear it."

"Do you remember those photographer studios at the mall where they would dress you in sexy lingerie, do your hair and makeup, and snap professional pictures?"

"Sure. It was the craze years ago. Women would get the pictures framed and present them to their boyfriends or husbands."

Sam smiled with a bit of smugness. It was a sheer brainstorm, even if she had to say so herself. "How do you think the women would like a framed sketch of them for their husbands?"

It didn't quite hit Jackie at first. Then her eyes widened. "You mean have Bryce draw them?" She slapped a hand against her chest. "That's brilliant." Then she stopped. "What kind of sketches? The ones you described to me are not what I want associated with my shop."

"Jake may not think he is capable of anything tasteful but I do. All he needs is someone to take his work, his real work, seriously."

Jackie thought about that for a moment. Then her enthusiasm returned. "I can bring in this young girl who is fantastic with makeup and hair. Bryce sketches so fast the customers can be in and out of there in a half hour. Although I should make them linger and shop awhile. I can schedule appointments between certain hours, serve wine and cheese." She clawed at the air. "The hell with that. I can schedule appointments all day long. People can watch as Bryce draws." Jackie grew quiet, her brows furrowed. "But do you think Bryce would go for it? He seems to be perfectly happy drawing on the beach. Besides, what if he ends up in prison?"

"Bryce isn't guilty of anything more than extreme artistic expression. Besides, he will need money eventually. His mother isn't going to support him forever." Sam laughed remembering the drawing Bryce made of her. "When Jake took a look at that sketch, I wasn't sure if he was going to drive over and punch the kid's lights out or make love to me again."

Jackie squealed with delight. "Do tell."

Sam shook her head. "You'll have to draw your own picture."

33

"I wondered when I might see you again." Sarah Whitcomb emptied the last of the water into a pot of pink geraniums. She led Jake to a bench fifty feet from the shelter. He carried a brown envelope and set it on the bench next to him. Frank remained at the office. Besides, Jake thought Sarah would respond better if she only had to deal with one of the detectives. "Figured the P.I. would talk to you."

Out of force of habit, Jake studied his wedding band of inlaid coral and turquoise, handcrafted by Alex. "We tend to share a lot," he said.

Sarah dropped her gaze to his ring finger and heaved a long sigh. "Of course." She clasped her arms around her waist as though hugging herself. "What else do you need to know about Amanda?"

"After she mailed the sketch to your husband, would you say your relationship changed?"

"Between me and Amanda or me and my husband?"

"Both."

Sarah nibbled at her bottom lip and stared off toward the playground. Jake wasn't sure how to read the look on her face. She was either very angry or ready to burst into tears. "Amanda opened up a whole new world for me. She proved that there was more to life than high neck blouses and listening to the whining of desperate, miserable women who did nothing to change the way they lived." She turned sad eyes toward Jake. "I miss her terribly. She let me see a side of myself I didn't know existed. Amanda loved life. She felt comfortable in any situation and she taught people that they can love living even if they hate the life they lead." Her gaze dropped to her hands which were wadding and twisting a hankie.

"Are you saying she hated her life?"

"Not hated. I don't think Amanda hated anyone or anything." Her hands stopped annihilating the hankie and she sank back against the bench. She smiled and shook her head. "Amanda once said you can have either love or money but life doesn't give you both. She settled for money because she didn't think she would ever find true love."

"But then she did."

"Yeah," she replied with a sad laugh. "I think she really did."

"So you didn't stay angry with her for long."

"No one could stay angry at Amanda for very long." She saw the look of skepticism on Jake's face. "What?"

"Did your husband stay angry at her?"

Amanda's face seemed to lose all color and her fingers started its intent on demolishing the hankie. "You think my husband could kill someone?" She shook her head vigorously. "He was more angry at me and Bryce. But he could never hurt me."

"You don't think your husband capable of murder?"

"No, never. He follows the Ten Commandments and loves his congregation. He would never do anything to betray their trust."

Jake picked up the brown envelope. Although Sam had told him he shouldn't look at the pictures, he didn't like being blindsided. He said, "My wife has a lot of contacts who owe her favors. She followed a hunch and thought you should know exactly what your husband is doing when he allegedly is out of town helping to build houses for the poor."

The hankie slipped from Sarah's fingers. She hesitated briefly, eyeing the envelope as though it contained some toxic chemical. Then she slowly pulled the envelope from Jake's grasp. He had a feeling Sarah was far too trusting of her husband and had argued with Sam that this could crush someone who was already fragile. Sam countered that the envelope contain a spine that Sarah desperately needed. Sam felt Amanda had helped to give Sarah a spine but then it crumbled when Pastor Whitcomb received Bryce's drawing and evidently laid down some strict laws or shamed Sarah into crawling back inside her shell.

Sarah stared at a photo of her husband holding hands with an attractive blonde woman outside of a resort surrounded by cacti in what looked like a southwestern state. Jake saw a tall man with a youthful face and graying temples. The picture was in color and his bright blue eyes were smiling at the petite woman.

"Please tell me he doesn't have a second family." She found a second photo with her husband and the woman lying by a pool. "He said his tan was from working outside building homes." One tear trickled down her cheek to her lips that were pressed tightly together.

"She is a sales representative for one of the bible publishing companies," Jake told her.

Sarah laughed, tears streaming down her face, and attracting the attention of the woman in the play yard. Her laughter increased as she thumbed through two additional photos of the pastor and the saleswoman sharing an intimate candlelight dinner on a veranda outside of what could have been their hotel room. Finally, a photo of the loving couple parting at the airport.

"Amanda warned me of this," Sarah said, swiping at the tears, her laughter reduced to gulps of high school giggles. "She said you had to watch out for the ones that were too good to be true. He said if I walked out of the house wearing makeup and revealing too much skin, it would be an embarrassment to the church. Yet here he is having an affair with a woman who looks like a...a." She broke out in a fit of giggles that changed to laughter again as she slid the photos back into the envelope. "That bastard."

Sarah stood and faced Jake, her shoulders back, head high. "To answer your question, Sergeant, no, my husband isn't capable of killing anyone. But I would have never thought he was capable of adultery. So if you want to haul him in and make him sweat, be my guest." She turned and walked back to the women's shelter.

Sam never ceased to amaze him. She actually did put a spine in that envelope.

"I think I need to go home and kiss Claudia," Frank said, "and be thankful I am NOT married to Sam. Whew, she is vicious."

"I think *effective* is the word, Frank."

They were in Jake's office waiting for a patrol car to bring in Pastor David Whitcomb. Although Jake had told Sarah she could join them in the interview, she declined to be driven in a patrol car. She told them she would drive herself and they didn't have to wait for her before beginning their interrogation.

Captain Robinson filled the doorway. "You did say Amanda started volunteering at the hospital and dressing conservatively. Sounds to me she might have fallen in love with a man of the cloth. Think the good pastor did it?" he asked.

Frank chuckled. "Should be fun finding out. You should get a front row seat, Captain. If anyone is guilty of murder, I think it will be Sarah Whitcomb killing her husband."

"Then we better have her patted down before she walks in the room," Robinson replied.

A very puzzled Pastor Whitcomb exited the elevator. The police officer led him down the aisle, past Jake's office, to the interrogation room. He wore a short-sleeved shirt open at the collar and dark slacks. He avoided Robinson's eyes and instead smiled reverently at the office staff.

"Kind of looks like milk toast to me," Robinson commented. "But I've said that about a lot of guys on death row."

"I think I'm going to join the captain in the viewing room." Jake patted Frank on the shoulder. "You are much better at quoting passages."

"Thanks a lot," Frank yelled at his back.

Frank walked into *The Box* and set two cans of Pepsi on the table. "My apologies for keeping you waiting, Pastor Whitcomb."

"It was a little embarrassing to be picked up by a police car." David Whitcomb popped the top open on the soda.

Frank studied the tanned skin and well-rested eyes of the good pastor while recalling how Mrs. Whitcomb had looked haggard and pasty white. Whitcomb had a clear and distinct voice, perfect for the pulpit.

"I'm sure the neighbors and parishioners would think nothing of a police car being at the church. After all, we have prisoners here that need ministering to." Frank smiled, laying on his own pastoral tone. Whitcomb nodded, his clear eyes smiling with understanding. "We understand Amanda Breyton helped out at the women's shelter and was a close friend of your wife."

The clear eyes clouded and he shifted uncomfortably in his seat. "Amanda was a very insecure young woman. Her influence on my wife and the women in the shelter was unfortunate."

"How about Bryce Breyton?" Frank watched the color rise in Whitcomb's cheeks. The pastor took a long swallow of soda before setting it down with what looked like forced control.

"Another insecure, misguided young person." He seemed to chew on those words, his jaws grinding.

"I don't know about that. He seems pretty talented to me."

Whitcomb pressed back in the chair in shock. "Talent? You call that ...?" His face flushed even more. "You've seen his drawings?"

"Sure. Most of them were of Amanda." Frank paused briefly before saying, "I didn't see the drawing of your wife, though. I understand you ripped it up."

"Vile. The picture...him. How she could pose like that I'll never know."

"Come on, Pastor Whitcomb. You seem like an intelligent man. Bryce uses his imagination. The women never posed for him."

"I find that very hard to believe."

"I understand it was Amanda who mailed the drawing to you, maybe in her playful way trying to get a rise out of you."

"Playful?" His face hardened, fingers clenched and unclenched. "It was destructive."

"Did it make you angry?" He watched the pastor carefully. Was he beginning to sweat?

"Angry?" He shifted in his seat. There was a hardness to his eyes that made him look like anything but a lover of his flock. "I could have …"

"Killed her?" Frank finished for him.

The door opened and Jake ushered in a new and different Sarah Whitcomb. Her hair was unleashed from its tight bun, falling loosely to her shoulders. Makeup was applied conservatively but the change was enough to make Pastor Whitcomb's mouth gape. The baggy dress had been replaced with a hip-hugging skirt that flared out to just above the knees. The cap-sleeved blouse was snug enough for the average man to notice this woman had breasts. Her calves were shapely and she wore jeweled sandals that matched the jewels at the neckline of her blouse. Her toenails and fingernails were painted. In her hand she clutched the brown envelope.

"Sarah?" David Whitcomb's eyes swept the length of his wife. "What are you doing out of the house dressed like that?"

"It could be worse," Sarah replied as she pulled out a chair and sat down. "I could be lying by a pool in a pink floral bikini." She placed the envelope on the table in front of her. It was obvious she was enjoying her husband's puzzled look. "Did I miss anything? Did we get to the part yet about where David was the night Amanda was *murdered*?"

"Sarah, you know I was out of town building homes."

"That might be true but I believe the detectives would need a list of all the people you were with. Isn't that right?" She looked directly at Jake.

Jake tossed a lined notepad on the table followed by a pen. "That's true. It would help us to eliminate you as a suspect."

"Me?" The pastor snorted. "How could you possibly suspect a man of the cloth?"

"Please, Pastor Whitcomb," Frank said. "We don't want to get into a discussion of children who have been abused by priests. Not all men of the cloth live up to the standards that their collars demand."

Whitcomb flushed and sputtered. "Why, talk to anyone in my parish. I am a man of honesty and integrity." He looked to Sarah as though expecting confirmation. "Sarah?" he prompted.

"I am confident that your parishioners *believe* you to be a man of extreme honesty and integrity."

"See?" Whitcomb said with a nervous laugh.

"Who would never lie or commit adultery," Sarah added, her fingers working the clasp on the envelope. Slowly, she slid the photos out and placed them one by one on the table in front of her husband. "If you are capable of this, David, how do any of us know that you weren't the one who killed Amanda? Maybe you were having an affair with her. I don't know what to believe any more."

The silence in the room was thick, choking the very air around them. Jake remained standing against the wall, arms folded across his chest. Frank had his elbows on the arm rests, hands clasped under his chin, a tsk tsking sound coming from his shaking head. Sarah waited silently, her eyes narrowed to daggers while Pastor Whitcomb continued to stare at the pictures.

"You had me followed?" Whitcomb finally charged.

"How like you to turn this around on me, David. Maybe I'm not the dutiful wife you think I am, sitting at home all drab, doing your bidding, wondering why you are spending more time away from me and your congregation."

"It's obvious from that drawing that you aren't the dutiful wife," Whitcomb hissed.

"Oh, can it. I didn't do anything wrong and I'm sick and tired of having to apologize for it."

Frank and Jake quietly slipped out of the interrogation room and into the viewing room. Robinson was sitting in the dark nibbling on a bag of popcorn. "Of all my detectives, I think you two put on the best show."

Frank dug into the bag for a handful of popcorn. They both took a seat and continued to watch the scene beyond the one-way mirror.

"You're the one who has to answer for your actions," Sarah was saying. "What were you thinking? Where did you meet her? How long has this been going on?"

David Whitcomb sank back against the seat, trying to keep his eyes off of the photos on the table. "She's a sales rep I met at the convention last year. She lives in Minnesota."

"How did you make it to Scottsdale?"

"She owns a condo there."

Sarah already knew all this. She had called Sam and Jake had overheard Sam filling her in on the woman's name, address, her full life history.

"Who is she?" Sarah demanded. She moved from the chair next to her husband to the one across the table that Frank had vacated.

"Does it really matter?" Whitcomb's voice was so low Robinson had to reach over and turn up the volume.

Sarah pulled a notepad from her purse and read from it. "Deanna Dawson. Sounds like a dominatrix. Please tell me whips and chains are not involved."

Frank took another handful of popcorn. "His ass is cooked."

Robinson turned slightly away from the one-way mirror and barked, "Jake, your wife's fingerprints are all over this lady."

Even in the darkened room Jake could see Frank tense, but then a slow chuckle rumbled from the front row seat where Robinson sat.

"God, I miss that woman," Robinson said.

On the other side of the glass, Pastor Whitcomb swallowed hard and avoided his wife's eyes. "Give me some credit. I'm not that perverted."

Sara folded her arms and stared him down. "Break it off."

"It's not that easy."

"Sure it is. You call her up, tell her it was wrong, it's over, finished, then hang up."

"I can't. She has videotapes."

"Uh, oh." Robinson shoved another wad of popcorn in his mouth.

Sarah was surprisingly calm which made Jake suspicious as to how much dirt on this affair Sam was able to dig up. Who did she know in Scottsdale? Then it hit him.

"Oh shit," Jake said under his breath. "Pit Goddard is now living in Phoenix. He probably still has his P.I. license and Sam asked him to look into this." Sam had worked with Pit on a case that cleared a man of murder just weeks before he was due to be executed. For now Pit had decided to stay near his deceased wife's parents.

Sarah looked over her notes. "Arnold Moore, Jim Holloway, Trey Cook. Any of these names ring a bell?" All David did was blink. Perspiration dotted the front of his shirt. "They are all pastors having affairs with Deanna Dawson, all paying her money to keep their affairs a secret. Is this why we couldn't build the addition to the school? How much money have you paid her?"

"I lost track."

"Lost track? You know to the penny how much I spend on food and household goods. Yet you don't have a clue how much you have paid her? I find that hard to believe. Skimming from your own parishioners. You are disgusting."

In the viewing room, Robinson shook his head and said, "I don't believe this wet sock has the balls to run over Amanda Breyton."

"Maybe he bedded her." Frank tossed a kernel of popcorn in the air and it dropped into his mouth.

As if Sarah could hear them, she asked, "Did you sleep with Amanda?"

He barked out a "No."

"Did you kill her?"

"No."

"The way I see it, you have three choices." She ticked off each point on her fingers. "You call her bluff and end it, you play the roll of Jimmy Swaggart and openly confess your transgressions to your parishioners, or resign your post. I can't guarantee that I'll be around for any of those options." Sarah gathered up her notes and photos and exited the room.

Jake came up from behind and kissed the top of Sam's head. "Since you seem to have an inside track, I take it you know what Sarah Whitcomb plans to do."

Sam watched him circle the wicker loveseat and settle down next to her. The jalousie windows were cranked open sending a warm, pleasant breeze through the Florida room. The large paddle fan overhead circulated the air. Jake had stripped out of his work clothes and donned a pair of shorts and a sleeveless shirt.

"She'll stay with him but she'll let the good pastor squirm a bit before informing him that Deanne Dawson won't be a problem any longer. Pit had a nice long talk with her, has all of her bank account information and is ready to share said finance information with the IRS seeing that Miss Dawson has neglected to pay taxes on her income. Naturally he didn't want to bring the police in on it. None of her victims wants to be dragged into court and have their names on the front page for family and friends to see." Sam watched him pop the top on the beer can and take a long swallow. "Do you think David Whitcomb is capable of murder?"

Jake shook his head. "Not at all. Not his wife either."

"So you still like one of the Breyton's?"

"They are persons of interest. Breyton is making a pitch again to get his construction back in operation. Murphy wants another meeting tomorrow." Jake filled her in on Benny's findings regarding the detection of decayed spruce found in the victims' bones and how they were able to narrow the search down to an area just west of Michigan City in a town called Pine Grove.

"And I suppose you are checking to see if Elton Breyton owns or did own a summer cottage in that area." Sam had a feeling she knew where Jake was going with this. "I really don't think Bryce killed Amanda and then dragged her body somewhere on the property of The Sanctuary to decompose without anyone being suspicious."

"An isolated enough house that the parents might have owned and didn't use any more, a teen who had access to said property… it all fits."

Sam didn't think it fit at all. "Did you call Nora Breyton and ask if her ex had a home or property there?"

Jake shook his head no. "She'd cover for the son so I can't trust her to be honest. Andy and Maury are checking the list of home ownerships in the town three years ago. They are also focusing on any abandoned homes, preferably someplace isolated."

"The four bodies have to have something in common. Anything come up in the missing persons reports? Dental records? Cause of death?"

"Other than arrow marks on the ribs, no."

"Well, it's hard to believe there is more than one killer and they just happened to have picked the same dump site. You already know neither Bryce nor Elton, nor Nora for that fact, know a thing about archery. Sure, someone could have stolen the artifacts for them and stashed them somewhere but you can't believe Elton would implicate himself by planting all the evidence on his own property. Not that I wouldn't be pleased if Elton were the guilty party, that self-serving, bigoted son of a…"

"I've worked many a case where it wasn't unusual for the killer to try such a move just to suggest someone was setting him up."

"Bryce isn't the killing type and I would bet you feel the same way. He might have had a crush on his stepmother but that's about as far as it went."

Jake pulled his arm around her shoulder and drew her close. "If I didn't know better, I'd say you had a soft spot for Bryce."

Sam smiled, knowing Jake wasn't the jealous type. "Still love me?"

"I'll get back to you on that."

34

The next morning Jackie received a call from Indy. Sam was to meet him outside the Administration building. The grounds were bustling with students rushing to and from class. Sam saw a familiar pimp-walking figure exiting the building.

He was all business as he said, "Let's walk." Indy led Sam down the sidewalk, away from the crowds. "Thought you'd be interested in the meeting taking place today with some alumni."

They walked in and out of patches of shade from the trees. Clusters of impatiens lined the walkway as they wove their way around knots of students. Indy was cute, in a Chris Rock sort of way. It was his manners that helped make him appear younger than his years. He could probably keep this gig for another ten years, or at least until the gray hair starts coming in.

He handed her a piece of paper. "This is the class your vic had enrolled in several years ago. Some of these alumni might be familiar with the class. You know how ladies like to talk."

Sam pulled the paper from his fingers and opened it. Her feet slowed to a crawl, then stopped as she read.

"See something you like?" Indy said with a wide smile. He wrapped an arm around her shoulder and practically dragged her the rest of the way, saying, "Why love of my life, let me show you'all to the library. It's the building with the large bell tower. I'd check the conference room on the second floor first."

Sam thinks she mumbled her thanks and good-bye but she was too busy staring at the piece of paper in one hand and dialing her cell phone with the other.

* * *

The outer office was in overdrive as every available man and woman devoted time to the various reports the baby dicks had coordinated. Robinson was up to his elbows in background checks on Breyton's employees, specifically his bodyguards. Janet was bent over newspaper photos from various museum exhibits, a magnifying glass in one hand. Jake was running through the names of homeowners in the Pine Grove area. And Frank was skimming through missing persons report for women in the age group of the victims found at the construction site.

Off in a corner Police Chief Dennis Murphy stood, arms folded. He started a measured stroll between the desks, as though he were a grade school teacher keeping watch as his students finished an assignment. Taped to one wall was the headline from this morning's paper:

Breyton Dig Cursed

The article spilled every detail about the four bodies found as well as a footnote on Greg Stiles. The reporter had even tried to interview Inga and Angel but they had retreated to their rooms and refused to comment.

Press releases flew in and out of Murphy's office all day yet he made a point of accusing every precinct of having a leak. It was Murphy's people who planted the stories. Jake sometimes wondered if they sold the tidbits of information. Headlines like these were Murphy's way of ramming a cattle prod through the departments. Negative headlines pissed off Mayor Jenkins which pissed off Murphy which gave him carte blanche on overtime budgets. There was a method to the chief's madness. Publicity put the focus on solving the case fast, which was all Murphy cared about. Breyton, one of the mayor's largest contributors, was getting antsy. An antsy contributor was slow to reach for his wallet.

Jake despised bureaucratic pressure.

Murphy checked his watch. "I have a meeting with the budget

department. Call me when you have something that makes your department look like they know what they are doing." With one last glare at Robinson, Murphy climbed on the elevator and out of their hair.

"Well, that was a real ball buster," Frank said. He stood and grabbed his cup. "Coffee anyone?"

There was a chorus of "yes, thanks, please." A few minutes later Frank returned with a carafe of coffee from the break room. He filled all the cups then set the empty carafe on the front desk.

Robinson stood and addressed the room. "I have to compliment all of you for the self control you exhibited during the past thirty minutes. I know it was difficult to sit here and have someone tell you your case was botched from the beginning, that we can't find our asses with both hands, that a third grader could have solved these murders by now."

"If that were the case, then the chief could have solved it," Frank said, much to the amusement of the baby dicks.

"You." Robinson jabbed a finger at him. "Were especially well-behaved. Makes me suspicious." This also added to relieving the tension in the room.

Jake's cell phone rang. He flipped it open and checked the screen.

"That better be a miracle worker," Robinson said.

"Mitchell." Jake kept it all business even though he knew it was Sam.

"Hi, hon. Guess where I'm at?"

Jake wasn't in the mood for guessing games. He said nothing.

"You obviously are having a bad morning. Let me brighten it for you."

He tried not to smile but his expression must have given something away because Frank said, "Uh, oh. Must be the missus."

"Sure, brighten away," Jake said.

"Guess what course Amanda took at Cal-Sag?"

More guessing games. He said nothing.

"Archeology," Sam replied.

This time, he not only said nothing, he hung up on her and looked at Robinson. "I think we might have just found a miracle."

"God, my head is going to explode." T.J. breathed out dangerous fumes.

Frank waved a hand at the air. "You're killing me here, T.J. I thought they gave you sufficient time at your hotel room to brush your teeth and use some mouthwash before escorting you to our beautiful office."

T.J.'s eyes were rimmed in red, matching the red lines in the whites of his eyes. Jake kicked a garbage can by the professor who looked down at it and winced. "I already puked up a kidney and half of my liver in my hotel room. I don't have anything more to donate." He saw Frank rise from the table. "And please, no more coffee. I have a bloody volcano erupting in my stomach."

"Good, then we can get down to business." Frank sat back down. "Let's go over it again. What were you and Greg arguing about?"

"Greg? Greg is dead." T.J. giggled at his rhyming.

Next to interrogating drug addicts, Jake hated interrogating drunks. Neither had much of a memory and there wasn't much cops could do to prove or disprove their lack of memory. He kicked a chair back and sat down. T.J.'s self-destructive behavior was made all the more clear now that Jake had this new piece of information from Sam.

T.J. rubbed at his face. Frank tossed him a piece of gum. "Bless you, my son." He unwrapped the gum and popped it in his mouth. "Can't remember now. It's been so long."

"I'm more interested in your over-indulgence, Professor," Jake said. "At first I thought it was because of Greg's murder. But the more I examine your actions, I believe you started sucking on the vodka bottle after Amanda Breyton's body was discovered."

T.J.'s face appeared to crumble. Even the chewing gum was given a rest. He tried to salvage some control but his eyes started to turn red and watery. "Of course. We've never had a homicide on a dig before. Anyone would have been upset, even hard-hearted Logan."

Jake pulled the paper from his pocket and flipped it open with one hand. "You taught classes in archeology at Cal-Sag College before splitting your time between Cal-Sag and Illinois Central."

"Old news. What's your point?" T.J. squinted as though that would help him read through the back of the note paper Jake held in his hand.

"Amanda Breyton was in one of your classes." Jake knew when someone was choking down words, hesitating to gather composure. This was one of those times. He waited the professor out.

"I had a lot of students over the years. You expect me to remember one in particular?"

"She was hard to forget," Jake reminded him. "Now, if we were to ask around, do you think we would find out that you broke the rules and dated your students?"

"Go ahead. Ask around." T.J. sank back against his chair.

Jake knew this was another long search they didn't have time for. The department was already up to its eyeballs in searches. "You left Cal-Sag around the same time Amanda disappeared. You wouldn't know anything about that, would you?"

"No." T.J. pressed his lips together. He blinked lazily, slowly coming out of his drunken fog.

Frank belted out a, "Nah," and then laughed. "The professor definitely wasn't Amanda's type."

Jake pushed a pad of paper and pen across the table. "I have a feeling you dated more than one student, and we have three other bodies besides Amanda's. We could start asking a lot of questions at the colleges or you can make a list for us of all their names. Pick your poison."

A new color rushed to the professor's face. He barely made it to the garbage can before vomiting.

35

It didn't take long for Sam to find the women. Only one conference room was occupied. The door was open and Sam stumbled in, looking confused. The tables were set up in a square with the women sitting on the outside seats. All heads turned her way.

"I'm sorry. I thought I was meeting my counselor in this room," Sam stammered.

The head table appeared to be the one with the most stacks of folders and papers. A woman with reading glasses tethered to her head by a beaded chain stood. "Who is your counselor?"

Oops. "The lady at the Administration building just said that one of the counselors would meet me in Room C," Sam said. "Is there a counselor in particular who covers the archeology courses?" She slowly approached the square of tables. At a quick glance, most of the women appeared older, not fresh-faced high school graduates. "I was hoping to narrow down my archeology class choices before I went on vacation. You know, get it all out of the way with early registration." Sam got within snicker distance as heads started pressing together.

The reading glasses dropped to the speaker's chest as she said, "Sounds like Carolyn Sobieski's area of expertise but I don't believe she will be at the college for another month."

Double oops. "I hope I didn't make a wasted trip." Sam tried for sympathy. "I was told the best class to take was Professor Logan's. Do you know him?"

Several sets of eyes danced around the table. Sam's ears picked up a "bastard" from a brunette in green sitting several feet from her.

"Listen," Sam said, "I'm really sorry to intrude. I'll just go back to Administration and have the receptionist check their records again." She backtracked out of the room, making a mental picture of the brunette in the green dress. Once outside, she located a bench under a giant oak tree. Sam wished she had brought a book to read because the women didn't start to filter out until thirty minutes later. She had already made one call to Abby to ask how Dillon was. Then a separate call to Jake to find out what was new with him only to get his answering machine.

Finally, a group of women filtered out, some in small groups, the brunette in green straggling behind.

"I'm sorry to bother you," Sam said as she approached. The brunette looked like a startled bird. She hugged her purse to her chest as though she were about to be robbed. Sam stuck a hand out. "I'm Sam Casey."

The brunette looked at her hand, making no attempt to reciprocate. "Erika," the brunette replied. "Erika Giles." She had an overbite that was just this side of cute.

"Could we sit for a moment?"

Erika looked at the bench where Sam motioned but her eyes showed suspicion. What could make this woman so distrustful?

"I'm sorry. This isn't easy for me to talk about." Sam's promise not to play games just went right out the window. "I noticed some negative vibes when I mentioned Professor Logan's name. I have had uncomfortable experiences with professors in the past. They have been a little," Sam struggled to find the right words while watching Erika's reaction. "Well, their actions bordered on sexual harassment. I don't want to get into that position again. Please tell me if I'm making a mistake taking his class."

Erika hugged her purse tighter as if it were some shield against evil. She glanced at the doorway to the library, then back to Sam. "I dated Professor Logan about four years ago. Naturally he wanted it kept hush-hush because of the rules. I was young and stupid and hopelessly in love. He dropped me as soon as I told him I was pregnant."

Sam's eyebrow jerked up of its own accord. "And he wouldn't

marry you."

The young woman shook her head and stared at her feet, as though eye contact made it harder for her to talk. "He paid for the abortion," she told her feet. "But from what I hear, I'm not the first."

"Any names you can share?"

"No one who's at the college anymore." Her head lifted, her interest no longer in her straw sandals. "I dropped out of college for a while. Professor Logan was handsome and a flirt, dangerous combination. So most people took him at face value. Trying to get the authorities to give our complaints credibility was hopeless. To his credit, he was basically discreet but somehow those of us caught under his spell didn't even want to share our experiences with anyone, least of all the authorities."

Sam showed Erika a picture of Amanda Breyton. "Do you remember seeing her with Professor Logan? This would have been over three years ago."

"Looks like his type," she offered with a shake of her head. "Of course, anyone is his type. Anyway, one thing really weird is that we all started receiving letters warning us about Professor Logan. The writer claimed he was responsible for killing her baby. She believes he pushed her down some stairs causing her to miscarry. She appeared to make it her mission to tell everyone about him. I understand she even wrote the college administrators."

Sam's visions of being pushed down a short flight of stairs started to make more sense. "The only way she would know the professor's girlfriends is if she had followed them. That doesn't sound good."

"Same thing we thought," Erika replied. "Those of us who received the letters would compare notes. Creeped us out."

"Does your pen pal have a name?"

"Linda, I think. Yes. Linda Vierk."

Sam was beginning to dislike T.J. more and more. But Erika was putting things into a whole new light.

"In case you are interested, Sergeant..."

Sam's attention snapped to Erika's face. *Damn. Does anyone in this town not know who I am?* "Yes?"

"Although Professor Logan spends most of his time in the field and at Illinois Central, he still has an office on the third floor." Erika gave a nod toward a red brick building to the left of the library. The Solomon Building was etched in stone over the archway.

"Thanks, Erika."

"I swear the door was open." Sam saw the beginning of a tiny crease between Jake's eyebrows. It was what she called his bullshit meter. "I could have gone in but I didn't."

Jake nodded toward a bench several feet down the hall from Professor Logan's office at Cal-Sag College. "Sit."

Again, she was being treated like Poco. If she heard one more command to sit out of Jake, she was going to scream. She slowly moved away from the door, her eyes tossing shards of cold blue ice his way. He was no longer bothered by the icy glares. As she moseyed down the hallway, she wondered what tactic Jake used to gain access to one of the college's offices. He must have threatened to inform the local papers that the college administrator covered up for the professor all these years. She imagined Frank waving a take-out menu at the administrator and telling him it was a long list of names from women willing to come forward.

Sam passed the bench with a pledge not to obey any more canine commands. Just beyond the bench was a glassed-in cabinet, a row of lights shining down from the top shelf. The cabinet contained trophies from football, baseball, hockey, swimming, and other sports. Medals with gold ribbons were placed on silk material in the blue and gold team colors. Along the walls were pictures of teachers, alive and dead, she assumed. There were pictures of team members in uniforms holding trophies, some hoisting their coaches on their shoulders. One photo was of an Olympic Archery

Team.

Sam took a closer look at the coach. She heard footsteps approaching, then Jake's voice.

"I don't see you sitting on the bench."

Sam pointed at the photo. "When I sit, we miss out on a lot." The coach of the team several years ago was T.J. Logan.

Robinson studied the sketch of Amanda. "She certainly was a beautiful woman." Frank had discovered a sketch of Amanda inside a brown envelope in T.J.'s desk drawer.

"Bryce must have drawn it before he got pissed at her," Frank said. "No chains, no blood." In the sketch Amanda stood against a pillar in a garden, the sun setting behind her. One rose was held in her right hand, barely brushing her cleavage. The drawing was tasteful. Amanda was dressed in a flowing white gown. Bryce hadn't signed the sketch but there was a note in flowery handwriting, written in red...*Love Always, Amanda.*

Jake jammed his hands into his pants pockets. "Wish she had written, *To My Darling Thomas.* Without it, T.J. could claim he found the drawing, that it wasn't meant for him."

Robinson dropped the sketch on the desk and clasped his hands. "Where are we on the list of women T.J. bedded? We need some names to match up with the other three bodies. In the meantime, Breyton is demanding his wife's body so he can have a proper burial. He insisted on confronting Professor Logan but I told him we had a jail cell with his name on it if he so much as set foot in this precinct."

The baby dicks approached carrying a thin stack of papers. "We have the reports on the names Professor Logan wrote down," Andy said.

"There are over twenty names," Maury added.

Andy held out the pages. It was Robinson who grabbed them first. "Our Australian wannabe was certainly a busy guy but all we need are three names."

"They were all from out of town," Andy said.

"Thanks." Robinson handed the pages to Jake. "How about the artifacts?"

The baby dicks shared a smile. "We blew up a few of the pictures Janet found from museum events. The few days prior to the artifacts being stolen, we saw a familiar face." Andy's freckles spread across his smiling face.

"Professor Logan is in just about every picture." Maury beamed a matching smile.

Robinson clasped his hands in victory. "Love it when things come together."

"However," Andy cautioned, "each of the museums is sending a rep here to take a look at the stolen items."

"They should be here by the end of the week," Maury said.

They said their thanks to the baby dicks and convened in Jake's office. Jake handed Frank the top five sheets, leaving himself with the bottom four. Janet brought them fresh cups of coffee.

"Better keep it coming," Robinson told Janet. "They'll be burning the midnight oil."

Sam felt the bed move. She had no idea what time it was but she felt a strong arm encircle her waist and drag her over. Another arm made its way under her shoulder and wrapped across her chest.

"Not now, Jake," Sam mumbled. "Tomorrow. I promise I'll be a real sex goddess."

She heard him cough out a soft laugh, then he kissed her shoulder. "I'm too beat for anything more than a kiss."

She gathered his arms closer, felt his body spooning behind her. "Any luck?"

"Spoke to three of the young women. They all agreed that T.J. was a bastard but their affairs were short-lived. Two refused to believe T.J. is capable of murder. One hoped to hell he fried. Those were Erika Giles' words. We did get a few more names from the women that weren't on T.J.'s list. Guess it's hard to keep track of all his conquests."

"Any of them named Linda Vierk?"

"Who?"

Sam reminded him of what Erika Giles had told her, how the women she knew had each received a warning letter from Linda.

"Now you tell me about a stalker."

Sam had completed a Nexus search on Linda Vierk earlier only to find a ton of Vierks, far too many across the country. She didn't have that much time to devote to finding the mystery letter writer. Indy had found three Vierks in the records but not one was named Linda.

Sam yawned and snuggled closer. "Probably now a dead stalker."

36

The next morning Jake and Frank sequestered themselves in one of the conference rooms after obtaining files and photos from the Administration Office at the college. T.J.'s list had proved reliable.

Jake taped photos of the women to one side of the whiteboard. In the middle column they had taped photos of three of the women they had located. Susan English was working back home in Scottsdale, Arizona. Jenna Michaels was working at an ad agency in Dallas, Texas. Erika Giles was working on her masters at Cal-Sag College.

On the right side of the board they tacked Amanda's picture under the heading of *Missing*. Although T.J. failed to list Amanda Breyton as one of his conquests, they added her name and photo to the list since they had found the sketch of Amanda in T.J.'s office. He didn't offer any explanation as to how her sketch ended up in his desk drawer and remained tight-lipped, under the advice of his attorney.

One other name missing on T.J.'s list was Linda Vierk, the former girlfriend who did her best to warn women away from the professor. His foggy state of mind couldn't conjure up what cities these women were from but at least the college administrator was cooperating.

Robinson walked in, a look of disgust clouded his face as he stared at the whiteboard. "The list just keeps growing and growing."

"This isn't all of them," Frank said. 'Just the ones that were at Cal-Sag."

Andy entered the office. "Got one that's missing." He searched for the photo among the group on the left and moved it to the column on the right. He grabbed the marker and wrote next to the name Marianna Bree, *Grand Rapids, Michigan*. Under the column heading, *Last Seen*, he wrote *May 2003*.

"Parents have dental records?" Robinson asked.

"The family dentist is sending them over the Internet to Benny as well as Miss Bree's medical history."

Robinson folded his arms across his linebacker chest. "If Miss Bree is one of the bodies in the pit with Amanda, then we just have two more to identify."

"Benny printed out his report on the three remains from the dig." Jake nodded toward papers clipped to the board. "One had a previous broken left femur. He guesses the girl was around six at the time. The second victim had several healed fractures on both arms. The third had a skull fracture he estimates happened at a very early age, probably as an infant or toddler."

The phone rang. Robinson punched Line Two and then the speaker button. It was Benny.

"Your boys might want to get down here," Benny said.

"Why," Robinson barked.

"I have some parents in my lobby. They saw the news reports last night and want to see if the remains we have are their missing daughters."

"Did they bring physician records and dental reports? Just see which of the deceased are theirs."

"Unfortunately we have three bodies and twelve sets of parents and they keep coming. One couple said they spoke to Sam more than a week ago. Drove all night to get here."

"What's the name?"

"The Korwins."

Sam arrived at the construction site just as Inga was slamming shut the side door to her van. The sifting screens and digging tools had been packed up. Angel wiped her hands against her slacks and nodded a hello to Sam.

"Are you leaving?" Sam asked.

"No need to hold up construction now," Inga said. "Our work is done. Greg is..." She halted in mid-sentence and looked at Angel. "And then there's the professor. I hope your husband is wrong about T.J. killing Amanda Breyton. All this time I thought Mr. Breyton or his son had killed her." She shook her head in disbelief. "I still find it hard to imagine T.J. could kill anyone. And the artifacts. What is this world coming to?"

Angel tossed a shovel into the back of T.J.'s truck. "I'm not surprised about the artifacts. He was so obsessed with them."

"You don't want to stick around for when the Smithsonian people show up?" Sam asked Inga.

"I need to get back to Springfield. Angel has offered to drive T.J.'s truck over to the police station, then we'll head back tomorrow. Shall I follow you over?" Inga asked Angel as she opened the door to her van.

"It's a nice day. I'll walk," Angel replied.

Sam waved as Inga drove away. She turned to Angel. "Where do you go from here?"

Angel raised the tail gate and slammed it into place. "Wait for the next dig. Maybe come back up here and finish my Master's."

"That is right. You went to Cal-Sag College." Sam shielded her eyes from the noon sun. "Did you know a Linda Vierk?"

"Yes, I do remember her. As a matter of fact, she used to tutor me."

"So she attended Cal-Sag?"

"Actually, she was a teacher."

Of course, Sam thought. Indy was looking through student files when he should have also checked faculty files.

"I took a literature class from her, the Classics. She wasn't much older than her students. Used to hang out at our dorms."

Sam gathered these were fond memories for Angel because her eyes took on a sparkle and her gloomy attitude had brightened.

"Any idea if she still teaches there?"

"Not during the summer," Angel replied. "She doesn't live too far from here."

"Really? Do you happen to have her phone number?"

Angel shook her head. "No, but I remember where she lives. Come on." She waved her over to the truck. "I'll drive. Hopefully she hasn't eaten yet and we can have lunch together."

Sam left her Jeep in the parking lot and climbed into T.J.'s truck.

"Does that give you good luck?" Angel asked, nodding toward Sam's medicine bundle.

"Yes, I believe so." Sam clasped her hand around it out of habit. "Guess it's all in what you believe."

Angel put the truck in gear and pulled away from the curb. A quick turn at the end of the street had them headed toward the expressway.

Sam asked, "Where does Linda live?"

"Pine Grove."

Tiny pinpricks exploded across Sam's shoulders and down her back. She dropped her hand from the medicine bundle and grabbed her phone. When she heard Jake's recording, she left a message where she was going and who she would be meeting with. She assumed Jake must be interrogating someone or he was in a meeting.

Angel said, "Why don't you call Information and see if they have a phone number for Linda? That way we won't make a wasted trip."

Sam preferred an element of surprise but said, "Good idea." She dialed the operator and waited. Once she told her the name and the city, the operator informed her that the number was unlisted.

"I'm not surprised," Angel said. "Linda didn't like to be bothered during her summers off. She took care of her grandfather, from what I recall."

Sam studied the landscape and billboards. Trucks sped past them oblivious to speed limits. The air was humid and dusty in the truck. Angel's window was open adding some tousle to her sun-bleached hair. Sam studied the interior of the truck and remembered her dreams, not of the victims being shot with a bow and arrow but of the victims being strangled by a man with a brown truck.

"How long has T.J. owned this truck?"

"It's not really his. It belongs to the college so I'm not sure how long the college has had it."

Sam wished she could remember more details of the interior of the truck from her dream. However, the exterior didn't match up. She had thought it had been a delivery truck, not a pickup.

Sam asked, "Do you happen to know if Linda dated Professor Logan?"

"No, I don't. I was pretty much a bookworm and didn't pay much attention to who was dating whom."

"T.J. seemed to be quite the ladies man, from what I hear."

"And look where it got him."

Sam wondered about Linda Vierk. Jake thought she might be one of the dead women. But if she were still alive, and if she was the one T.J. had pushed down the stairs, could she be driven to do more than just warn the women he dated? Was she jealous enough to have been the one to kill Amanda and the others? But how did she get her hands on the stolen artifacts?

As they passed the sign for Michigan City, a chill spread through Sam's body. The closer they got to Pine Grove, the more those tiny alarm signals started going off in her head. She wished Jake would return her call.

Robinson joined them in the interrogation room. He struck a pose against the wall, arms crossed. Jake and Frank took a seat across from the professor.

Silently and methodically, Jake laid out the photos of the women T.J. had written on his list. When he was finished with the last one, Jake rested his elbows on the table, chin on his folded hands, and waited.

T.J.'s gaze swept the faces of the women. "So? I gave you these names already. What do you need now?"

For almost a full minute Jake stared at the professor. Then he moved the three pictures at the center of the table closer together and pointed at them. "These three women's remains were found along with Amanda Breyton's."

Frank said, "You probably knew from the start that the entire dig wasn't an ancient burial site. Our medical examiner could tell they didn't have the features of Native Americans. The artifacts were items previously stolen from various museums." They saw T.J. swallow hard. "But that's not the worst of it."

Robinson finally moved away from the wall to stand behind his detectives. He placed one hand on each of their chairs and glared across the table at T.J. "You were probably the last person to see all four of these women alive. The way I see it, you are going away for a very long time."

They could see realization sinking through the fog in the professor's head. He pushed away from the table. "NO!" he yelled. "I'm a lot of things but I am not a murderer."

"Convince us," Robinson said. "Certainly explains why you kept those bones away from the prying eyes of our medical examiner."

Jake remained stoic, preferring to eyeball the professor over the top of his clasped hands. Frank leaned back and smacked a hand against the table. "Seems like a slam dunk to me."

"NO!" T.J. yelled again. He forced his eyes to view each picture separately.

Jake opened the folder and placed Amanda's picture on the table. Anguish marred T.J.'s handsome face.

"Okay," he whispered. He took several minutes to compose himself. He pressed the heel of each palm against his eyes for several seconds then shook his head as though clearing his thoughts. "Okay. Amanda and I were in love. I never thought it would ever happen to me but I fell hopelessly in love and she felt the same way. I was taking the job at Illinois Central and she was going to come with me. She was going to leave her husband."

"What happened?" Robinson asked.

"She never showed. She was supposed to come by my apartment where I was packing up my things. I tried calling her cell but she didn't answer. I figured she changed her mind. After all, how could I compete with that kind of money?"

"You never went to the police?" Frank asked.

"What? And admit I had been dating a student, something that is against the rules? I couldn't call her house, couldn't call the police, couldn't call her friends. I drove down to Illinois Central University and licked my wounds, took on a dig site in South America for a year. Didn't even date for six months. Guess you can say I became a little bitter after I lost Amanda. I probably haven't been the most pleasant guy to be around for the past three years."

Frank snorted out a laugh. "Ya think?"

"Maybe you have been taking in out on other women," Robinson suggested.

"No." T.J. shook his head. "Go ahead. Give me a lie detector test, anything. I may be a heartless bastard, but I'm no killer."

Jake tossed a notepad across the table. "A lot of this could have been avoided if you had just been truthful from the beginning. Now what about the artifacts?" He hoped T.J. got writer's cramp from writing his entire involvement in this case.

Another sigh escaped the professor. "Yes, I stole one item at a time from every museum event I attended. I figured they wouldn't miss them. It made me feel good knowing that when the museums returned the items to the tribes, at least they weren't getting everything. But then someone stole them from me."

"Where had you kept them, before they were allegedly stolen?" Robinson asked.

"I had rented a temperature controlled storage unit. Someone got into it. I don't know how. Maybe they copied my key. Maybe the owner of the storage facilities stole the items."

"You didn't report the theft?" Frank asked.

"Right. And how do I explain to the authorities where I got them? The thief knew I'd have to keep quiet or implicate myself."

Everything was sounding a little too logical but Jake still didn't trust the professor. Jake asked, "Who would have access to your keys?"

"Anyone basically. At the college I hung them on a hook in my office. At home, I tossed them on a table by the front door."

"So any woman you brought home who wanted to get back at you would have had access," Robinson said.

"Impossible. No one knew about the storage facility." Sudden confusion filled the professor's face as he eyed each one of them. "The question you don't seem to have an answer for is, how did the artifacts and the bodies get onto the property owned by Amanda's husband? What if his goons had me followed and knew about the artifacts? How do you know he didn't order those goons to kill Amanda?"

"We've already confronted Breyton with those questions," Jake said.

"Did he pass a lie detector test or didn't you give him one?"

Robinson said, "We haven't found any proof that he was involved. The bodies were moved to the dig site from an area that is filled with decayed spruce. Breyton is known to buy property and commence construction immediately."

T.J. slowly straightened, a sickening realization settling behind his eyes. "There was a practice dig we conducted in unincorporated land years ago. We dug about as deep as Breyton's workers did. It's possible it was the same area."

"Who worked the dig?" Jake asked.

"Oh, God. That was so long ago. I don't remember." He ran his shaky hands through his hair.

"You better start remembering because you've got a lot of

murder indictments hanging over your head." Jake reached into the brown envelope, pulled out a final picture and tossed it across the table. "You may say you're a lover not a killer, but how do you explain Greg's death?"

"I told you, one of the Natives had to have killed him." He picked up the photo. "What's this?"

"Outside your office at Cal-Sag College is a photo of you with the Olympic Archery Team. Isn't that you in the photo?" Frank asked.

T.J. studied the photo and shrugged. "I said before. A lot of the faculty went to support our team."

Robinson looked puzzled. "Weren't you the coach?"

"Coach?" T.J. laughed. "I wouldn't know the front end from the back end of an arrow. Never shot one in my life." He pulled the photo closer and studied the faces of the team members. "From what I recall, the best archer in the group was…" His finger rested on one picture and whatever color was left in his face faded. "Oh my God!"

37

"This place is really isolated, isn't it?" Sam climbed out of the truck and studied the two-story house.

"Linda said her grandparents have owned the land for decades. It's supposedly the largest piece of property in this area, stretches all the way to the lake."

The road leading to the house had been a winding stretch of asphalt at least two blocks long. Tall pine trees bordered the road. Angel had to unlatch a wooden gate to gain access. Sam had noticed a barbwire fence stretching as far as the eye could see. Beyond the house was a sea of pine trees, patches so thick that barely a slice of sunlight could cut through.

"Are both grandparents still alive?"

"Just her grandfather."

Sam took several steps, then stopped. The walkway was made of cobblestone. The house loomed at the end of the walkway, as cold and uninviting as in her visions.

"What's wrong?"

"Nothing." Sam took a deep breath and continued up the walkway. Each step sent a jolt through her body.

"Linda used to leave the front door open. She is way too trusting." Angel turned the doorknob. "Still careless."

They walked into the living room. The hardwood floors echoed their footsteps. "Hello," Angel called out. "Linda? Anybody home? It's Angel, Angel Morgan." She looked at Sam and shrugged.

The room was neat and tidy with leather furniture and cherry wood tables and bookshelves. Sam noticed dust on the bookshelves and unopened mail on a desk. Her eye caught the name of Lawrence Vierk on one envelope. It looked like a Social Security check.

Angel said, "I think I'm going to check outside. There's a

garden out back. Maybe Linda is weeding or planting new flowers. I'll be right back." Angel made her way down a hall.

Sam heard the back door open and close. She scanned the living room with its wall-to-wall carpeting and chrome lamps. The leather couch had that new leather smell. The furnishings looked modern rustic. All that was missing was a moose head on the wall.

A beam of sunlight sprayed the carpeting and crept across the floor. Sam took a step back as if the beam were made of molten lava. The light traveled to an antique roll-top piano. A pair of bifocals rested on top of the piano, as though Lawrence Vierk took a walk out to get the mail and planned to be right back. Did he not need glasses to drive? Or was he out back with his granddaughter? The tiny pinpricks spread through her body as she thought about the man in her visions. She never did get a good look at his face. The light settled on the worn foot pedals, finally finding a place to rest. Sam gave the bifocals one last quizzical glance before making her way down another hall to a wide, arched doorway leading to what looked like a den. Trophies filled a bookcase along with red ribbons and medals. Sam noticed an Olympic gold medal next to one of the trophies. The far wall was filled with framed certificates and photos.

Jake tried Sam's phone again. It wasn't connecting. "She must be out of range." He turned to Frank, "Call down to Communications. Give them her cell phone number and have them track her location." He pointed at Janet. "Call the Pine Grove police and tell them we need their assistance and to meet us at whatever location Communications gives us."

Robinson held a phone to his chest and said, "Jake, the fire department helicopter will meet you on the roof in five."

Andy rushed off the elevator with a tube of paper. He unrolled it on Frank's desk. It was a map of Pine Grove. Maury joined them with a list of the homeowners from the Village Building Department.

"Yes," Frank spoke into the phone. "Between Cedar and Highland Dunes. Can you be more specific than that?" He watched as Andy finger-walked the map, locating the two dunes. "Locust Street."

"Lotta houses on Locust Street. South Locust, North Locust?" Maury shook his head, his eyes feverishly searching.

"North Locust," Jake said. "Has to be close to the lake."

"Wait." Maury jammed a finger on the paper. "Vierk. There's a Lawrence Vierk at 102 Locust."

"That's it." Jake ran to the stairway with Frank close behind.

A cold swept down her spine as Sam scanned the wall of photos. There was an array of pictures—infant, toddler, and grade school. An older man who must have been the grandfather was showing a young girl the proper way to hold a bow and arrow. Sam tried to mentally place a baseball cap on his head. The build looked the same although the man in her visions had been slightly younger. She spotted more pictures from the Olympics. But these were dated pictures and it was the grandfather at a young age wearing the gold medal. In more current Olympic pictures an older version of the young girl was being taught by her grandfather. She looked vaguely familiar. Then she saw a picture of the grandfather leaning against a dark brown truck, a truck with worn letters but she could make out *Arctic Ice* imprinted on the side.

Sam's left hand pulled the phone from her pocket. She checked the display. *No Service.* A whisper of air circled the room, sped around Sam's body like a tornado as her finger touched the picture and moved up to the face of the Olympic gold medal winner in the individual category. A rush of wind blew past her head and an arrow slammed into the wall just one inch above her finger.

Sam gasped, jerked her hand away, and fought the urge to

scream. Slowly she slipped her phone back into her pocket while giving herself time to regain her composure.

"You are good," Sam said.

"I know."

"There really isn't a Linda Vierk, is there Angel?" Sam turned slowly, pressed her back against the wall. Angel stood twenty feet away. "You were the one T.J. pushed down the stairs so you would lose your baby."

This brought a startled look to Angel's face. "How did you know that?" With a well-practiced move, Angel pulled another arrow from the quill on her back and reloaded.

Sam took a step away from the board. Another arrow whizzed past her shoulder. She flinched and held her breath. "I've had visions of you being pushed down a flight of stairs."

Angel cocked her head as though she didn't believe Sam. "He dumped me after one night. Said if he hadn't been drunk, he wouldn't have looked twice at me."

"So if you couldn't have him, no one could."

A strange veil slipped over Angel's eyes. It was a veil Sam had seen before in suspects with maniacal tendencies. She could only hope Jake was able to trace her location through her cell phone. There was a sliver of doubt, though. If he were still in a meeting he might not have had time to listen to his messages.

Something didn't make any sense. "Why Greg, though? Why did you kill him? I thought you two had something going?"

Angel blew out a puff of air. "In his dreams. Greg's suspicions about the artifacts got him into trouble. He thought he could dangle the reward money in front of me and I'd fall right into bed. I was going to alter the reports so no one would know they had been stolen. I was going to do it for T.J. But if Greg announced it to the press just to collect the reward money, it would have screwed up my plans. If T.J. knew all that I was doing for him, he'd take me back."

"But he is the primary suspect in multiple murders. How is

that helping him?"

"All circumstantial evidence. There isn't any proof that he killed them. I would testify on his behalf."

Angel was grasping at straws, making it up as she went along. Sam could hear the desperation in her voice. Her arms had to tire sometime. She couldn't keep holding the bow and arrow forever. Keep her talking. Maybe once Angel tired Sam would be able to talk some sense into her.

"How did you know T.J. had stolen the artifacts?"

"I followed T.J. and was curious what he kept in the storage unit. He used his birth date for everything and I was right that he used it for the code to access the building. All I had to do was make a copy of the key to his lock."

"You could have just turned him in if you really wanted to get back at him."

"I wanted him to love only me. I tried to warn the other women, but they wouldn't listen."

"So you could have him to yourself?" Sam was trying to figure out Angel's motives.

"Of course. But they wouldn't, not all of them."

"So Amanda wasn't the first."

"I took something away from him that he loved. All the others were just play things. But Amanda, she was different." Angel started to tremble and her arms slowly lowered. "I took away the one precious thing in his life, just like he took my baby." Suddenly, that glazed look returned. Angel raised her arms and nodded toward the door. "Outside. Now."

Sam reached down to get her purse. If she could only get to her gun.

"Leave it. You won't need it."

Everything about Angel had changed. She no longer had the face of an innocent girl-next-door, much less the pitiful look of a woman scorned. Her eyes had a sinister glare, her mouth unsmiling. She lacked any hint of emotion.

"MOVE."

"You would have made a wonderful mother."

"Don't patronize me. I saw the way T.J. looked at you. He couldn't keep his eyes off of you, even with your husband sitting there."

"He looks at every woman that way. I didn't do anything to encourage him. I love my husband."

"Eventually, every woman gives in to him. I'm saving you. Don't you see that?" Her body relaxed and she pulled back on the arrow. "You have two seconds to start moving."

Sam mentally pounded her head against the wall. How did she miss this? How did she not pick up on Angel's guilt? The only thing she could think of was that Angel had two personas. She only showed the Angel side in public. In private, that second personality came out.

Thoughts of her dreams came to mind, dreams of being chased through the woods, of being shot in the back with an arrow. It was all going to come true. Sam moved slowly to the back door, trying to buy time, hoping Jake was picking up on her phone message, that somehow he was going to piece all of this together in time. She tried to appeal to Angel's maternal instincts again.

"You really seemed to like Dillon. You wouldn't want to take his mother away from him, would you?"

"He has Abby to take care of him."

The dense ceiling of tall pines permitted just a scattering of sunlight to penetrate. In the distance Sam could see a break in the forest where sunlight streamed through. Sam wondered if it was an entrance to the beach area. The path she walked looked worn. Off to the right was a dirt road leading deep into the property. Besides trees, there wasn't anything else in view except weeds and underbrush. Were the other three women attracted to the sunlit opening in the distance? Is that where they ran to? It had to be. The bones were bleached white by the sun. That was not where Sam wanted to head.

It was cooler in the shade. Sam shifted her gaze from side to side, looking for another route, a thicker patch of trees where she could hide, someplace where she could circle back to the house, back down the road to the main street. Then another thought assaulted her.

"Where's Lawrence Vierk, Angel?" Sam imagined him behind one of the trees. As if Angel wasn't enough to worry about.

"Oh, he's around."

Sam didn't like the sound of those words, the inflection in Angel's voice. "Did he have anything to do with Amanda's death?"

"Quit talking about my grandfather," Angel said. "Now run."

Run. That's exactly what Sam was doing in her dreams. That's exactly what Angel had the other women do. Sam stopped and turned. Angel was a safe twenty feet away. She probably wanted her to run toward the open area where she could leave her body to decompose and bleach in the hot sun. Angel couldn't weigh more than one-hundred and twenty pounds. She wouldn't be able to carry a body that distance on her own. But maybe she didn't act alone. Sam had yet to see the mysterious Lawrence Vierk.

"I SAID RUN!" Angel yelled.

Sam felt a breeze charge around the trees, encircle her body. The underbrush to her right bucked and swayed. Abby had always told her to watch for subtle messages from the spirits. She ran, darted to her right. Sharp branches of the underbrush slapped against her naked legs. She zigzagged between the trees, trying to avoid giving Angel a clear shot.

"Pretty clever of you, Sam."

She could hear Angel's voice, the pounding of her footsteps. It sounded as though she were running, and in order to run, Angel had to have lowered her weapon. That should buy Sam some time.

She dodged to her right, around a tree, then to her left. The ground made a sudden drop so she dove into a ditch filled with leaves, landing face down. She scrambled to her feet, the leaves crunching, making far more noise than was safe. Crouching low, Sam stepped above the bank of leaves and navigated the wall of the gulley, making as little noise as possible. Dried pine needles poked at her fingers as she tried to grasp at some tufts of grass. The scent of pine and mold mingled with other smells she couldn't readily identify. After several feet, she stopped, listened for several seconds, then peered over the edge. Angel was about fifty feet away, the loaded bow at her side.

"I'll find you eventually, Sam. There's no way out."

Dropping back down Sam listened as her heart drummed in her ears. She took deep breaths to calm herself. A loud chattering and cawing echoed through the trees. Then came the whispers, soft voices that circled around her. Indistinct words jumbled together in a cacophony. The breeze picked up, scattering the leaves, sending them swirling. They gathered into clusters like platoons awaiting orders. Just as quickly, they divided and spun off in different directions.

Again those images from her dreams filled her head. The expressway, the disabled car, the truck driver with his hands around her neck.

Where was Lawrence Vierk?

38

"How far is it?" Jake asked. He was sitting in the passenger seat of a Pine Grove squad car. Frank was riding in the back. Three squad cars and two state police cars had met the helicopter in the village square. From the air it had been the only piece of open land the pilot could use.

"Just around the corner." Deputy Oliver Banks barked out answers as though he were still a marine drill sergeant. Also a member of the Army Reserves, he had served two tours in Iraq and was none to shy to admit he was itching to go back. "Like I said, Lawrence Vierk is a recluse. From what I understand, he isn't afraid to arm himself and dare people to trespass."

"Arm himself with what?" Frank asked from the back seat.

Banks lifted his face to catch Frank in his rearview mirror. "Bow and arrow. He's got medals up the whazzoo for archery."

"I'd like the other cars to hang back and give us at least ten minutes." Jake pulled his gun out and checked the clip. "What do you know about the granddaughter?"

"Not much. I've only been in this town for five years. I can honestly say I've never met her. Only seen the grandfather one time." A siren wailed from behind them. Banks picked up his mike and pressed the button. "Boys. We're going in blind so cut the lights and the noisemakers. Don't advance past the entrance until I call you."

The voices multiplied in numbers and volume. Sam wanted to clamp her hands over her ears. She pulled the cell phone from her pocket and checked the display. Still out of range. Another odor mingled with the dried leaves and damp earth. It was unmistakable—

death. And it was getting stronger. Keeping her head down, Sam scampered through the edges of the ditch, successful at avoiding the leaves and making as little noise as possible.

Stealing another peek over the edge, Sam scanned the area. She didn't see Angel. Couldn't hear footsteps. Maybe Angel was in hiding, waiting for Sam to make a move toward the lake, or the house. All Sam knew was that she couldn't stay here. If she had any hope of getting out alive, she had to move now.

Moving to her right, Sam stifled a scream. Flies were buzzing around the decomposing body of a deer, shot through the heart with an arrow. Sam moved quickly past the corpse and came across another dead animal, this time an owl. Five feet from the bird lay a squirrel. Both had been killed by arrows.

How sick, Sam thought. Angel and her grandfather used the woods as their target practice. Sam shook the memories of the man's hands around her neck. If he was as dangerous as she thought, no wonder Angel was screwed up.

She remained still and listened. Animals were chattering in a branch overhead. Birds were flitting from tree to tree. Sam was wearing bright colors. She may as well have had a flashing neon sign across her chest. It would be hard to make a move without Angel noticing, but she had no choice. It was either now or never. If Angel were keeping her focus on the sunlit area, maybe she wouldn't notice Sam creeping back toward the house.

She dashed toward the first tree, then halted. Her eyes swept the surrounding area. Where was Angel? There were too many patches of shadows. Angel could be anywhere.

Pine trees shared the property with tall oak and cottonwood. The ground was thick with needles and dried leaves. It would be hard to make a run for it without making a lot of noise. But that was a chance she had to take.

Sam tore off toward the house, keeping a zigzag pattern to her run. If Angel were chasing her, Sam wouldn't be able to hear her footsteps. There were too many voices in her head.

Don't leave us.

Come back.

Help!

Sam's feet slipped out from under her and she fell on her ass. It felt as though someone had pulled the ground out from under her. And it was a good thing because just as her ass hit the ground, an arrow slammed into the tree. The last place Sam expected Angel to be hiding was in the trees. Forty feet ahead, Angel jumped from one of the branches, landing on her feet, her bow already raised and loaded.

Sam slowly stood, took a step back. To her right an arrow quivered in the tree trunk.

A mocking smile flashed across Angel's face as she advanced. "You're a little harder to catch than the other women."

"Comes from chasing criminals," Sam replied. She had to keep her talking. Sam moved her hand slowly toward her chest, then grasped her medicine bundle tightly. "Why did you run Amanda over with a car if you could have had fun chasing her through the trees?"

"That would have been too easy for her. Of all the women, I wanted to feel the impact, to feel her bones crush. For good measure, I backed over her body." Her smile broadened as she added, "Several times."

Sam squeezed the medicine bundle tighter and flashed a sly smile of her own.

Angel nodded toward Sam's hand. "Do you really think that's going to help you?"

"It provides protection, either in the way of emotional support or police backup."

Angel's eyes darted to her right where Jake and Frank crept, guns pointed at her. "Well, well. Sergeant Mitchell to the rescue." She pulled back harder on the bow.

Sam had never seen Jake in full riot gear. Muscles pressed against a white shirt which was worn under a Kevlar vest. A holster was strapped to one leg. One arm of his mirrored sunglasses was looped over the shirt collar. That exposed his eyes...cold and deadly.

"Put it down, Angel." Jake's voice was as cold as his eyes. He and Frank were thirty feet away and closing in.

"One more step and she's dead. I mean it," Angel yelled. "This arrow travels at three hundred feet per second. Do you really want to test me?"

Frank, in matching swat gear, cocked his head. "Well, gee. Let's see. A 357mm bullet travels about thirteen hundred feet per second. Three hundred vs thirteen hundred. Helllloooo."

Angel lowered the bow a couple inches. "I'm aiming right at her heart, Sergeant. Now back off. Sam and I are going to go for a little drive. If you stop us, she dies."

"I don't think so. The driveway is full of squad cars and more are on the way."

"Then you better start moving them."

Sam's heart quickened. Angel's grip never wavered and Sam doubted Angel would miss.

"Ball's in your court, Sergeant," Angel taunted. "What are you going to do now? Count to three?"

Sam looked at Jake whose eyes didn't leave Angel's face.

In a quiet voice, with just a hint of amusement, Jake said, "What makes you think I ever bother counting?"

Sam saw Angel's brows scrunch in confusion, giving Jake that one second of hesitation he needed.

Two guns exploded followed by screams. Angel fell to the ground, blood pouring from her left hand where the bullet from Jake's gun had torn through it. The bullet from Frank's gun had clipped Angel's right shoulder. Sam had slid back down on her ass, her arms shielding her face. She hadn't realized one of the screams was hers.

Lowering her arms, she saw Angel writhing on the ground. In the distance the trees appeared to come alive, but it was just the local police advancing from their positions. They inceased their pace, breaking out in a run, weapons drawn.

Angel stopped flailing and jerked her head toward Sam. There was a gleam in her eyes Sam didn't like. Angel wasn't done yet. Oblivious to her injuries, she started clawing through the dirt and dried leaves, trying to get to Sam.

Jake walked over to block her path. He aimed his gun at her head.

Frank said. "Jake, I've got her. Go check on Sam." Frank waved the approaching officers over.

Jake reluctantly holstered his gun, then ran to Sam's side. She took a few seconds to assess her body for injuries. Her legs were shaking as Jake helped her to her feet. She wasn't sure how long they would hold her up. Jake gathered her in his arms.

"I didn't know if you were going to get my message. I didn't know until I got here that it was Angel."

He finally released his hold and held her at arms length. "Your legs are bleeding."

"Thorny bushes and a hard-packed ground." Sam noticed her top was also torn. Jake pulled twigs and leaves from her hair. There was commotion all around but all she wanted to do was get away from Angel, away from all the voices swirling in her head.

"Come on." Jake wrapped an arm around her. He led her through the underbrush and back to the dirt road that led to the house.

They passed a cop who looked more like a drill sergeant than Jake. His name badge read *Banks*. "You okay, miss?"

Sam shook her head yes. "Thanks for getting here in the nick of time."

"We've got an ambulance coming."

"Save it for her. I'm fine, but thanks."

They reached the driveway and Sam breathed a sigh of relief. Jake opened the door to the deputy's squad car. "Sit."

"Another canine order," Sam said under her breath, but she sat down anyway.

Jake's hands cradled her face. He turned her head one way, then the next, checking her eyes.

"I'm okay, honest." She wrapped her arms across her body as though even the sun couldn't warm her. "There's a man, too, Jake. Lawrence Vierk."

"We know."

Two EMTs rolled a gurney from the back of the ambulance. "Where are they going to take her?"

"Probably to a local hospital until we can get a court order to take her back to Chasen Heights."

"I'm losing my touch," Sam admitted. "You would think with three other women in the grave with Amanda that I would have picked up something more."

"We haven't been able to locate a couple other women on Logan's date list but it's possible they just don't want to be found."

Frank waved from the edge of the pine trees. "Jake, we need you for a few minutes."

"You going to be okay?"

She assessed his appearance again from the flat stomach to the muscular body under the Kevlar vest and said, "I never knew you looked so hot in Kevlar."

The right side of Jake's mouth twitched. He pulled out his sunglasses, slipped them back on, and leaned in close to Sam's ear. "No…I'm not wearing Kevlar to bed."

She watched him leave and smiled, but then thoughts of how close she came to being killed made her shudder. She was thankful Jake was such a great shot. After taking several deep breaths she closed the door and slowly made her way to the front of the squad car where a state police vehicle was parked. The two crime scene investigators leaned against their van looking bored. Word must have circulated to the surrounding towns because the place was beginning to be overrun with uniforms of all colors. They obviously didn't see much action in their small towns.

Sam gazed into the forest of trees that stretched endlessly in front of her. Where did Angel keep the bodies where they could decompose so quickly? Beyond the woods there was probably a high dune, a place with full exposure to the sun. She took a step closer, then another. A sigh of whispers filled her head, words she couldn't decipher, voices she couldn't identify. It sounded as though she were eavesdropping on a committee of angels conferring among themselves. Her gaze drifted to the pine trees which stood tall and motionless. The voices were beckoning her. But whose voices and where were they coming from?

She walked over to the state van, grabbed a handful of evidence flags and followed the dirt road.

"Hey," the drill sergeant yelled. "We don't have a search warrant."

"I'm not a cop. I don't need one," Sam called out over her shoulder.

How far should she walk? What was she supposed to find? Behind her she heard the sound of legs moving through the brush. She wanted to tell them to step lightly.

Sam followed the dirt road for several minutes, then stopped to watch for telltale signs, listen for voices. The rustling of footsteps faded, replaced instead by the sounds of nature as she blocked out all other distractions. A branch of underbrush bent back and forth in a slow tempo. Brown needles covered the ground and dried cottonwood leaves were caught in the underbrush. Sam bent down and placed a flag in the ground.

She continued, stopping every so often to see if anything moved in her peripheral vision. A squirrel chattered from a branch several yards away. It dropped down and pawed at the ground. Sam stayed motionless, not sure if the squirrel was just looking to bury a piece of food. It turned its head and stared at her with one eye. It continued patting the ground, then scurried off. Sam studied the spot where the squirrel had sat. A small tornado of leaves spun in a tight spiral, then settled down. She walked over and placed another flag.

She heard Banks ask Jake, "What the hell is she doing?"

Jake replied, "What she does best."

A cluster of tiny tornadoes assembled one by one until it filled a large area. The group waited as though making sure they had her attention. Quickly, they spun off in different directions. Sam felt herself turning, trying to watch each one to determine what each wanted to show her. But it was impossible. The woods were spinning now, circling around her along with objects that looked like jewelry—an ankle bracelet with palm trees, earrings, a chain with a dolphin pendant. Sam felt light-headed, her legs like rubber, too weak to hold her up. The canopy of trees overhead appeared to press down until her legs gave out. The evidence flags floated from her hands and her knees dropped painfully to the floor of damp leaves and pine needles.

"There are too many," Sam sobbed, her eyes barely able to see through the tears as men rushed to her aid.

She heard Jake's voice. "Sam, what's wrong?"

"I don't have enough flags."

The drill sergeant was barking something about "What the hell did she say?"

"Sam?" Jake knelt in front of her, his hands gripping her forearms.

She stifled another sob as she said, "There are too many bodies."

39

It had been three days since the grizzly discoveries on the Vierk property in Pine Grove. Jake had used his connections with the FBI to convince them to use their plane equipped with infrared to detect any remains on the property. Sam had wanted to stick around but Jake pleaded with her to return to Chasen Heights. When the press started showing up, Jake didn't want Sam anywhere near a camera.

The FBI search plane had detected twenty-three bodies. Jake and Frank had also made a surprising discovery under a pile of tree branches—a dark brown delivery truck. Forensics had a field day going over every inch of that truck.

By removing the piano and the living room rug, Bank's men had found a door leading to the cellar and the bones of the late Lawrence Vierk. All press releases now came strictly from the FBI and anyone else caught talking to the press or giving out information would be terminated, according to Banks. That made Jake happy. At least for now the papers wouldn't be putting Sam's picture on the front page. The media was too busy speculating that these women were abducted by the I-80 killer. The FBI wasn't forthcoming with details on what was found but Banks had told Jake they discovered trophies in the cellar along with a scrapbook of all the press clippings on cases involving women believed abducted along Interstate 80 since the 1980s.

Jake and Frank had practically lived in Pine Grove for the last three days as the investigators dug up the graves and Angel Morgan recuperated from surgery in a Michigan City Hospital. She was transported to the hospital in Chasen Heights this morning. According to Deputy Banks, Vierk had always been a recluse. His wife, Linda, had divorced him ten years prior and died from a heart attack two years later.

Sam stretched and lifted her face to the sun. The heat rose off the patio but she welcomed the warmth. She was feeling some bad vibes about the arraignment, which was where Jake was this morning. Angel was clever. She had minored in Drama and Psychology. It wasn't a stretch to assume Angel was putting her training to good use. Doctors had patched up her shoulder but the surgeons were unable to do much with her left hand other than stitch it up minus three fingers.

A car rumbled up the drive, followed by the grinding of one of the garage doors. Sam opened her eyes just as Jake climbed out of his Riviera. His sportscoat was hooked on one finger as he made his way with slow, deliberate steps toward the patio. This didn't look too promising. With his other hand he dug at the knot of his tie, then pulled it off. He tossed both on one of the patio chairs.

Sam grabbed two Pepsis and set them on the table. "I don't like the look on your face." She opened both, taking one for herself.

Jake fired up a cigarette and took a long drag. He looked as though he had lost ten pounds. There was a tinge of gray to his face. Hardly anyone had much of an appetite after staring at all the decomposed bodies.

"Angel pled not guilty. Naturally, she blames her grandfather for all the murders including Greg and the four women at the Breyton Dig."

"That's a little hard for her grandfather to do from the grave." Sam set the soda can down and straightened. "Wait. What about me? She tried to kill me. You and Frank witnessed it."

Jake smiled through the smoke. Sam didn't like what that smile implied.

"Temporary insanity due to post-partum depression."

"What?" She sank back against the chair. With a smart lawyer, there was a good chance Angel could get away with this. "This is a nightmare."

"What they are finding with the other victims so far is that they died of asphyxiation. Strangulation is a man's choice of murder. Plus Angel was too young at the time most of the women died. Banks also found souvenirs in the cellar belonging to the victims—wallets, rings, necklaces, watches. All they have to do is match the bodies with the names."

Sam remembered the jewelry she had worn in one of her visions. "Did they find an ankle bracelet with palm trees and pineapples?"

"Yes. Why?"

Oops. "Besides the woods and bows and arrows I also had visions of a truck driver helping to change my flat tire." Sam winced as she added, "After spiking my water he tried choking me."

"And you were going to tell me this when?"

"I didn't want to confuse the cases. I had no way of knowing one was related to the other. Besides, since when do you listen to me?"

Jake pondered tha question with a shrug. "Guess I better start."

"About time," a voice bellowed from behind the birdbath. Alex stood and added, "Took you long enough." He disappeared again. Jake jammed his cigarette into the empty soda can.

Sam remembered Fran and William Korwin. "Now that I think of it, all of that happened after I spoke with the parents of Alison Korwin and after I held Alison's necklace."

"Korwin? I think her wallet was in the cellar." Jake fired up another cigarette. Sam wondered how many packs he smoked over the last three days. His frustration level could also be measured by the number of cigarette butts. "It's going to take time for the authorities to sort through everything. We'll never know how Vierk picked his victims, how long it had been going on, or if there might be victims buried elsewhere. There isn't any record of Vierk living anywhere else but Pine Grove. The company he worked for will release his delivery logs so that might help the FBI coordinate Vierk's movements with the dates the victims were reported missing."

"How did someone Angel's size, though, get the bodies to Chasen Heights?"

"The only way Angel could handle the bodies on her own was to let them decompose on the property. Female body can be reduced to about twenty pounds of bones, easy enough for a woman Angel's size to handle," Jake offered. "Same might have happened with the grandfather. She obviously couldn't have carried him into the cellar."

"No, but she could have pushed him."

"Unfortunately, unless we can get her to plead guilty so the case doesn't go to trial, you will have to testify."

A courtroom was one place Sam didn't want to be. Her testimony centered around visions and voices she heard, enough for any defense attorney to file for a mistrial.

"Why don't you take a nap? You look beat?"

Jake shook his head and wiped the fatigue from his eyes. "Just have time for a couple aspirin and then I have to get back to the precinct. Professor Logan is our only hope of getting Angel to trip herself up."

"You're going to get him to talk to her?"

"And he'll be wired for sound."

"Well, well." Frank circled T.J. as though the professor were on the auction block. "You clean up rather nicely."

Earlier, two officers had escorted T.J. to his hotel room and waited while he showered, shaved, and dressed. Room service had delivered a steak with all the trimmings and a full pot of black coffee. A communications technician had wired T.J. for sound and was monitoring his conversations from a van in the parking lot.

"I can't believe you are putting me in a room with a serial killer." T.J. pulled on the sleeves of his sportscoat.

"Hell, man. You slept in the same bed with a serial killer," Frank said.

"Don't remind me."

"Let's go over it one more time." Jake picked up his notepad as T.J. rolled his eyes. "Hey, if you fuck this up…"

"I heard already. My suspended sentence for stealing the artifacts is contingent on my cooperation. I get it. It's just hard to not convey my utter disgust of Angel when I'm in her presence."

Frank checked the small microphone under T.J.'s collar. He tapped his own earpiece. "Testing. You read us, Bobby?" He turned to T.J. "Say something to Bobby."

"Something."

Frank listened for a few seconds, then told T.J., "Stay close to a window when you are in there."

Jake sank into one of the upholstered chairs. "As motivation, whatever you can get Angel to admit to will guarantee she will be put away for life for Amanda's murder."

"Right." T.J. took a deep breath and repeated, "Right. Okay. I'm to mention her grandmother, Linda Vierk. Get her to talk about her grandfather and the women he murdered."

Frank added, "If you can get her to toss in a few details about the Breyton Dig and Greg, we'll definitely show our gratitude."

"That's a lot to remember." T.J. wiped perspiration from his forehead.

"Show concern and compassion," Jake said. "And it better be genuine because Angel is smart. Don't go in there accusing her of anything. That will put her on the defensive. Just get her talking."

"But above all," Frank warned, "don't get near her. If she sees the bug, if you say something to set her off, Lord only knows what she might grab and swing at you."

"No worries about that."

Frank pulled the sketch of Amanda from a file folder and held it up. "Incentive."

Tears sprang to T.J.'s eyes.

"That's good," Frank said. "Keep Amanda in your head and let Angel think those tears are for her alone. Remember, Angel is still in love with you."

T.J. groaned. "Enough to make me join a monastery. Let's get this over with."

40

The door to the hospital room opened softly. T.J. wished the cop was sitting inside the room rather than on a chair outside the room. Angel was lying on her side, eyes closed. He walked over to the windows and pulled the drapery cord. Sunlight splashed across the bed.

Angel's eyes sprang open. "T.J.?"

T.J. tried not to stare at her bandages. He still couldn't believe she had actually tried to kill Sam. Remembering Detective Travis' suggestion, he thought of what Amanda's last day, her last minutes and seconds of life must have been like. Tears sprang easily.

"I've really made a mess of things, haven't I?" His voice was barely above a whisper. He heard the technician's voice in his earpiece telling him that reception was good.

Angel pushed the controls and the bed rose to where she was in a sitting position. "Yeah, you have." Her eyes narrowed as though she were inspecting him under a microscope.

He reined in his anger. There was so much he wanted to say to her, to scream at her, but he had to force himself to stay on script. T.J. dragged a chair over to the side of the bed, out of arm's reach of Angel. Where does he start?

"No matter what you might think, I did not push you down a staircase and cause you to lose your baby."

"OUR BABY!" Angel screamed.

Wrong subject. T.J. could see the spark of insanity in her eyes. "I never even knew you were pregnant until after you lost it."

Her hands moved to her mouth and she chewed on a bandage as though unaware some of her fingers were missing. "Would it have made a difference?"

T.J. could see the maniacal light switch off in her eyes. Should he lie? Tell the truth? Sergeant Mitchell said she was smart and could tell the difference. Finally he replied, "No, Angel. It wouldn't have." He watched her shoulders slump and her eyes fill. "I'm an ass of the highest degree."

She turned her attention back to the windows and the dark clouds hovering in the distance. "He didn't like the rain."

"What?" He followed her gaze, heard the low rumble of thunder.

"My grandfather. He didn't like the rain."

"What about your grandmother?" He watched her face change. Instead of a twenty-five-year-old woman, her demeanor changed to a petulant juvenile.

"She was a bitch. Never wanted my grandfather to take me in. Thought I had something to do with my family's house burning down."

Whoa. This was unknown territory T.J. was stumbling into. Why hadn't the detectives filled him in on Angel's past?

"Your entire family?" He found himself scooting his chair back ever so slowly.

"It was just a small fire. How was I to know it was going to go out of control? And then Gram hated the fact that Gramps and I used wildlife for practice. Birds, rabbits, deer." She studied his face, then smiled. "Do you find it appalling?"

Holy shit. You're damn right I do. T.J. tried to hold down his steak lunch. "Not quite the practice I would envision for an Olympic champion." He hoped the detectives were getting everything they needed because he didn't plan to go through this again if they claim some equipment failure. "What I really find appalling is what your grandfather did to all those women. It must have been a shock to find out he was a murderer."

Angel leaned forward, the fingers on her good hand pinching her lips as though trying to prevent them from smiling. In a sick and twisted voice, she whispered, "Sometimes, he'd let me watch."

T.J.'s face, his entire body froze, then he slowly pressed against the chair back in an attempt to distance himself further. Was Angel only trying to get a rise out of him? Did she suspect their conversation was being taped and she just wanted to solidify an insanity plea?

"Did your grandmother know?"

"Gram." Angel pushed at the air. "She was so stupid. Once she wandered onto the back property when Gramps was burying someone but he told her he was burying a deer that I killed. She never went out into the forest again. Filed for divorce soon after. Good riddance. Gramps and I celebrated."

"You were so young," T.J. gasped. "How could you not be repulsed by what he was doing? Did he ever say why he killed them?"

A flash of lightning lit up the sky. Angel turned back to the windows as the sky churned. Thunder intensified as the storm advanced. Her expression took on almost a childlike wonder.

"Grandfather always said, 'there's pain in the rain.'"

"I'm done. I did my bit," T.J. said. "There's 'pain in the rain.' For Jesus-fucking sake I was ready to blast out a chorus of *the rain in Spain*. She is a fucking psycho!"

"Thank you for the obvious assessment, Professor," Jake said. He looked at Frank who was listening to the technician on the earpiece.

"Bobby says it's good."

T.J. breathed a sigh of relief. "Will be great to get my life back on track."

"It won't be quite what you are used to," Frank said. "You won't be permitted on digs or invited to museum exhibitions."

They pounded down the metal stairwell to the first floor.

"Guest Lecturer has its upside. And, believe it or not, I have a literary agent who is shopping around a book deal. Who woulda thought?"

"Only in America," Frank said.

They poured out the front door and into the humid air. Jake shoved his sunglasses on to hide the eye-drilling he was giving the professor. Dark clouds bullied their way in, blocking out what little sunlight was left. With T.J. in the back of the Ford Taurus, Frank peeled rubber out of the west side parking lot.

On the north side of the building, a young woman stood on the third floor ledge. It had been the only room available when she was admitted. How stupid for them to give her a room with windows that opened.

The storm approached rapidly as a drizzle dotted the pavement. It pelted the young woman's face. She looked up and smiled, as though welcoming a good cleaning. The wind whipped her hospital gown around her legs, the fabric clinging like cellophane to her body. In the parking lot below, visitors were charging into the building, faces hidden under umbrellas. Not one person looked up to see the patient hovering on the ledge.

Lightning struck with a loud crackle, followed by a rumble of thunder that sounded like a sonic explosion. The woman could feel the vibration beneath her bare feet. From the parking lot it appeared as though the thunder had shaken a delicate figurine off of a shelf. With arms outstretched the young woman fell, bandages flapping in the wind like broken wings.

Overhead the storm clouds opened.

And it poured.